TH

A

By

Doug Dandridge

BIRTHDAY 2016
FROM LAURA

"What the hell are you?" he screamed as the weapon clicked on the empty chamber. He reached frantically into his jacket, trying to fumble another magazine, then tried to ram it home. But as his hands shook the new magazine refused to go where the old one still resided.

Lucinda took off in a sprint toward the man, moving faster than humanly possible, faster than the swiftest sprinter. She lowered her shoulder and took Carlos in the ribs, feeling the bones crack as she lifted him into the air. The man struck his right shoulder and arm against the wall, grunting out his breath. Lucinda was past him and into the living room as he slid down the wall to the floor, the machine pistol falling from nerveless fingers as consciousness fled.

Lucinda pivoted on her right foot, turning toward the family room, as more bullets whizzed past her, the sound of cracking plaster and breaking porcelain sounding to her sensitive ears. One large man, with the mass of a football player, came straight at her from the glass doors, lowering his shoulders and reaching his arms out into a classic tackle. Lucinda leapt into the air and brushed the ceiling as she flew over his form, which was falling to the floor after not meeting the resistance it had been preparing itself for. The vampire did a turn in the air, as she thanked herself for the gymnastics lessons her mom had insisted that she take, and landed lightly on her feet.

She could sense that the door before her was locked, and she didn't have the key. So going into a crouch and out again she sprung toward the double doors and crashed through the glass, leaving jagged hanging splinters behind her. Women screamed as she propelled her naked form across the flagstones. One man dropped his drink and made a grab for her, but a strong backhand lifted him from his feet and into the pool. By the time he hit the water with a splash Lucinda was speeding across the grass lawn, reveling in the cool passage of the night air over her bare skin.

From ten feet out she went into a quick crouch and sprung into the air, her feet clearing the ten-foot privacy fence as more rounds cracked past her. Dogs barked at her as they struggled to catch her and were thwarted by the fence. Her feet hit lightly onto the grass of another lawn and she sprang ahead, swerving to avoid another large dog that was coming at her across the lawn.

Lucinda leapt into the air again, spreading her arms as she arched up to twenty feet. She willed the transformation again, feeling her limbs shorten and the fur thrust out through her skin. She gave a screech to the night as she flapped her wings and disappeared into the darkness.

Dedication

This book is dedicated to my mother, Hazel Angelina (Roy) Dandridge, 1920-2009. You believed in me when others didn't.

BrotherofCats@gmail.com
http://dougdandridge.net
Copyright © 2011 Doug Dandridge

ISBN: 1468155431
ISBN-13: 978-1468155433

Chapter 1

The hunger gnawed at her, a craving that suffused her very being. Lucinda had to have it soon. She wouldn't die without it, not immediately, but she would wish she were dead. She could feel the sweat beading on her forehead, the cramps in her stomach, the quivering of her muscles. Without it she would go mad, and her actions would make the rest of the world wish she were dead. Make them try to make her dead, for real this time.

Lucinda looked down from the roof of the building to the man standing across the street. Her target for tonight. A tall, muscular black man, the streetlight glinting from his shaven head. His girls were walking the street around him, looking for the men who would give them the money they needed to support their own habits. The men who would keep their lord and master from beating them within an inch of their lives.

Lucinda remembered, looking at the man with the heat of hate rising from her gut. Remembered the nights when she had not done enough Johns. Had not made enough to score what she needed, and keep heavy hands from beating her into the ground. Until the night they had beat her to the brink of death, and cut her throat, leaving her to bleed out.

"Come here, bitch," she heard the man call, breaking her out of her thoughts of the past. A white woman with stringy blonde hair framing a pale face came running toward him, her mouth and eyes twitching with terror. Lucinda could smell her from here, the musky scent of fear that made the saliva drip from her mouth.

"What the hell you doing, bitch?" Leroy McKinnon yelled as he grabbed and jerked her arm behind her, twisting her around as his other arm came around her neck. "You need to shake that ass, bitch. How the hell you expect to suck the Johns if you don't give them something to lust after."

The woman nodded her wide-eyed head as she went still in his grasp. Her lips moved as she tried to speak, to say the right thing to keep the big man from hurting her.

"And you want your rock, don't you bitch?" growled Leroy. "You better shake your ass if you want your rock, cause it don't come for free."

Leroy released his arm lock around her throat and pushed her away. The woman scrambled to keep her feet. Failing, she fell to the hard concrete of the sidewalk. She lay there for a second, her breath coming ragged. Leroy took a step and raised a leg to kick at her. The woman pushed herself to her feet and walked quickly away, blood oozing down the scrape on her right knee. She staggered away from the big black man, looking over her hunched shoulder to see if he was following her. Then with a resigned shake of her head she started to shake other parts of her body, trying to draw in the flies to her honey. The flies that would pay to sample her honey. And pay for her next fix.

Lucinda felt the hunger grow as she watched, threatening to make her mad. A mother pushing a baby carriage walked on the sidewalk directly below the building. She felt the pull of the hunger, the thought of young baby blood, and the vital energy it contained, coursing through her veins. The dark side of her soul trying to drag her back into darkness. Shaking her head and pushing the dark side to the back of her mind, Lucinda brought her concentration back to the crack dealer/pimp across the street, ignoring the mother who must live in such a rundown area of town.

Another woman came up to the man, a black woman as thin as pipe stems. She whispered something to him and Leroy nodded, a smile coming to his lips. A smile that did not go as far as his eyes. He motioned to the alley across the street and the woman led the way. Lucinda's eyes followed them as they entered the semi-darkness of the narrow space between the buildings.

Lucinda pushed her hearing up to hyper, listening in as the deal was being made. She knew she didn't have much time, as these kinds of deals didn't last long. Going over the top of the rooftop she placed her fingers on the rough brick and scrambled like a lizard onto the wall. With a quick motion of arms and legs she moved silently down the five stories of wall into the end of the alley, coming to stand behind some barrels filled with the foul smelling remnants of people's lives.

Her eyes focused and the darkness faded in front of her. She could clearly see Leroy and the skinny black woman concluding their deal. Money went into the dealer's hand and a small package of foil was placed in the woman's. She nodded and smiled, then ran out of the alley, to head home and blast her sorrows from her tortured mind. Leroy watched her go, waited a moment, and then started to walk out himself.

Lucinda came around the barrels then, into clear sight of the dealer. Her hair was now long and stringy, her body thin, looking the part of the crack whore in search of a fix.

"Hello, sugar," she said in a husky, seductive voice that pulled at the lust inside of all men.

Leroy spun around very quickly for a big, muscular man. A gun appeared in his hand, a heavy .40 caliber automatic that an instant before had been stuck in his waistband.

"Easy, honey," purred Lucinda, no fear in her voice, only pure seduction. Her eyes looked into Leroy's, and she could see the blank glassy look that came into his gaze as she gained control. She walked slowly toward him, and the gun dropped to his side.

Leroy shook his head for a moment as he shoved the gun back into his waistband. His eyes remained glued to her face, but he had broken some of the spell.

"I only want a little of what you got to sell," said Lucinda, moving closer to the man.

"Who you work for?" asked Leroy, lust for a new piece of meat taking control of the man.

This is not going to be as easy as I thought. Lucinda looked at the man and realized that her hypnotic spell was not taking charge. *But it will happen.*

"I'm an independent," she replied, moving closer to the man. "I work for myself."

"The streets is dangerous," he said. "You need someone to protect you."

"I'm safe enough," she replied. "I just need some of that good stuff."

"Bitch," growled Leroy. "These streets is mine. No one works them without coming to me."

Leroy swung a hand toward her face, animal lust and anger shining in his eyes. Lucinda brought up an arm in a blur of speed, stopping Leroy's blow like the swing of an errant child. The hunger swelled in her chest, and the deceptive appearance of human fell from her face.

"What the hell are you?" screamed Leroy, trying with all his strength to pull his arm out of Lucinda's grasp. His other hand reached toward his waistband, closing onto the grip of the gun. With a twist and a flick of her arm, Lucinda sent Leroy flying through the air and into the barrels at the end of the alley. The pimp hit hard, in a clatter of metal hitting concrete and brick.

Fear kept Leroy conscious. And fear made his movements swift. The gun came out of the waistband and swung toward Lucinda. His finger squeezed the trigger quickly, over and over, sending death streaking through the foul air of the alley.

The first bullet missed, cracking through the air close to her ear. The second went through her chest, continuing intact after meeting no resistance. Baring her elongated canines she walked to stand over the now shivering man.

"What the hell are you, bitch?" screamed Leroy. "What are you?"

"Your worst nightmare," hissed Lucinda, reaching down and pulling the man up to his feet. Leroy struggled, trying to get away, but Lucinda held him like a child and pulled him close. She could hear voices at the opening of the alley now, people talking about what they thought was going on in the passageway. But no one brave enough to do anything. The faint sound of sirens told her that it wouldn't be long before people showed up who would be brave enough to try the alley.

Stretching her jaws wide, wider than humanly possible, Lucinda plunged her canines into her victim's neck, puncturing his jugular vein. Jerking the teeth out of the holes she sucked at the pulsing blood, feeling it slide down her throat. Feeling the life force that the blood symbolized flooding into her body. To feed the hunger within. Within minutes she had drained the energy from the now lifeless body. Still holding it up with one hand, she pulled a long knife from a sheath on her back.

Never again, she thought, as she swung the knife with all of her strength, aiming the blade at the corpse's neck. She would never leave another of the scum intact, to come back from the dead and hound her. The blade sliced through the neck with the inhuman strength behind it. The head flew from the body as the last bits of blood in the corpse splashed into the alley. Lucinda tossed the body through the air with a one armed push, to smack limply against an alley wall.

"This is the police," called a voice from the alley entrance as the beams of flashlights stabbed into the darkness. "Stop what you're doing and put your hands up."

Lucinda ran swiftly to the blocked end of the alley as shots rang out and bullets struck brick walls with showers of sparks. She stopped at the far wall and turned back, her undead eyes showing her the trio of cops coming up the alley with drawn weapons. She bared her fangs as her instincts bid her to attack.

Not these, she thought. These were not her enemies, though they would think themselves such.

She reached her arms into the air and felt the pleasure of change come over her. Limbs shortened, body shrank in on itself, as clothes were absorbed and short fur grew from every pore. Flapping her wings in the cool air, screeching her call to the night to generate the sound needed to sense surrounding objects, the vampire flew into the sky, leaving the alley far behind.

*   *   *

Tampa Police Department tried to wave him away. A push of the badge out the open window of the Mustang had the cops shaking their heads as they waved him into the crime scene. He pulled between a police cruiser and a forensics van and got out of the car as another uniformed cop, with sergeant stripes on his sleeves, hurried over to the car.

"I know you don't want me here," he said in his best Ivy League accent to the tall, white police sergeant. "But I am claiming jurisdiction in this one, sarge."

"Since when is the FBI interested in a local homicide?" asked the sergeant.

Agent Jeffrey DeFalco ran a meat hook of a hand through his short brown hair, and looked the sergeant in the eye. He wasn't as tall as the sergeant, but he figured he definitely had him in the muscular development department. DeFalco was proud of his body, with his heavy shoulders, chest and legs, joined by a narrow waist. He used his athletic image many times to cow the local boys, while his Law Degree from Princeton was enough to gain the respect of the non-law enforcement professionals he had to deal with.

"If this murder has the earmarks I think it has," said DeFalco, "there's a chance this was performed by the same killer who has left a trail from Boston to Atlanta."

"OK," said the sergeant. "But you need to talk to Lieutenant Smith. He's the officer in charge here."

"He was," said DeFalco. "And where can I find him?"

"Where the action is," said the sergeant, gesturing toward the alley where the shadows of people moved in the powerful lights set on stands around the scene.

"OK," said DeFalco as he walked toward the entrance of the alley. He looked over to where plain clothes cops were questioning some street scum and pointed at them as he walked. "Don't let anyone go until I have a chance to see their statements. I might have some questions you haven't thought of."

DeFalco swaggered into the alley to the sound of loud voices arguing. He saw a wiry man as black as night standing over a headless body, arguing with a man wearing a blue vest, *Forensics* lettered on the back.

"There's not enough fuckin' blood," yelled the forensic tech, pointing a black light at the wall. At a gesture the tripod mounted spots dimmed to darkness.

"Look here," said the tech in a loud voice, pointing to the splatter of glowing red on the wall. "Here's the blood from where the body hit. There should be a shit load of it, not a couple of small spatters."

"And here," the tech said, pointing the light toward the floor of the alley. "Here's where the blood from the decapitation poured out before he was flung against that wall. There's not enough."

"And here," he said while pointing the light to another section of alley wall. "Here's the splatter from the blade taking the head off, and flinging blood into the brick. A little better than the others, but still not enough."

"Shit. So what are you telling me?" asked the black detective as the light came back up to reflect from the shaven head. "Someone took the blood out of him before they cut his fuckin' head off. Is that what you're telling me?"

"Did you find any puncture marks in the neck?" asked DeFalco, walking up to the men.

"And who the fuck are you?" asked the detective in a voice brimming with anger.

"Are you Detective Smith?" asked DeFalco.

"I asked first," growled the detective.

DeFalco raised his ID for the man to see and waited for a reply.

"Yeah, I'm Jamal Smith. Lieutenant of Homicide in this beautiful sun drenched city. What the fuck has the FBI interested in a local murder? I could see the World Inquirer. But the FBI"

"Were there puncture wounds in the neck?" asked DeFalco again, a trace of Brooklyn creeping into his voice as his frustration grew. He hated dealing with local cops. Always the unwelcoming attitude when they found out that he belonged to a higher order of law enforcement than they did.

"Couldn't tell," said the tech. "There are ragged edges on the neck where the blade cut through, could have covered up puncture marks I guess."

"Why ragged edges?"

"Because, agent" said Smith, "the experts believe that it was a dull blade that was used to separate Mr. Leroy McKinnon's head from his body."

DeFalco shrugged and tilted his head in a questioning gaze.

"Mr. Leroy McKinnon was the resident scumbag of this section of the City," said the detective. "Lord of a six-block area. No dope or pussy moved here without his permission."

"And someone used a dull blade to cut through his neck. How many swings would that take?"

"That's the thing, DeFalco," said Smith. "The experts," he nodded at the forensics man, "think from the single blood splatter that it was one."

"And it covered up the puncture marks," muttered DeFalco. "Girl's getting smarter."

"Couldn't have been a woman," said the tech. "You know what kind of strength we're talking about here. I'm thinking maybe a body builder. Or some kind of professional fighter."

"And what did your officers see when they came in the alley. I heard that they thought the perp was still in here when they started their sweep."

"Couldn't have been," said Smith. "Look at those walls. The shortest is four floors. And we didn't find any ropes or hand holds."

"I didn't ask about what you thought," said the agent. "I asked what the cops saw when they came down this alley?"

Smith glared at the agent for a moment, his lips moving in a silent curse.

"The cops thought they saw someone at the end of the alley. They said it looked like the person blurred, changed somehow. Then they weren't there."

"Anything else?"

"One of them saw something fly up to the rooftops. A bird, or…"

"A bat?"

"I know you now," said Smith. "You're the man they call the vampire Hunter. I hear that the FBI isn't too happy with you right now."

"I'm still an agent in good standing," said DeFalco, more Brooklyn coming out of his voice in his anger. "And as the agent in charge here I want all the information you have. At police headquarters. First thing tomorrow."

"You really believe it's a vampire?" asked Smith. "I heard the Inquirer called her the *Avenging Angel*. Only kills the scum of the Earth."

"You tell that to Francine Lopez," said the agent in an angry hiss. "She was no scum of the Earth. She was an innocent person who was in the wrong place at the wrong time. And this *Avenging Angel* killed her just as dead as Mr. McKinnon here. Drained her of her blood and left a young, vital woman a corpse in an alley in Philadelphia."

"Well, avenging angel or no," said Smith, "we'll get her. I read she only works at night. The night is my shift, and I'll get her if she keeps killing in my town."

"You can't get her in the night," said DeFalco over his shoulder as he walked from the alley. "You can only hurt her in the day."

*   *   *

"Crazy motherfucker," said Detective Jamal Smith as the FBI Agent walked out of the alley.

"You think that he might have something with this vampire thing?" asked the forensics man.

"In sunny Tampa?" asked Smith, shaking his head. "I don't believe in ghosts or goblins either. No, this was done by a living breathing human. Probably a big strong male human. And the cops who arrived on the scene let their imaginations get away from them."

Still Jamal felt himself shivering as a chill ran up his spine. Like something monstrous was watching him at this very moment. What if the FBI man was right? Could there be something to this. The Inquirer seemed to think so.

"Shit," said Smith. "No fuckin' way."

"What was that lieutenant?"

"No fuckin' way that this is supernatural. You just find everything you can find, and make sure that a copy of it gets on my desk. We'll find this mother. And he'll go down in a Florida prison."

*   *   *

Marcus LaMons watched from the top of a building across the street from the alley, his supernatural vision looking through lights and darkness alike. His supernatural hearing listening in on the conversation. *So one of them knows*, he thought, watching the human in the cheap suit getting into the black Mustang. One who would bear watching. One who might lead him to the renegade. And one who would finally feel the fangs of the one once known as Marcus of Alexandria.

He could feel a touch of the hunger now. An urge to go into the alleyway across the street and begin the slaughter. But with a thought he suppressed the urge. An ancient like he was no longer a slave to animal instincts. He could go for weeks without feeding, with little discomfort. Or hibernate for decades without the life force of another.

His blue-green eyes glowed in the night as he looked up and down the street, wondering where the fresh meat had gone after doing her work. *At least she is doing a better job of covering her tracks with the humans*, he thought. Not that it would do any good. Mistakes would be made. And the humans would catch on to the mystery that was his race.

Just as the Vandals and the Goths had destroyed the people of his birth, the humans were a threat to his present race. The race of night stalkers had power, it was true. But the humans had progressed in their abilities in the last two thousand years, to the point where they could destroy the planet if they so desired. And if a great number of humans knew of the race that lived on the fringes of their society, that fed on them like the cattle that they were, they would demand a war against the race. A war that the race could not win.

Marcus reveled in the feel of the night breeze flowing through his long, sand colored hair. He looked at his artist's hands, beautiful in their clean, manicured perfection. He had been large for the people in his time. He was not so large as the people in this time. But the blood of patricians flowed through his veins. And the strength of the warriors of the night dwelled in his muscles.

It is time to go, he thought. The sun would soon be on the horizon. The first rays of dawn could destroy even an ancient like him, if he were caught unawares. Later, after a sleep in the soil of his resting place, he would be able to walk the streets in comfort, contrary to the popular belief of most of the mortals. But he would lose his special abilities, and be no more than one of the blind, deaf, crippled creatures who walked the streets of this city. No, the night was the time to walk the streets, with no fear of the mortals.

A mist began to gather around Marcus, a mist that soon engulfed his form. A fog coagulated on the roof top, thicker and thicker. The predawn breeze from the ocean blew through the mist, spreading it out, breaking it up, until it was gone. And gone with it was the ancient vampire named Marcus of Alexandria.

*   *   *

This is a nightmare, she thought as she walked in the ankle high water of the storm drain. *I hide like a rodent in the earth during the day, not like a human being. Because I am not a human being.*

She could feel the imminent rise of the sun, when she would lose all of her powers and become as the mortals. With a difference. They were alive, living and pursuing their lives under the powerful light of the sun. While she had to hide in the bowels of the Earth and wait until the night, or at least the afternoon, when she could walk as a mortal. While in the night she was almost invulnerable. Almost unstoppable.

I felt him tonight, she thought. *He's here.* The Vampire Lord had followed her to Tampa. She had sensed him in Atlanta as well, but had been able to avoid him while she made the city streets safe for the innocent. And a terror for the truly evil. She had gotten out of there before she had to face him. A confrontation she was sure to lose.

But here he was again. Before she had even made her presence known to the city. Every time he got closer. And he was only one of many who sought her death.

I would welcome death, she thought as she crawled through the small opening in the side of the storm drain. *An end to this hellish existence.* A selfish thought she knew. Wallowing in a sewer of pity and regret. She had so much to do.

I'll never be done, she thought as she finished the crawl and stood up in the small side chamber used by maintenance crews to store equipment. This one had the look of not being used for years, and the manhole cover overhead was rusted in place.

There would always be street scum preying on the desperate and hopeless people of the cities. No matter how many she killed there would always be more. A feeling of hopelessness washed over her. She realized that her best efforts would be like thrusting a hand into a bucket of water. No matter how hard she pushed her hand in, or how often, the water would always return to fill the hole. Just as new scum would always come to fill the roles of those she killed.

Lucinda looked down on her coffin sitting in the middle of the chamber, her supernatural eyesight penetrating the total blackness of the chamber. *The hated bed. My prison on this Earth. I don't know if there is a hell, but this is close enough.*

She could forgo her sleep for this day if she wanted. She felt some fear at the thought that Marcus might be here, looking for her. She could use the day to get away, get out of town, go someplace he would never think to look for her. But if she didn't sleep she would not regain her strength, and she would be weaker when the night came. And then she might have to face Marcus, or one of the others, when they were at the height of their powers.

No, she thought as she climbed into the coffin and lay down on the soil of her resting place. The soil of the grave that she inhabited in the three days that passed before her rising.   The pauper's grave in the city that she called her home.   *I've just come to this place.   I've only begun my work here. They have not yet come to fear the night.   They think it is their cover, and their playground.   But soon they will learn it is mine.   And they will come to fear the streets.*

With that final thought Lucinda laid her head on the loamy earth, closed her eyes, and fell into a deep sleep.

Chapter 2

Lucinda screamed a silent scream as the dealer, her pimp, punched a rock like hand into her stomach. The slim contents of that stomach surged up her throat as she vomited on her pimp's shoes.

"Bitch," yelled Derrick. "You fuckin' whore. Don't you dare to came and ask for dope until you sell enough ass to pay for it."

Lucinda felt the hunger through the nausea of her retching. The dope sickness that came with withdrawal from the Heroin. A hunger that only one thing could feed. And this trash in front of her was the only person who could give her the food she craved.

"Please, Derrick," she whined through coughing up what little food she had eaten that day. "I need a fix. I need one now. Please give me a fix. Then I'll sell ass all night long for you. You know I'll pay you back."

"You know the deal, Lucinda," he said with a smirk on his dark tan face. "No credit. You wouldn't sell yourself for credit, now would you? So the answer is no, you whore. You can have a fix when I have my money."

Derrick turned to walk away, out of the tenement building and back to the street where he usually conducted his business. Lucinda felt the pain of the hunger coming over her, and knew that she couldn't move from this spot until she had fed it. And her source was walking away from her.

"Wait, Derrick," she cried as she lurched to her feet and stumbled toward him. He turned to look at her and she slammed into his legs with all of her little bit of strength. She clasped his legs tightly with her arms and felt him fall under her tackle. He hit the floor with a grunt as the loose floorboards vibrated from the impact.

"I have to have it now," she screamed as she crawled up his body and clawed for his eyes. "Now Derrick."

"Bitch," he yelled as her nails scratched his face. "You fuckin' bitch. You're dead."

Derrick grabbed her wrists and roughly pulled them from his face. With a roar he let go of her left wrist and brought his hand back, then swung it straight into her face. Lucinda could feel the cartilage of her nose shatter as the fist hit her. Then she was falling off of him to land on her back, the air pushed out of her lungs. She struggled to draw a breath and get back to her feet. Derrick stood up, pulled a knife from his pocket, and flicked it open.

"You're dead," he repeated, reaching down and grabbing her short red hair, locking his finger into the strands. With a jerk that brought tears to her eyes he lifted her to her knees.

"No one touches me bitch," he growled into her face as he leaned over her. "No one."

He brought the sharp knife up to her throat, pressed it hard into the flesh, and drew it across her windpipe. At first she thought the blade hadn't cut in. All she felt was the pressure coming across her throat. Then she was gagging on blood as it flooded into her air passage.

Derrick shoved her head back and let her fall to the floor.

"You're dead, bitch. And I hope it takes you a long time to die. You'll be an example to all of the others."

With that Derrick turned and walked out of the room. Lucinda could hear his footfalls in the hall as he walked to the entrance to the building. The door swung open with creaking hinges, then slammed hard.

Lucinda lay on the floor trying to draw breath through her flooded airway, and failing. She could feel her life's blood flowing down her skin to add to the pool under her head. She knew she was going to die, and there was nothing she could do to prevent it.

Lucinda yelled out as she sat up in the coffin. *The dream*, she thought. One of the dozen or so horrible dreams that rotated through her sleep periods. And this was, in her opinion, the worst.

She looked around the room, but now the darkness was complete. Her night vision was gone with the night. She reached over the side of the wooden box, fumbling to find the electric lantern that she had left there. She closed her eyes as she flicked the switch, then slowly opened them to allow them to adjust to the light. The chamber looked different in man-made light, not quite as surreal as it had in night vision.

There was her chest of clothing about ten feet away on the farthest wall. It had been almost as much of a problem pushing it through the crawling man sized opening as it had been to bring in the coffin. Next to it was the small kitchen chair, the only furniture in the chamber. The rest of the chamber was bare except for a tall metal locker that contained some of the maintenance tools used in the storm drain system.

Lucinda pulled herself up and stepped out of the coffin, brushing the back of her head with her hand to knock the soil back into the box. She removed her shirt and did the same, making sure that the precious dirt of her burial place remained where it would do her the most good. While there was still some earth in boxes at the local Amtrac office freight storage, she made it a habit to be conservative with the soil. Because when it was gone, she would be unable to rest or restore her powers for the coming nights.

Placing the light on the seat of the chair, she stripped naked and laid the stalking clothes on the backrest. She then opened the chest and rummaged through the clothing within, coming out with a summer suit and white blouse, along with some sandals and a purse. She transferred her ID and some toiletries, put everything in a gym bag, and climbed back through the opening and into the storm drain system.

She rubbed her hands over her skin and it was instantly clean, free of the dirt that had gotten on her when she had brushed up against the many dirty surfaces on the way out of the chamber. She sniffed at her underarms and gave a satisfied shrug as she smelled the neutral odor that resided there. *One of the advantages of being undead,* she thought. She stayed clean and sweet smelling pretty much no matter what. Her breath stank of death and stale blood, but a shot of breath mint would cover that up for the short periods of time requiring close contact with mortals.

Lucinda walked naked through the ankle deep water to an exit chamber of the storm drain, a chamber with a man tall door and a painted ladder leading up to a working manhole cover. Lucinda pulled on the clothes and strapped on the sandals, then climbed up the ladder and listened for a moment at the manhole. The alleyway above sounded quiet, so she decided to risk it and pushed the manhole cover up and away from the opening. She raised her head into the shadows of the alley and looked around. There was no one observing her exit, so she climbed nimbly out of the hole and pushed the cover back over it.

It took a moment for her eyes to adjust to the light of day that flooded the street the alley opened onto. Once she could see fairly well she stepped out of the alley and onto the sidewalk. An elderly couple stared at her as she flashed a warm smile at them. They muttered to themselves as they turned and walked the other way.

The skin of her face, hands and feet were stinging a bit as the warm sunshine impacted on her. She knew it would continue to sting as long as she was in the sunlight. But unlike in the movies, books and TV programs she would not burst into flame and fall to the street a blackened skeleton, at least not from the afternoon light. Nor would her strength be any greater than that of a normal human, and she was susceptible to injury from a variety of sources, though still hard to kill.

Lucinda wandered down the busy street, looking at the vehicles in the asphalt, many expensive luxury cars and convertibles. The sun was gleaming off of the cluster of high rises surrounding the downtown skyscrapers. A pair of hot air balloons floated lazily through the blue sky, while a trio of military fighters from McDill flew high in the air, leaving white contrails behind them. A line of thunderheads gathered over the bay.

The sidewalks were swarming with people. Some sweated in suits and dresses, many were in states of unclothing that would have garnered stares in northern cities, shorts, tank tops and sandals. Sunglasses were the norm. There was a diverse group of people, happy and sad, rich and poor, prospering and declining. White, Black, Hispanic and Asian. But all living relatively normal lives, not unlives.

Lucinda turned down a smaller side street, then stopped and stared at the headlines displayed in the newspaper machine by the wall of the bank. *Man found dead in alley, drained of blood*, screamed the headline, while the story below right said *Vampire in Tampa?* She felt a rage come over her at that moment. If blood had still pumped through her veins, she knew that her heart would be pounding. If she still had body heat her face would be hot. But instead all she had was the cognitive sensation of rage.

The fools, she thought. *Don't they know that I'm doing this for them?* This would bring the others here to hound her. The tabloid writers, the supernatural *experts*, the law, the church and all of the others that sought to destroy her. Now things would become more dangerous for her.

But she didn't know how else to kill the scum that were her targets. Sure, she could kill them in a way unrelated to her state. She could push them off a building, crush them under a car, shoot or knife them. But she had to feed, every night. And they were the source of her food. If not them, then who? The innocents that she was trying to protect?

She looked up finally after wandering many blocks. She was in a seedier part of the city, off of the main thoroughfares. The buildings were mostly two to three story brick low rises, some with boarded up windows. The people were shabbier as well. Crack addicts stared at her from the steps in front of the buildings, sizing her up in their need for the money to buy still more drugs. One young man, tall, gaunt and feral, tried to stare her down. One glare from her deep blue eyes, reflecting red from the sunlight, turned his face away. *He recognizes a predator when he sees one*, she thought.

She turned down another street and made her way back toward the business district. *He's why I do this?* she thought. Not just for the respectable people who lost sons and daughters, nieces and nephews, grandsons and granddaughters to the dark side of the city. But to the direct victims of the scourge. The addicts and hookers who fed the beast as their lives went from bad to disaster. The old people, living in poor housing on small pensions, while worrying each night that their lives might be threatened, their meager belongings stolen by the desperate souls seeking to relieve their hunger.

She looked up and down the busy street as she came back to the more prosperous section of town. A young businessman in an expensive suit whistled at her, winked her way, and followed her with his eyes as he walked by her. She looked back, feeling a smile tug at her lips. The smile turned down in a frown as she turned and continued to walk down the sidewalk.

I never thought I would miss sex, she thought. *The touch of a gentle hand, the breath on the hot spots on my neck, the sigh as I let the feeling take me.* She had thought that the years of selling herself on the street, the shame and the guilt of using her body to get money from sick people to feed her own sickness, would have made her revolted at the thought of the hands of another on her body. But having death as a constant companion had made her yearn for the life-affirming act that other people took for granted.

How would he feel once he smelled breath as musty as the grave? Hands as cold as ice? Didn't feel a heart beating in my breast? Could he stand the gaze of a hungry predator staring at him?

She shook her head as she walked down the street. She couldn't get that close to any mortal. She would be endangering them, and she would be putting herself at risk. She couldn't do that to anyone, or to herself. She had a mission, she couldn't let her personal feelings or desires get in its way.

Before she knew it she was back at the alleyway that led down to her world, the world of darkness. The afternoon had passed faster that she had realized, and the sun was down behind the big buildings. She could feel that it was touching the horizon now, and would soon disappear. She waited for that moment patiently, leaning against the wall of a building.

Lucinda could feel it happening, the last sliver of the sun disappearing around the curve of the world. She could feel the strength suffusing her muscles; the dark shadows could no longer hide what they covered from her vision. Quiet conversations on the street came clear to her ears. She could smell the aftershave on a man on the other side of the major thoroughfare. She could smell the stench of urine and feces blocks away in the seedier section of town. She could smell lust and anger and fear. She relished the least feeling, a feeling she would raise to terror in some lucky mortal tonight. And the smell of fear brought just a little bit of the feeling that she dreaded, the hunger that she must quench before the night was over.

With a thought she triggered the change. Mist began to form around her, as she felt her own body begin to fade, becoming mist itself. The mist billowed, filling the alleyway thick as it rose above the first floors of the surrounding buildings. Then it started to thin as suddenly as it had filled the alley. It flew through the tiny openings of the manhole, gathering in the storm drain below, which filled with white moisture as the alley became clear again.

The mist swirled down the storm drain, making its way from junction to junction, until it reached the opening of the unused access chamber that Lucinda had made her own. The fog poured through the tunnel into the access room, twisting into a vortex of mist that got thicker toward the center. The mist condensed in the center as it thinned at the edges. And then it was gone as a human figure stood in the center of the room.

Lucinda felt a shiver course down her spine as she reveled in her power, the abilities of a super heroine. Then she shuddered in revulsion as she thought about where her powers actually came from. They were a gift from Satan, bestowed upon her that she might bring hell on earth. *But he is not my master*, she thought. *He might get my soul when I die. But until then it is my soul.*

Lucinda dressed for the night, dark clothing that would look normal on the street, but blend into the night when she wanted it to. Black shirt, black skirt, and black stockings into black boots. She attached the sheath with the large dull knife to the back of her throat collar, hanging the sheath down the back of her shirt. With a thought she changed her physical appearance, red hair lengthening as it flowed down her back to cover the bulge of the knife. Her face rounded, her eyes darkened to hazel and her lips became fuller.

With another thought she began the transformation back to mist, flowing out of the room and down the storm drain. She flowed quickly down the miles of drain until she came to another chamber that she had scouted the night before. The mist turned up as it flowed through the holes of another manhole cover. Filling the alley it rose into the air and settled on the rooftop of a three story low rise. There it began to once again coalesce, forming into the human shape, until Lucinda stood on the rooftop, looking over the bright lights of the city of Tampa.

*   *   *

Marcus' eyes opened as the sun went over the horizon. He had felt no need to wake this day. The odds of finding her in the city during the day, when all of his infernal abilities were inactive, were remote to say the least. So he had slept through the daylight to make sure that he was at his strongest this night.

Marcus sat up in the marble sarcophagus and let his gaze settle on the quartet of naked thralls kneeling beside his resting place, their foreheads to the floor. Two large men and two petite women, they guarded him in his sleep. And provided food when he wished to hide his presence from the world. Marcus climbed from the coffin and onto the floor, allowing his thralls to continue to grovel for a moment. He savored the rank smell of their fear, for it was a sure indication that they would continue to serve him to the best of their abilities.

"You may rise," he said in his deep resonant voice. The thralls came to their feet, their wide eyes locked on his face.

"Any news of the quarry?"

"Yes, master," said the large black male, Frederick, handing Marcus the newspaper he had been holding.

Marcus snatched the paper from his hand. His lips curled back to bare his fangs as he read the headlines and the story beneath.

She has again given us away to the mortals, he thought. *So far the idiots, or most of them at least, think it is nothing but a human playing at vampire. But how long before they begin to believe? And begin to seek us out and destroy us?*

"Frederick. You are to continue monitoring the media for news of the quarry. Matthew," he ordered of the muscular blond man standing next to Frederick. "I want you to shadow the dealers and the pimps of the city, so I may know their daily movements.

"Tonya, Gloria," he said, turning to the shrinking females. "I will need to feed at nights end. If I don't find a source tonight in the city…"

He knew what they were shivering about as he made the statement. They would provide his food tonight if he didn't think it was safe to make a kill. They knew that he would not kill them. He would bring them to the brink of death, and then let them heal for several days, building up their blood levels and life force for his use again.

Marcus turned away from the mortals, sure that they would follow his wishes to the letter. He walked from the room with the heavy draperies to one that overlooked the bright night sky of the city, thinking of where the quarry might go tonight. To one of the high crime districts, he was sure. But there were many in every city, and he must guess correctly if he was to find her. Not the neighborhood she had frequented the night before. Of that he was sure. She would worry about police patrols staking out the streets, and the other hunters she had attracted.

He looked at the map of Tampa tacked to the wall, a red pin showing where she had hunted last night. There were nine other areas outlined in red marker. The high crime districts of the port city. The places where drugs were dealt, women were sold, and life was cheap.

So much like the cities of my time, he thought. *Despite the superficial changes in technology. Still the scum of the empire congregate on its streets, while the rich dwell in their guarded enclaves and ignore the problem, as long as it doesn't land on their doorsteps.*

Tonya and Gloria came into the room with his clothes for the evening. Marcus raised his arms over his head and allowed the thralls to undress him, until he stood naked before them. Gloria rubbed her hand over his tight body, and Marcus wished he would feel himself stirring physically, even as psychological lust grew in his mind.

It is not to be. The hunt is the only thing that arouses me. Only the feeding leads to satisfaction.

Marcus nodded and the women began to dress him. Soon he was clothed in something that would pass as normal in the warm night streets of the Florida city. Khaki slacks, boat shoes, and a green Izod shirt. Tonya handed him a silver headed cane to complete the ensemble.

Marcus twisted the head of the cane and pulled the slender sword from its sheath, slashing it through the air to his front. Satisfied that he was prepared he pushed the blade back into the cane proper and twist locked it into place.

Marcus walked up the stairs to the rooftop. He had rented the entire building through Matthew, so he had no worries that anyone would be on the roof. He came out into the soft night air under the full moon on the horizon. Pulling the sweet smell of crowded humanity, his cattle, into his nostrils he bared his fangs again.

Marcus spread his arms wide and willed the transformation. He could feel his bones changing, growing smaller and changing shape, as his skin and muscles followed suit. He could feel the clothing absorbed into his skin, even the cane, as fine hair grew all over his body. He made to roar his pleasure and a hypersonic screech came from his throat as he flapped his wings in the cooling air.

Marcus clawed the air with his fur-covered wings as he gained altitude, until he was high over the city, looking down on the streets filled with cars below. He wheeled around his building for a moment, getting oriented to the city. Then, with a strong flap of wings he headed to the northwest, reveling in the freedom of flight.

* * *

Julio Rodriguez cursed softly under his breath in Spanish as he watched the girl wiggle her ass as she walked up the sidewalk. *I could break her fucking neck*, he thought as Carla crossed the street and homed in on a John, an elderly man who was looking as Carla walked as if he wanted a little of that. She sidled up to him and ran a hand down his chest, laughing at something he said. He nodded to her question and looped his arm into hers. They turned and walked into the building he had been standing in front of. Carla's apartment was in the building, as well as her three children.

Julio knew that Carla was holding out on him. The whore had been one of his best producers until recently. He was sure that he still made the money she had. She took too many Johns into her apartment. Too many of them left with smiles on their faces. She was still taking in money, no matter what she had told him. So she was putting away his money and not giving it to him. That was like stealing as far as he was concerned.

In fifteen minutes the man was out of the building, a smirk on his face. Five minutes later Carla was back on the sidewalk, her dress not mussed and new lipstick on her face. She walked up and down the sidewalk, shaking her ass and smiling at the men who walked up and down the street. She waved at a man in an expensive car who rolled down his window and called to her. The buxom woman leaned into the window and talked in accented English that Julio could hear from his station at the front of his building.

"Julio," called out another of his girls, as he watched the man pull the car over to a curb and get out to follow Carla back to her building.

"What is it, Maria?. You got my money?"

"I'm a little short, Julio," said the short, dark skinned woman in Spanish.

Julio glared at her, towering over her as he clenched his fists, his biceps standing out on his bare arms, his chest heaving under his wife beater shirt. *They're all holding out on me*, he thought. *They're all a bunch of thieves.*

"Come inside, Maria," he said through clenched teeth. *Time to get rough, to make an example for the other girls.* Maria cringed and backed up, as Julio reached out and grabbed her arm. The woman cried out as his grip tightened and he dragged her up the steps and into the building.

Julio flung her into the living room as he slammed the door behind him. Maria fell to the floor on her hands and knees, crying as her skin burned on the rug. Julio flexed his arms, reveling in his strength, gained from hours each week in the gym. He walked heavily over to Maria, feeling a rush of adrenaline as he looked down at the frightened woman, smelling the sweat of her fear. He reached down and gripped her hair and pulled, lifting her up.

"Please no," she cried as tears came to her eyes. She rose up as he pulled. He had hoped to pull some of her red hair out of her head, but she was frustrating his effort by her quick scramble. His rage flared as his face grew hot. His right hand struck before he could think, slapping her hard in the left cheek. She grunted and cried as he brought his hand up over his shoulder and then backhanded her on the right side of her face.

"Puta," he growled. "You don't hold out on me, you hear. What you get with your pussy is mine. You hear me."

"Please," she cried as he released her hair and she fell back to her knees. "The ninos."

"I could care less about your brats, woman," he hissed as he stared down into her eyes. "Your pussy is mine. What you make is mine. And you will give me all of it. You hear, whore. I'll give you what I think you deserve. And if you don't have enough for the ninos then you must work harder."

He grabbed her arm and jerked her back to her feet. He grabbed the purse from her grasp and opened it, rummaging around and pulling out a small wad of twenty-dollar bills. He quickly counted the money and shoved it into his pants pocket. Then he grabbed her arm again in a tight grip, bringing tears to her eyes that ran down the bruising flesh of her face. He then jerked the arm hard, spinning her toward the front door.

"Now get out of here," he yelled. "If you ever hold out on me again you're dead, you hear me. Dead."

Maria fumbled at the door for a moment before pulling it open and stumbling outside. She left the door open in her haste to get away from him, and Julio cursed under his breath as he walked to it and looked at the woman walking quickly up the sidewalk away from his house.

"And close the fucking door next time," he screamed at her back. "I'm not trying to air condition the world."

He slammed the door behind him as he walked down the steps and onto the street. As he looked up he met the eyes of Carla, standing by the car that was beginning to pull out into the street. Her eyes were wide with fear. *Your turn next, bitch*, he thought, motioning her over with a finger.

* * *

Lucinda stared down at the giant of a man who was crooking a finger at one of his girls, while another of them stumbled down the street with tears streaming from a face quickly swelling from the abuse it had received. She had listened in on everything that had gone on in Julio's apartment. She had gripped the lip of the roof wall so tight that concrete had crumbled, wishing that she could burst into that hovel of despair and rescue the woman Maria. But she was bound by the ancient restrictions of her kind, and could not enter any dwelling for the first time uninvited.

The prey was motioning to one of his women to come over to him. *Probably so he can beat the hell out of her*, Lucinda thought, feeling the rage build up in her, battling to crowd out the hunger that had been taking hold of her for the past hour. She started to turn to go to the backside of the building when a snatch of song came from the man's pocket. She stopped and turned to watch the prey pull a cell phone from his pocket and put it up to his ear, waving the woman away. Lucinda sharpened her hearing to listen in on the conversation.

"Yeah," said Julio.

"How's things going, Julio," said the tinny voice on the other end in Unaccented English.

"Very good sir," said Julio, his voice instantly losing its normal sarcastic undertone. "What can I do for you tonight, sir?"

"Just calling to make sure my boy is OK," said the voice. "You read the paper today? Or watched the news?"

"No sir," said Julio. "I've been kind of busy with the girls tonight. And you know I sleep during the day."

"Well, someone out there is killing my people," said the voice. "You watch yourself. And make sure to call me if you see anything suspicious on the street, OK. You're one of my sets of eyes out there."

"Sure thing, boss," said Julio. "Maybe I'll even get the fuck for you."

"You just watch yourself and let me know if you see or hear anything. I've got people to take care of this kind of thing. People I pay very well to get rid of…, nuisances like this. You take care, Julio. And stay in touch."

"I will, Mr. Giovani. I will. Bye now, sir."

Julio folded the phone and put it back in his pocket. He glared for a second at the girl across the street before walking up the short steps to his porch stoop and opening the door, walking into his house and slamming the door behind him.

Lucinda walked to the back of the building she was on top of and climbed to the top of the wall, looking down at the small fenced in yard below and the triple line of laundry hanging over some cheap plastic children's playground toys. She listened for a second as her eyes scanned the yard. Nothing moved, to her sight or her hearing. She sniffed the air for a moment. She could smell the dog howling at the night a block down the street. But the dog in the building she stood on was not out in the yard, but still barking in the second floor apartment its owner lived in.

Lucinda leaped into the air and fell the two stories to the ground, landing lightly on her feet. She ran and leapt at the eight-foot privacy fence, grabbing the top and swinging herself over, landing on the grassy patch between two buildings and waiting for just a moment. After making sure that no one had seen her from the street she walked onto the sidewalk and crossed the road between the sparse traffic. She walked up the steps to her prey's building and pushed the ringer.

"What do ya want?" called a harsh voice from the first floor apartment to the left.

"I need to talk to you, sir," said Lucinda in a quavering voice, trying to put into it a feeling of fright that she did not feel.

A curtain was drawn and she saw Julio's face at the window, looking out at the porch and breaking into a smile as his eyes landed on her. Lucinda knew she was beautiful to men, and that she attracted them as a snake attracted a bird. She tried to look nervous as she gazed back at the man, setting an alarmed look on her face. The curtain fell back into place and moments later she heard a door opening and footsteps coming down a hall and up to the door. The door swung open and she found herself looking up at the tall, muscular man.

"Senorita," he said to her, licking his lips. "Ain't you a little young to be out this late at night."

"I ran away from home, sir," she said in her frightened, teenage voice. "My daddy was raping me and I couldn't get mama to believe me. So I ran away from home and came to the city."

"You don't have a place to stay?" asked Julio. "Maybe you're looking for one?"

"I heard that you can help girls get..., established on the street," said Lucinda. "I scared, sir. I would do anything, sir. Anything at all."

Julio motioned with his hand and turned to walk down the hall. He turned back when Lucinda did not follow. Lucinda felt as if she were rooted to the spot. She wanted to follow Julio. The Hunger was almost overwhelming at this point of the night. But she couldn't, yet.

"My mama taught me to wait until I was invited in before entering a man's home," she said, licking her lips nervously.

"Come in, chica," said the man. "My casa is su casa."

Lucinda felt the barrier that was between her and the house come down as she hurried into the hallway, her movements still showing her to be a frightened child looking for a refuge. She followed the man to the first door on the right of the hall as he pulled it open and motioned her in.

As she entered the living room she almost gagged on the stench coming from the kitchen. The living room itself had bags of garbage piled up by the door, beer bottles and overflowing ashtrays on the tables. A high-end stereo system on the bookshelves filled with CDs played Latin music, while a baseball game played on the wide screen plasma TV against one of the walls. A couch and a weight pulley machine completed the furnishings. A large mirror was on another wall, and Lucinda looked at it in fascination as it portrayed an image of the room. An image she did not occupy.

"So," said Julio, turning as he loomed over her. "What can I do for you? And more important, what can you do for me?"

Lucinda could smell the lust in him as he looked down at her. See the hunger in his eyes, the hunger that almost matched the hunger that was growing in her. She smiled up at him, a feral smile that made him recoil and step back a bit.

"Who the hell are you, chica?" he said, reaching behind his back to pull an automatic pistol from his waistband. He started to raise it toward Lucinda in a side reaching gangsta pose.

Lucinda exploded into a burst of speed. The man seemed to slow to a standstill in front of her. She pulled the gun out of his hand like jerking a toy out of the hands of a child, and then threw the weapon at the mirror. The speed left her and the world returned to normal, as the man backed up from her.

"What the fuck are you?" he yelled, stooping to pick up a heavy dumbbell from the floor. With a roar he flung it at her, aiming at her head.

Lucinda reached for the dumbbell and caught it as it flew toward her, tossing it over her shoulder. She took a step toward him as he backed into a corner.

"I'm your worst nightmare, chico," she said to him, her hand grabbing the front of his wife beater shirt and twisting the fabric, pulling him toward her. The fabric ripped apart at that moment, exposing the small silver crucifix on the dark skinned chest.

A feeling of panic overwhelmed her. She dropped the grasp she had on the remnants of the shirt as she stumbled back. Her eyes burned at the sight of the holy symbol, and she flung her hands up to cover her face as she hissed in terror. She wanted to kill him, to drink his blood and feed her hunger. But the holy symbol on the unholy man put a barrier between her and the man. A barrier of animal fear that overrode all of her other instincts.

"Are you on drugs, cunt," yelled Julio, grabbing another dumbbell as he watched her out of frightened eyes.

Lucinda backed away till she was near the door. Her instincts told her to go through the door, to flee into the night. Then her heel struck the dumbbell that had been thrown at her moments before. She fought down the fear for a moment and reached down to grasp the dumbbell, picking it up as she turned back toward Julio. She lifted it over her head and threw it at him with all of her might.

The dumbbell hit Julio in the stomach, blasting the breath from his body. He went down to his knees, grasping at his stomach as he coughed up the contents of his gut. In that instant the cross on his chest was covered up.

Lucinda felt the panic ebb as the holy symbol left her sight. The hunger grew in her, building with the rage that was directed at those who enslaved other humans for their own greed and lust for control. She took running steps toward Julio, her left hand grasping his long hair as she pulled him to his feet, her right hand flying to the cross around his neck as she felt the panic begin to come over her again. Her hand enveloped the cross, which burned into her flesh like hellfire. A high pitched scream erupted unbidden from her mouth as she pulled hard with her right hand, jerking the cross from the chain and tossing it behind her. She looked down at her throbbing hand, the red shape of the small cross burned into her palm.

"You have no right to wear that symbol, you unholy scum," she growled as she bent his head back with the iron grip she had on his hair. "Now tell me who you work for, scum. Tell me."

"Lucian Giovani," grunted the pimp through pain tight lips. Julio swung a heavy hand into Lucinda's face, followed by another. Lucinda rocked from the to her feeble punches and pulled his head to the side, exposing his neck.

"Now I send you to your true master," she hissed, baring her fangs. With a thrust of her head she buried the fangs into his neck, her instincts driving the canines unerringly into the pulsing jugular vein under his skin. Blood spurted into her mouth as she closed her lips over the wound, drinking the life force from his body. The life giving fluid flowed down her throat, feeding her hunger.

He was a big man, and she felt satiated before the last of the blood was sucked from his body. Still she continued to drain him as she sensed his heart fluttering to a stop. She held the heavy man up with her one hand as she sucked till nothing more came into her mouth. She moved her mouth away from the neck and jerked on his hair as she lifted the lifeless body high into the air, his toes trailing the floor. Then she reached her left hand over her shoulder and grasped the hilt of the big knife, pulling it free.

With a measured swing she took the head from the body. She held the head in her hand by the hair as she kicked the falling body into the weight machine, where it hit limply but heavily and fell over the bench. She tossed the head on top of the piled bags of garbage near the door and walked from the room.

There were loud voices on the street, people talking about the commotion that had come from Julio's apartment. Soon there would be police, as well as other hunters, all intent on finding and destroying her.

The door swung open onto the back yard behind the building and she strode out into the night. She was physically and spiritually satiated as she walked away from the building and into the darkness. She could hear the sirens in the distance as she ran through several yards, putting distance between herself and the site of the murder. In one yard she dodged as a dog on a long chain lunged at her. She fought down the urge to kill a beast that was only doing its job, protecting its master from a perceived threat. She left the barking dog behind as she slowed to a walk and headed down the empty neighborhood street.

* * *

Detective Lieutenant Jamal Smith swore softly to himself as he looked at the multitude of gawkers standing on the sidewalks, lit by the rotating blue and red strobe lights of the blue and whites at the scene. *Why do these fools always have to come out and get in the way*, he thought.

Uniformed officers were out on the sidewalk taking statements, three quarters of which he knew were going to result in a waste of time and manpower.

The forensics van was parked close to the entrance of the building, and a muffled flash seen through the curtains let him know that the cameraman was at work inside. Smith pulled a pad of paper out of its holder in the car and put a couple of mechanical pencils in his jacket pocket. A sergeant walked toward his car as he got out.

"What's the word, McCraw?" asked Smith, the sergeant falling in beside him as he walked toward the building.

"We have several statements from people who were on the street at the time of the murder," said the sergeant. "Two of them are going to come down to the station tomorrow to do pictures with the police artist."

"And what did they say they saw?" asked Smith, stopping to look over the gathered crowd. *Whore, addicts, dealers and pimps*, he thought. *Not the most reliable of witnesses, but all that we're gonna get.*

"A red haired woman entered the dwelling after talking with the victim," said McCraw. "About five eight to nine, slender, in solid black clothes that were not too expensive nor too cheap."

"And they saw no one else enter the place?"

"Not until the first unit arrived and the men went inside to find the body."

"Decapitated, I assume," said Smith as he walked up the step to the front door to be waved into the building by the officer guarding the door.

"Yes sir," answered the sergeant. "Stephens thinks that it had to be a large, strong man. Not a woman."

"Ok," said Smith, looking back over the crowd as a flash bulb flared, causing him to squint his eyes for a moment. *That's just great*, he thought. *Now I'll be on the front page of the Tribune.* "Keep the press clear. We don't need them stepping over our evidence."

Smith stepped over the yellow tape that blocked the doorway and walked the few steps into the hall. There were several officers in the hallway, talking about vampires and werewolves and other such nonsense. Smith shook his head as he walked into the ground floor apartment, to the sight of uniformed officers and plainclothes forensics men bustling through the room. He noted that the doorknob had the white powder used to dust for fingerprints, and one of the techs was snapping a picture of a dumbbell near the body that had already been prepped for prints.

"Lieutenant," said a soft voice behind him. Smith turned to look into the eyes of *Doc* Stephens, the chief of the forensics unit, bagging a head as if he were putting his lunch into the plastic container. "Two nights in a row, huh."

"Still think it was a man, doc?" asked Smith. "We have witnesses saying that a woman entered the premises about the time this happened."

"No way it was a woman," said Stephens, pointing with his free hand at the chalked outlines of where the body had lain on the bench. "I believe that whoever took our boy's head off was holding him up high, above his normal height. With one hand, because they needed the other to swing the knife. I got that from the splatter marks on the wall. And then they pushed the falling body against the weight bench. He didn't fall from where he stood. He weighed about 230 or so, before his head came off. It took a strong man to lift him up by the hair and take his head off with a single swing."

"So no way a slender woman could have done this?"

"No lieutenant. Maybe she let the killer into the house through the kitchen door, which was wide open when the uniformed officers got here, by the way. But a slender woman has nowhere near the strength to do this."

"She's not a normal woman," said a gravelly voice from the doorway. "I've been trying to tell you that."

Smith swore under his breath as he turned around to the sight of Jeffrey DeFalco. The agent looked like he hadn't slept since last night's murder. His eyes had bags under them, and there was beard stubble on his face.

"Still sticking with that vampire nonsense, eh Agent DeFalco?"

"It's not nonsense," growled DeFalco as he staggered into the room and closed with Smith. Smith could smell the rancid odor of alcohol on the man's breath. He frowned in disgust at the agent.

"It's not nonsense," repeated the drunken man. "And she'll look different the next time she strikes."

"It's a man, Agent DeFalco," said Smith in DeFalco's face. "And you are a disgrace."

"It's the dreams," said DeFalco. "I need to deaden the dreams."

Smith waved a uniformed patrolman over to him while he stared at DeFalco's bloodshot eyes.

"Take this man back to his hotel," he ordered the officer.

"I'm an agent doing his justifiable duty," slurred DeFalco. "You have no right to send me away from this crime scene."

"And place him under arrest if he refuses to go," ordered Smith. "Drunk and disorderly. And public intoxication."

"Just make sure that you send copies of all the transcripts to my office, detective," said DeFalco in the Brooklyn accent that had taken the Ivy League right out of his voice. The uniformed officer took his arm and started to lead him away. "Everything, you hear me. Don't you be holding out on me."

"A real nutcase," said Stephens.

"Yeah," agreed Smith. "But you don't think there might be something to what he's saying, do you?"

"Vampires," said Stephens, shaking his head. "I don't believe in them, or Werewolves, Zombies and Ghouls. No, this was done by a living, breathing human being. A large and strong human being."

"OK, doc," said Smith with a nod. "It was just a thought. Now I'm counting on you to give me what I need to get this sick bastard."

"The prints are being sent to the FBI in Washington as we speak," said Stephens. "If our boy left his prints on anything, and he's been in the military or has an arrest record, we'll find out who he is at least."

"And if he doesn't have a military or arrest record?"

"Then you're just going to have to catch him in the act, detective, before he can leave the scene."

And to do that we're going to have to establish some kind of pattern, thought Smith, *in a city of four hundred thousand. And that's not counting the million and a half people in the entire bay area. Our jurisdiction ends at the city limits. But the killer has no jurisdiction. So we're probably going to have to count on luck to get this boy.*

"Just find me what you can, doc," said Smith. "Just find me what I need to catch this maniac before he decides to kill some upstanding citizens."

*   *   *

Marcus stood outside the building, blending in with the crowd. He knew he appeared calm on the outside, but inwardly he fretted about all of the police in the neighborhood allowing the trail to go cold. He could smell her. The scent of the hunter that he needed to track, before she caused too much damage to the race. But he couldn't get into the building to pick up the start of the path she had trod. And there were too many police wandering around the neighborhood looking for clues to risk a circumference of the scene to pick up a trail that was getting colder by the minute.

Marcus growled low in his throat as a reporter tried to stick a microphone in his face. The man turned away to find another victim, as Marcus smelled the fear in his sweat. Marcus cursed to himself as he turned away from the reporter and pushed his way out of the crowd, listening to the protests of the mortals that got in his way.

I need to be more careful, thought Marcus. *Humans get curious about that which makes them afraid. And I can't afford to bring any more attention to our kind than is already being offered to them on a silver platter.*

Marcus circled the crime scene from several blocks out, blending into the shadows whenever a roving police car or foot patrol came near. At three blocks out and to the north he came across the scent he had been looking for. The scent of a hunter like himself. He followed the scent through backyards and across streets until he came to an alley, where he could scent the change that she had gone through. As a bat she had lifted into the sky at this point, and severed the trail that had been leading the Vampire Lord on.

Marcus growled into the night, his anger building, and with it the hunger that he had controlled for many days. Tonya and Gloria would not feed him tonight. He needed to kill something, and his thralls were too valuable for that kind of treatment. But he must be careful. It must be someone who would not be missed, and the body had to disappear. A shadow stumbled down the street, and Marcus focused his night vision to see a shambling hunched over man in dirty clothing, a paper bag grasped in one hand.

No one will miss a wino, he thought, as he began to silently trail his victim.

* * *

The sun was just coming over the horizon when the 7:03 express from Atlanta came into the renovated Union Station in downtown Tampa. O'Connor had been able to sleep most of the trip in the comfortable seat, but had woken an hour before the dawn and stared out into the darkness as the train made its way south. He had watched the lights of towns and lone dwellings go by the windows, wondering about the people that lived there. Their ordinary lives passing by, with no knowledge of the terrors that inhabited the fringes of the world.

O'Connor had an easy time spotting the welcoming committee on the concourse. Picking out a black cassock and white collar among the few people waiting for family and loved ones was relatively simple. *I wonder if this will be the red carpet*, he thought, *or the cold shoulder.* He knew that the Bishop of the Diocese of St. Petersburg would not let him come into town without questioning his motives.

O'Connor grabbed his carpet bag and walked to the exit of the car, making his way down the steps and out onto the concourse. The young priest was looking at a photograph in his hand, looking up at the people coming out of the train, then back to the photo. The priest did a double take as O'Connor walked out, put the photo into a pants pocket, then hurried over to O'Connor with a bowed head.

"Your excellency," said the young priest, going down to one knee with his hand out to accept the hand of the man he had come to meet.

"No longer," rumbled O'Connor in a resonate voice that had kept the attention of congregations through the years. "I'm officially just a Monsignor, though I prefer to go by the name of John."

"But you were the Archbishop of Washington excellency, on your way to becoming a Cardinal."

"That was a lifetime ago, my son," said O'Connor. "Now I am a simple priest, father…."

"Johnson. Timothy Johnson," said the priest, standing up and holding out a hand, this time in the traditional sign of greeting between two men of almost equal rank. O'Connor took the hand in a firm grip.

"John O'Connor. Glad to meet you. You have a car I assume?"

"Yes Monsignor. I've already arranged for your bags to be at your hotel. Can I take that?"

"No," said O'Connor. "I need the exercise. Lead on."

Father Johnson led the way through the station and onto the street to stop at a late model Taurus with a clergy plate on the front. He opened the passenger door and motioned for O'Connor to get in, then closed the door behind him, moving around the car to get into the driver's seat. With a beep of the horn and the twist of the wheel Johnson accelerated into the flow of traffic, to the honking of horns and curses of other drivers.

"You're not from around here, are you?" asked O'Connor after saying a quick prayer.

"No sir," said Johnson with a chuckle. "I grew up in the City, New York. Lost the accent at Notre Dame."

"You know you could have stayed at the Diocese Cathedral in St. Pete," continued Johnson. "You didn't have to spring for a hotel room."

"Then I would have too many people asking questions of me," said O'Connor. "You know how people like to talk."

"About vampires," said the young priest. "That's what everyone has been talking about the last couple of days."

"No comment," said O'Connor with a frown. "My mission is my mission. And I require no cooperation. Only that people get out of my way."

Johnson turned his attention back to the road as O'Connor gave a satisfied grunt. *The young man might think me a nutcase*, thought O'Connor. *But being thought a nutcase serves me well.*

* * *

Bishop Wislowski's Tampa office was nowhere near as opulent as his abode at the Cathedral in St. Petersburg. But the Bishop was known as a very hands on ruler of his domain, and an office in the other major city of the Diocese was keeping in character. He stood up as O'Connor was ushered into the room, coming around his desk and holding his right hand out. O'Connor went to one knee and took the Bishop's hand in his, bringing the signet ring of the church hierarchy to his lips.

"Have a seat, Monsignor," said Wislowski, moving back to behind his desk, as O'Connor took a seat in the upholstered chair set in the center of the room.

Like the chair of a victim of the inquisition, thought O'Connor. *And where are the inquisitors?*

"I'll get right to the point, Monsignor O'Connor," said Wislowski, looking over his steepled fingers. "I don't want you here. The Council of American Bishops doesn't want you here. The police and the city officials would not want you here if they knew of your presence."

"But I have the permission of the Holy Father," said O'Connor, playing his trump. "He puts more faith in me than all of the rest of you combined."

"Because he was raised a peasant in a land of superstitious peasants," said the Bishop. "A man who was raised with stories of vampires and werewolves with his mother's milk."

"Are you so sure that they are untrue?" asked the priest. "The Holy Father believes that there is evil in the world. Do you not?"

"Oh yes," said the Bishop with a nod of his head. "There is evil enough in the world without bringing fantasy into the mix. Men have become experts at the doing of evil through the centuries. I am sure that no imaginary creature of the night can compare with some of the men in our jails. Or roaming our streets."

"The Holy Father believes in my quest," said O'Connor, standing up from his chair to walk toward the desk. "As long as he gives his blessing to this enterprise you have no say in where I go or what I do."

"I knew you would have an attitude," said the Bishop, standing himself and glaring at the priest. "Yes, you have the permission of the Holy Father to engage in this witch hunt. And I will put no obstacles in your way. Nor will I allow any of the resources of this Diocese to aid you in this insane quest. Do you hear me, Monsignor O'Connor?"

"I hear you, Bishop Wislowski," said O'Connor, placing his hands on the desk and leaning to bring his face close to that of the Bishop's. "I ask for no aid or comfort from your precious Diocese. But I also will still put my life on the line for you and your parishioners, as well as all of the other innocents who live in this city."

"Just remember what I said," cautioned the Bishop, drawing back from the intensity of the man. "If you land afoul of the authorities it is on you to get yourself out of the trouble you caused. If you land in jail then you will have to make bail, or rot in a cell until they decide to let you go."

"Fine with me, your Excellency," said O'Connor. "I prefer to work alone. Are we through here?"

"The audience is ended," agreed the Bishop. "You know I don't approve of your methods, but I have no power to make you leave. So go with God my son."

The Bishop held his ring hand out one more time, over the desk. O'Connor took the hand and brought the ring to his lips, showing his respect for the office if not the man. Then he turned and walked out of the office, his footfalls sounding heavy on the polished wooden floors.

O'Connor picked up his rental car outside of the offices, a late model Thunderbird. It was a short drive to the hotel near I4, and O'Connor was in his room minutes after the end of the audience. His laptop was out of the carpetbag in an instant, even before he had taken the time to unpack his other bags. With a couple of keystrokes he was at the Vatican Website. A password and a couple of more strokes granted him access to the hidden areas of the site, and the database that he was one of the few on Earth privy to.

*   *   *

Tashawn Kent didn't have access to any sophisticated databases. But his instincts were normally good enough to get him what he wanted. Especially since he had become one of the undead.

"I don't understand, Tashawn," said his boy Marvin as Tashawn pulled himself out of his coffin. "We had it going up in Philly, man. With you as enforcer we had no problems with any of the other players. So tell me again why we're here in this little burg."

"I want her blood," said Tashawn, flexing his twenty-one inch thick arms. He had tried to stay in shape in the years since the Eagles cut him from the squad. It had been difficult to keep his defensive tackle's body in that kind of shape. But since crossing over it had been no problem at all.

"Her blood will make me stronger. Her blood will make me invincible."

"My god," said Marvin. "You can already lift a luxury car over your head. How much stronger do you need to be."

"I am still a child, brother," said Tashawn. "You know the thing about living forever?"

"Sure," said Marvin, twisting the top off a bottle of beer and offering it to his lifelong homeboy. Tashawn shook his head and Marvin brought the bottle up to his own lips to take a swig. "You live forever as a vampire. But most of you actually die before the first year. Cause you're stupid."

Tashawn bared his fangs and laughed as his friend blanched at the display.

"I don't mean you're stupid, brother," said Marvin. "I mean your kind is when you first start walking the night. So for most of you the eternal life thing is so much BS."

"But we can gain the strength of the vampires we kill and drain," said Tashawn. "We get stronger, and gain their experience too."

"But she hasn't been around all that long," said Marvin. "You told me that yourself. Why not find someone with more time under their belt?"

"Because they might be too much for me," said Tashawn. "And with her it's personal."

"She made you a vampire," said Marvin. "I thought you liked being a vamp. I mean man, you are the shit on the street. Weren't no one would take you on."

"Do you want to join me?" said Tashawn, baring his fangs again. "I could bring you over easy."

"Not me man," said Marvin, backing up till his back hit the motel room wall. "I like being alive, man."

"Your choice," said Tashawn. "The bitch didn't give me a choice. And she was trying to do me for good. If something hadn't interrupted I wouldn't be a vampire. I'd be rotting meat in a Philly graveyard. So it's personal, and I want to return the favor to her.

"But enough of that," said Tashawn. "I'm hungry. Let's go get me something to eat."

Marvin nodded his head as he put on his jacket. Tashawn could smell the fear in his friend. The fear that one day he would be on the menu of his old friend. *Maybe that day will come*, thought Tashawn. *But not now.* Now it was nice to have a mortal who could think for himself, unlike the thralls he had seen in other vamps.

Chapter 3

"You're gonna love this, Lieutenant."

Jamal Smith hated hearing those words as he entered the station house. He had only been up for an hour, after only sleeping four hours during the height of the day. Sometimes he thought that the only sunshine he saw was that of sunrise over the bay area. He turned a baleful glance over at the young female detective, standing there with a folder in her hand held out in offering to her superior.

"You read it to me, Justine," he ordered as he took a sip of the strong coffee that was part and parcel of police work on the overnight shift. Smith tried to adjust his blurry eyes to take in the paper lying on his desk. *Vampire? Strikes Again?* stated the headlines.

"We got a match back from the FBI and one of the sets of prints we sent them. The smaller set from the dumbbell and the back door knob."

"The woman we assumed?" said Jamal. "And I guess we got a match on the victim's as well?"

"Yes sir, and it matched the ID that we came up with from the remains," said Justine, brushing a stray blond strand from her forehead. "But the woman is the interesting one."

"OK. Give me the short version."

"We have the prints of one Lucinda Taylor, AKA Lucinda Porter. Porter being her maiden name. Born in Hershey, Pennsylvania. Yeah, the chocolate town. She got a BS in History at the City College of New York and was working on her Master's at Stony Brook when she started having trouble."

"What kind of trouble?"

"Police called to her apartment for several domestics. She refused to press charges on her prince of a husband. And then he threw her out on the street. Fell in with the wrong crowd and got picked up on some drug charges. Then she got hooked on Heroin and ended up doing tricks on the street for her drugs. Several arrests for hooking."

"God," groaned Smith, thinking of his own daughter at Florida A & M. Such a promising future, lost to drugs. "So how'd she get down here? And what's her connection to Julio Garcia?"

"None that I can figure, lieutenant," said Justine. "But here's the part that gonna mess with your head."

"Hit me," said Smith, taking another sip of coffee.

"Ms. Taylor was killed by her pimp six years ago."

"What the fuck," said Jamal. "Are they sure?"

"Sure enough to have pictures of her laid out on a slab in the Buffalo morgue. DNA match, fingerprints, the works. She was killed, alright. But her fingerprints have turned up at other murder scenes up and down the East Coast."

"So how'd they end up in Tampa? If she's laid out in a New York grave."

"Actually Hershey," said Justine. "Her parents flew her home for the funeral. And I have no idea."

"Because she rose from the dead," said Jeffrey DeFalco, walking up to the pair.

Smith looked the agent over with a sneer. But tonight the FBI man looked the part. Clean pressed suit over starched shirt and dark tie. His eyes looked clear as well, like he had gotten a good day's sleep and had stayed away from the bottle.

"Don't give me that undead crap, agent," said Smith. "There's got to be a rational explanation."

"So you tell me why her grave was found empty the day after the funeral," said DeFalco. "You come up with a rational excuse."

Justine shook her head in agreement, holding the folder out for Smith. The detective took the folder and laid it on his desk, open to the photo of a pretty girl in a casket.

"Sick people robbing a grave," said Smith. "It happens."

"And two years later that sick fuck came back," said DeFalco, "and stole three cubic yards of soil from the gravesite."

"And why would they do that?" asked Smith.

"Because the undead must sleep in the soil in which they were laid to rest," said DeFalco, a wild look in his eye. "And our girl is smart. She wanted to have lots of the soil she needed, so she could have a number of bolt holes, now and in the future."

"I don't know, DeFalco," said Smith. "Sounds pretty nutty to me. But here. You have a look over this folder. It came from your agency but it's part of our case now. So you can have access to it."

"Thanks," said DeFalco, sticking out a hand to refuse the folder. "I've memorized it. You might want to also, so you can understand what you're dealing with."

DeFalco turned and walked away, muttering something under his breath.

It's bad enough, thought Smith, *to have to deal with the normal freaks who called in information to the cops. But to have to deal with a Fed who's one of them.* Smith shook his head again, then looked up at the expectant young detective whose training he had taken upon himself.

"Let's deal with the impossible later, Justine," he said. "Let's make our plans for tonight. Now where do you think our boy is going to strike?"

* * *

The thing that really sucked about being a vampire, Lucinda thought as she woke up, were the vivid horrifying dreams that haunted her each and every night. And they replayed like a movie of her life, one after another after another, in sequence, each and every night. Lucinda shuddered as she recalled tonight's.

She thought about the dream for a moment. How she had woken in total darkness, reaching up and hitting hard wood with her fingernails. She could feel the panic begin to take hold of her. She scratched at the covering overhead and kicked her feet. She didn't know where she was, but it wasn't a place she wanted to be.

And then the second feeling came over her, even stronger than the fear. The hunger. The ravening hunger that gnawed at her guts, and drove every other thought out of her mind. She grimaced as she thought of how the hunger controlled her in those days, completely suborning her actions to her instincts. She struck out with her fists, and was surprised when her hands went completely through the strong thick wood overhead. Surprise again turned to fear as musty earth fell through the hole.

With strength born of desperation, and something else that she couldn't name at that time, she pulled the wood overhead into a series of small slats and splinters. Then she dug at the earth above. She could smell the stale air of the coffin, for she had figured that much out, and couldn't understand why she wasn't short of breath. Then she noticed that she wasn't even breathing. She redoubled her efforts and dug and dug with her claw like hands. Then a hand broke through into the air, and she pulled herself out of the ground, spitting the dirt out of her mouth and wiping it from her eyes.

It was dark in the cemetery, but her eyes seemed to cut through the darkness to reveal the grave markers as if a diffuse illumination existed in the air itself. Lucinda looked over at the closest marker, her eyes opening wide as she saw the name on the stone.

Lucinda Porter Taylor
Born March 11, 1976
Died March 17, 2000

So it hadn't been a dream, she thought. She had died on that cold Philadelphia night. She had died, or was dying, when the other face came into her narrowing field of vision. A face with lips moving in speech, but she could not hear. And then the face moved nearer, and she felt a sharp pain in the side of her neck that paled to the pain of her cut throat, but had a sweetness that cut through the feeling of death that was coming over her. She could feel the darkness growing over her visual field, and the fear of dying had left her.

And now she was here, in a cemetery. But how could she be here if she had died in Philadelphia? She looked down at the dirty gown, a garment she would have never chosen for herself. She concentrated her awareness onto herself, as her hand went to her throat. But the wound was gone, not even the ridge of scar tissue that would be expected if it had healed. And she noticed again that her chest was not rising and falling, that she was not breathing, but felt no need for the air that surrounded her.

Lucinda put her hand on her chest under the dress, and cried out. She felt nothing. Her heart was not beating. But how could she be alive and walking above ground without a heartbeat, without breath in her body.

Then all thought of life or death left her as the hunger hit her in her guts, doubling her over. Like going cold turkey on heroin, but a hundred times worse. She felt like she had to eat, something. She didn't know what it was she needed, but knew she needed it, now.

She heard footsteps in the distance, coming to her ears as if they were within feet of her. Her instincts told her to go toward the steps. That what she needed would be given to her if she went to the footsteps. So she hurried into the night, jumping the high fence that surrounded the cemetery, concentrating totally on the hunger now, with no thought to the impossibility of her twelve-foot leap into the air.

She smelled the woman before she saw her. A sweet smell that told her she was near what she needed. The smell of the blood pulsing in the stranger's veins. Then the middle aged woman was within sight, walking down the sidewalk that skirted the cemetery. Lucinda could hear the beat of the woman's heart, the pulsing of her blood, and knew what she needed to do. She ran toward the stranger, coming at her out of the darkness.

The narrow faced brunette looked at her with wide eyes as Lucinda came at her like a projectile. Lucinda ran into the woman and carried her to the ground, clamping a hand over the woman's mouth before she could utter a scream. The smell of the blood was overwhelming now, and Lucinda felt her lips curls back as she brought her face to the woman's neck. Lucinda's jaw opened wide, and she bit down hard with her extended canines, as the victim groaned in terror. The sweet blood spurted out, its iron smell strong in her nostrils. Lucinda placed her lips over the wound and started to suck, feeling the blood and something else, something intangible, flood into her body. Feeding her hunger.

In minutes the woman lay limp on the ground, as Lucinda felt the hunger ebbing, then retreating in her consciousness. She felt sated. Then she looked into the dead staring eyes of the innocent woman she had taken the life from. And she sat on the ground next to the woman and tried to cry the tears that would not come.

* * *

Lucinda cleared her mind of the past as she looked out over the city from her perch upon the roof of the high rise hotel. Below her lay the Port of Tampa, where freighters and cruise ships alike were docked, while a number of cranes and forklifts unloaded the products of the world for the people of Florida. To the north a set of blinking lights lifted into the air, as the sounds of jet engines came to her ears. A flight from Tampa International, taking tourists and businessmen back to their homes. To the south another set of blinking lights, as a transport lifted from MacDill, taking equipment and personnel to some far-flung outpost of the nation.

I must be the hunter now, she thought. She could sense the presence of her mistake in the city. The scumbag she had killed but not finished, who had risen to stalk the world. He was hunting her, as was the ancient one she had sensed before. As she hunted him, to try and rectify her mistake. Unfortunately her senses only told her that he was somewhere in the city, not his exact location. Fortunately they could not pinpoint her location either.

There were other hunters on her trail as well. The priest had to be in town by now. And she had smelled the scent of the Government Man the night before. But she couldn't do anything about them but avoid them. She had pledged when she had gotten her freedom, made a pact with God, that no innocents would fall to her fangs. No matter what they tried to do to her. But she did not trust her instincts, and felt that she might harm them if push came to shove.

Lucinda raised her arms to her side and willed the transformation from woman to animal. She felt the change come over her, faster now with the practice she had in the years she had been a night stalker. Where at one time it had taken minutes to change, now she was fully into the change in seconds, flapping her wings as she left the rooftop and flew over the city.

She knew where she was going tonight. She could see the luxurious house from the air as she headed northwest. It was time to go for bigger prey tonight. Prey whose death would make a bigger difference than the deaths of those subordinates who had preceded them. A few minutes of night air over her fur and she was there, over the sprawling one story in a gated community where the leader of scum lived protected from the effects his criminal activities brought to his community.

She wheeled over the house, looking down into the brightly lit backyard, where people gathered about the large swimming pool. Closed top barbeque grills wafted smoke into the air, Latino music blared from loudspeakers facing inward from the edges of the property. Respectable looking men stood talking in casual clothing with drinks in their hands, while women watched the many children swarming in and out of the pool. She quickly spotted the hired muscle; the men wore jogging suits with bulges under the zip up sweatshirts. There were a half dozen of them scattered about the property, a few walking security around the ten foot tall privacy fence.

Lucinda swooped lower, looking for a place of concealment. There were none near the fence. She could tell that the yard had been laid out with observation and fields of fire in mind. But there was a gazebo near a stand of rose bushes, where the light was diffuse. A rendezvous for lovers, where they could have the illusion of privacy in the stronghold of Lucian Giovani.

She landed on the rail of the gazebo, using her heightened senses to make sure that no one was looking her way. Her bat form hopped onto the floor, and she laid herself out as she willed the transformation back to human form. She slowly stood up as she looked around the yard, seeing no one looking her way. Feeling confident that she had entered the midst of her enemies without their awareness, she walked out of the gazebo and headed toward the pool.

Men could see a tall, stately redhead walking gracefully toward the pool. Her blue eyes caught the light in a hypnotic manner; her long hair flowed behind her in the night air, while the black cat suit and short black skirt accentuated the curves of her body.

Lucinda could feel the eyes of the males in the party staring her way as she walked across the yard. She was counting on the numbers of party goers to cover her appearance. That though no one would remember her coming to the party; all would figure that someone had let her in and that she belonged there. And seeing the lust in their eyes made her realize that most would not care how she got there. Most would be trying to figure out how they could get her into their beds at the end of the night.

A trio of dogs growled at her, then began barking as the hair rose on the backs of their necks. The two biggest crouched and started for her

"Shut up," yelled one of the muscle, pulling at the leash of a big German Shepard that tried to join the pack.

Lucinda bared her teeth and she gazed at the dogs. The barking stopped as they whimpered, then slunk off with their tails between their legs. Lucinda ignored them and turned her attention back to the humans at the party.

So many targets, she thought as her sandaled feet hit the flag stone deck around the pool. The death of any of them would improve the world. But one in particular would make the greatest impact. And her eyes locked on him as she walked toward the largest group of men.

Lucian Giovani was a man of moderate height, with the arms of the longshoreman he had begun his career as. In his early fifties, with graying hair and intense green eyes, his yachtsman's tan gave the man a healthy glow.

Lucinda could feel the beating of the man's heart as she walked up beside him, licking her lips and smiling as she felt the heart rate increase. She snatched a drink from a passing tray and brought it to her lips as she looked deeply into the man's eyes. She could taste the flavor of good rum over coke, and took a hefty swig of the drink that would not affect her in the least.

"You might want to go easy there , miss…"

"Lucinda. Lucinda Taylor. And I can handle my liquor."

She again ran her tongue lightly over her upper lip, moistening it. She knew that she would most likely vomit the liquor up later. Not because of intoxication. Her body did just not accept most things she could put down to her stomach. It only accepted the fluid that she craved so much. She could feel the hunger for it growing as she looked at Giovani, but she pushed those feelings down. There would be time enough for them later, when they were in private.

"We haven't met before, have we?" asked the crime boss, flashing her a smile. "I would never forget a face like yours."

"No," she said, shaking her head. "We never met. But I've heard all about you. And I've so wanted to meet you."

She could feel the man being drawn into her eyes. Feel his soul becoming hers.

"Who did you come with?" asked one of the other men.

"Who cares who she came with," said Giovani. "She's over here talking with us now."

A scrawny six year old came running up to the group, water falling from his hair to splatter the flagstones. He ran into the legs of Giovani, clasping the bare legs below the shorts in a tight grip.

"This is my grandson, Gino," he said, rubbing his hand through the child's hair.

Gino looked up at Lucinda with a smile on his face. The smile fled as he met the vampire's eyes, and he edged away from his grandfather and turned, running back to the other children with a wide-eyed glance over his shoulder.

"I don't know what's wrong with these kids these days," said Giovani, looking back into her eyes.

Children know when there's a danger about, she thought, as she felt the hunger rise in her at the proximity of the pure life forces that were the younger members of the human race. *And they don't feel the sexual fascination we exude.*

"I don't really care all that much about kids," she said, laying a hand on his forearm. "I prefer, adult, activities."

Giovani looked down at the Rolex on his left wrist and whistled.

"I think it might be time to get these kids to bed," he said. There were groans and shaking heads from most of the children. Gino held onto the legs of a woman who looked like his mom and stared at Lucinda. "It's a school night. They need their sleep."

Parents began to gather the children up and make their way to the side gate, where a pair of muscle positioned themselves. Several of the men noticed their boss' fascination with the beautiful woman and said their farewells, following the women and children out of the yard. A few of the people continued to stand around the pool and drink.

"Why don't we go inside and talk about adult activities," said Lucian Giovana, putting his arm around Lucinda's shoulder ad steering her toward the house. Lucinda let herself be directed to the glass doors, where another muscle was standing. The man held up his hands.

"Carlos is a little too protective of me sometimes," said Giovani, pulling his arm off of her shoulders. Carlos took her purse and ran his hands inside. "I'm sure you understand."

"Of course," agreed Lucinda, as Carlos ran his hands over her body, feeling for any concealed weapons. She smiled at Giovani as Carlos ran his hands down one leg, then another.

"I think she's safe enough, Carlos," said Giovani, putting his arm back around Lucinda and steering her toward the open glass doors. Lucinda stopped in her tracks and looked at Giovani.

"My home is your home," he said. She smiled at him and allowed him to lead her through the door.

To Lucinda's eyes the back room of the mansion looked like it was lit up with spotlights, though she knew to the humans in the room it was elegantly darkened. Good paintings hung on the wall, and a large arched opening led into an enormous kitchen. Giovani moved her into an even larger room to the front of the house, a room with a huge fireplace and expensive looking vases on antique furniture. And then they were in a hallway.

Giovani opened the first door on the left and led her into a large bedroom. He dimmed the lights and took her hand, leading her to the huge round bed in the center of the room.

Lucian Giovani let go of her hand and grabbed her shoulders. Lucinda shrugged him away as a look of confusion awoke in his eyes. She smiled at him as she pulled a breath spray from her purse and squeezed a couple of squirts into her mouth. She then grabbed the crime boss by his shoulder and molded her body against his, pressing her lips fiercely onto the sensuous lips of the man.

Lucian moaned as he ran his hands over Lucinda's body. She caressed his shoulders and ground her groin against him. Her hand went to his shirt and pulled open the buttons. Then she stepped back from him with a smile and pulled her skirt down to the floor as he fumbled off his pants and briefs. She pulled the cat suit over her shoulders and shrugged down out of the tight black garment, till she was standing naked before him.

His breath caught as he looked at the pale beauty of her body. Her eyes grew wide as she saw the erect size of the man. He grabbed her arm as he lay back on the bed, pulling her onto the mattress with him. She reached her hand down and grasped him, stroking her palm up and down. Giovani hissed and jerked for a second and she released him.

"Your hands are so cold," he said, a frown on his face.

"I have a little medical condition," said Lucinda. "My hands and feet can get really cold. But other parts of me are very warm, and wet."

Giovani moaned as she kissed him on the neck. A hand reached down and caressed her breast. She pulled away and looked into the man's eyes, and knew that he was hers.

Lucinda kissed him again on the neck, dragging her canines across the tanned flesh. Lucian moaned, and she drove the canines into the flesh and to the vein below. The man stiffened under her for a second, then moaned and relaxed as she planted her lips on his throat and began to suck. As she felt the life force drain out of him the hunger rose in her. The beast was taking over. But she still had information to gather. It took all of her will to pull her mouth away from the neck as she pushed her fingers into the wound.

"Who is your boss, Lucian?" she asked, staring into his blurry eyes. "Who gives you all of this?"

"George Padillas," he answered in a strained voice.

"The shipping magnate?"

"Yes."

"Thank you," she said, then planted her lips back on the neck and began to suck the life out of him. When she felt his heart flutter, then stop, she drained the last of the fluid from his body. She released him as she stood up from the bed, feeling unclean from the touch of the man. She forced the revulsion down as she looked around the room. That was when she noticed the security camera in the corner, sweeping her way with a red light on.

* * *

Carlos had gone to the security room after letting his boss and the boss' woman for the night into the house. He thought that she was as gorgeous a woman as he had ever seen. That was someone he wouldn't mind having sloppy seconds with. So he decided to look in on the boss and see what she looked like while she was being fucked.

"What the fuck," said Carlos as the camera panned toward the bed. The boss was lying on the bed with his eyes wide open, unblinking, while the fine looking naked woman stood over him. The woman looked at the camera and Carlos felt a chill go up his spine as the red eyes met his. The woman snarled and Carlos quickly made the sign of the cross when the elongated canines came into view.

He only came out of his shock when the bitch jumped onto the body of his still boss, straddling him with her athletic legs. She grabbed the sides of his head and started twisting, turning it around until the face was turned into the bed at an impossible angle. She continued to twist, and the microphone on the camera brought the sound of cracking bone to the security room. Carlos slammed his hand down on the panic button as the woman heaved with her arms and the head came off. She threw it at the camera. The last thing Carlos saw in the room was the head flying up toward the camera. Then the camera went dead as the decapitated head smashed into it.

* * *

Lucinda was starting to reach for her clothes as the door to the room was flung open. She came out of the stoop, her clothes and purse forgotten, as the two large men burst into the room, big automatic pistols leading the way. She bared her fangs as she looked for a way out. But the room had been constructed with the security of the boss in mind, and the only way out was through the door, and the two men.

The guns tracked onto her as she glanced left, then right. They barked their first shots as she made up her mind. She moved straight ahead, blurring with her speed. A large slug cracked past her left ear. Then another hit her left shoulder. She could feel a moment of resistance as the bullet passed through her undead form. Then it was out and flying into the wall beyond.

Lucinda closed a hand onto the jacket of the man to the right, jerking up with all of her strength and lifting the thug from the floor. She twisted and flung him through the air with the strength of ten women, sending him toward the far wall. The vampire turned her attention toward the other thug who was bringing his pistol down on her head as she heard the meaty thunk of the first man hit the wall. Her sensitive hearing could make out the crack of breaking bones just before the heavy automatic hit her in the temple.

Her head rocked just a bit from the strike, as she grabbed the man's lapels and jerked his face down. She brought her knee up and into the downward moving face, feeling the shock radiating through her thigh as the facial bones of the man broke up under the hard strike. She released his lapels and let the limp body fall to the floor, leaping the man and landing lightly on her feet in the hallway.

A burst of rounds flew through her, each one causing a slight jerk of her body as they passed through her as if she were made of cobwebs. Lucinda looked up with a snarl as she turned toward the source of the rounds. Carlos stood at the end of the hall with a small machine pistol in his hand, bucking as it sent rounds down the hall.

"What the hell are you?" he screamed as the weapon clicked on the empty chamber. He reached frantically into his jacket, trying to fumble another magazine, then tried to ram it home. But as his hands shook the new magazine refused to go where the old one still resided.

Lucinda took off in a sprint toward the man, moving faster than humanly possible, faster than the swiftest sprinter. She lowered her shoulder and took Carlos in the ribs, feeling the bones crack as she lifted him into the air. The man struck his right shoulder and arm against the wall, grunting out his breath. Lucinda was past him and into the living room as he slid down the wall to the floor, the machine pistol falling from nerveless fingers as consciousness fled.

Lucinda pivoted on her right foot, turning toward the family room, as more bullets whizzed past her, the sound of cracking plaster and breaking porcelain sounding to her sensitive ears. One large man, with the mass of a football player, came straight at her from the glass doors, lowering his shoulders and reaching his arms out into a classic tackle. Lucinda leapt into the air and brushed the ceiling as she flew over his form, which was falling to the floor after not meeting the resistance it had been preparing itself for. The vampire did a turn in the air, as she thanked herself for the gymnastics lessons her mom had insisted that she take, and landed lightly on her feet.

She could sense that the door before her was locked, and she didn't have the key. So going into a crouch and out again she sprung toward the double doors and crashed through the glass, leaving jagged hanging splinters behind her. Women screamed as she propelled her naked form across the flagstones. One man dropped his drink and made a grab for her, but a strong backhand lifted him from his feet and into the pool. By the time he hit the water with a splash Lucinda was speeding across the grass lawn, reveling in the cool passage of the night air over her bare skin.

From ten feet out she went into a quick crouch and sprung into the air, her feet clearing the ten-foot privacy fence as more rounds cracked past her. Dogs barked at her as they struggled to catch her and were thwarted by the fence. Her feet hit lightly onto the grass of another lawn and she sprang ahead, swerving to avoid another large dog that was coming at her across the lawn.

Lucinda leapt into the air again, spreading her arms as she arched up to twenty feet. She willed the transformation again, feeling her limbs shorten and the fur thrust out through her skin. She gave a screech to the night as she flapped her wings and disappeared into the darkness.

* * *

Monsignor John O'Connor could smell the telltale odor of the lair from down the tunnel. He had been walking through the miles of accessible storm drains for many hours, starting before the sun had disappeared. The priest had some trepidation at going underground in search of a creature that made the night her home. But, as he put his hand on the large, ornate cross hanging from his neck, the cross that had been personally blessed by the Pope, he felt armored in his faith. The vampire that touched him would be a creature of Satan struck down by the power of the almighty.

O'Connor was dressed in his normal short-sleeved black shirt and white collar, but wore a thick set of black denim jeans and black high top athletic shoes. The better to work his way through the close confined of the tunnels. A holstered PPK was attached to his belt, his untucked shirt over the top of the pistol. The concealed weapon's license the Papal legate had arranged for him sat in his wallet. He took comfort in the pistol, and in the seven bullets that sat in the magazine. Each round was tipped with an inlaid silver cross, and the leads had soaked overnight in holy water and then blessed by O'Connor himself.

His other weapons and equipment were in the common student's backpack he carried over his right shoulder. O'Connor knew that he was as well-equipped as a man could be to hunt the undead. Whether that was equipped enough remained to be seen, but the Monsignor was sure that the Papal Authority would not have sent him into a situation where his soul would be imperiled beyond his ability to protect it.

O'Connor switched off the powerful police flashlight as he pulled the night vision goggles from where they sat on his brow to back over his eyes. A flip of a switch powered up the Starlight lenses. A slightly grainy image appeared to his view, as the glasses amplified the tiny amount of ambient light in the tunnel ten thousand times. The flashlight would have given a clearer picture, but also would have given him away to anyone waiting in the tunnel.

The sickly sweet smell hit his nostrils again. He had smelled it many times before. It had permeated the lairs of the dozen vampires who had fallen to him. And it had lain like a miasma of death over the lairs he had reached too late, after its occupant had already moved on.

O'Connor stopped and listened for a moment at the small entrance to the service chamber that led off of the tunnel. He pulled the PPK from the holster and made sure the safety was on, then hunched over and shuffled the couple of feet into the chamber. As he made it through the entrance he stood and raised the pistol in front of him, sweeping it back and forth to cover the chamber.

When nothing moved he let out the breath he had been holding, taking in a deep breath that almost gagged him on the odor. He walked slowly to the coffin, and breathed another sigh as he saw that it was empty. He reached his left hand into the box and felt the thin layer of soil within. He scanned the room one more time, feeling a bit of disappointment come over him, even though he had known that she would be out and about her evil tasks.

With his left hand O'Connor pushed the Starlight glasses up to his forehead and turned them off, then pulled the flashlight from his belt and flipped it on. He swept it around the chamber, wondering yet again why there were never any bodies in her lair. Every other vampire home he had been in had at least a body or two hanging from the ceiling or lying in a corner. But her lairs were always well ordered, clean even, with none of the detritus normally found among the undead.

If she's out then she is going for another victim, thought the priest. He said a quick prayer for the soul of the man she was going to kill tonight, wondering how much good it would do. Unlike other vampires this one didn't allow her victims to rise. And the people she killed tended to be the ones that were on their way to hell in the first place. Which didn't make her any less the evil spawn of Satan, and his sworn enemy.

O'Connor pulled the backpack off of his shoulder and placed it against the coffin, unzipping it open. After digging around for a second he pulled a small flat metal container from the bag and twisted it open, revealing a number of small discs of unleavened bread. The hosts he had blessed himself after an all-night vigil mass he had said for no one.

He took a couple of the wafers out of the container and twisted it shut, placing it carefully back into the pack. Standing back over the coffin, O'Connor began to break one of the wafers into small pieces and place them on top of the soil in the box. When one was gone he started to break the other one, until both wafers were spread among the soil, sterilizing it against the undead and making it useless as a resting place.

Next O'Connor pulled a spray bottle from the backpack and walked over to the large chest that sat against the wall. The priest opened the chest, cringing for a moment as the hinges squealed. He looked around the chamber, which was still empty, then turned his attention back to the chest, which was filled with women's clothing. He pulled some of the clothing from the chest and aimed the spray bottle at the remaining clothes, squirting liquid over the clothes. The fabric absorbed the holy water quickly. O'Connor then put some of the clothing on the floor back into the chest and sprayed it, repeating the procedure until it had all been treated. When the vampire returned she would find nothing in the chamber of use to her.

O'Connor flipped the flashlight off and pulled the Starlight glasses back over his eyes, engaging their power.

He moved to the far side of the chamber and sat down against the wall, placing the flashlight on his lap. The priest moved his lips silently as he said a series of prayers and prepared to maintain a vigil through the night, waiting for the return of the vampire.

*   *   *

Lucinda could feel a presence over her lair as she spiraled out of the night toward the asphalt in the alley floor. She couldn't tell what the presence was. It didn't feel like one of her kind. There wasn't the foul taint to the presence. It could have been the FBI man, or even the priest, or just some random person who had stumbled across the lair by accident. But whoever it was, they had found her secret resting place, so it was not a secret any longer.

As she transformed back to human form and landed on her feet she thought about her options. Other vampires would have stormed back into their lairs, using their powers to surprise and then terrify the intruder. Other vampires would kill whoever had the gall to encroach on their resting place. But Lucinda was not like other vampires. She would not kill what she had not identified as an enemy of the society she no longer belonged to. She might still sneak into the lair and get a feel for who was there, and then make a decision on what to do.

As she made up her mind to do just that, to convert to a smaller size that could slip through an opening in the manhole cover, she felt the tingle of warning. She could feel that the area was off limits to her now, and that she would be destroyed if she tried to use anything she had left in the chamber. It was a serene message that entered her mind, not the angry hate filled messages that many vampires tapped into from their ultimate lord and master. The message did not have an evil taint to it. It had the feel of the divine, protecting her from that which would harm her.

Time to make use of another bolt hole, she thought.   She remembered back to her Junior ROTC class in high school, when Gunny Ramirez told the class about his experiences as a private in the Nam.   How the Gunny told them that a smart guerrilla fighter would have escape routes planned from any hide out they might inhabit.   And how they would always have alternate refuges to go to whenever the enemy discovered where they were hidden.

Lucinda transformed back to her bat form and flew back into the night, heading toward the southern part of the city and the house she had rented near MacDill.

*   *   *

Detective Lieutenant Jamal Smith was getting tired of driving to murder scenes every night.   He could barely get through processing the information he already had without getting yet another scene every night.

The gate guard of the community had looked at his badge carefully, even though a dozen emergency vehicles had already gone through the entrance.   He didn't have to ask directions.   The multitude of flashing lights pointed the way.   A uniformed officer waved the crowd back and motioned for the detective to drive onto the grass.

Smith pulled up into the yard of the large house set among other large houses on the curving street.   A trio of ambulances sat on the yard close to the door, almost blocking the path of the forensics van and coroner's vehicle. Smith opened the door as a uniformed officer approached.

"Lieutenant," said the female patrolman.   "It's a madhouse in there.   Nothing seems to make sense."

"Story of my life," said Smith as he walked past the ambulances, stopping for a second as a gurney was wheeled out of the house with a filled body bag on it.

Smith looked around as he entered the house.   A Latino man was sitting on the couch, a paramedic wrapping his ribs with tape, as a plain clothes officer stood over him writing on a pad of paper on a clipboard.

"Detective Frazier," said Smith as he approached the other man. "What is vice doing here at this hour?"

"You kidding me," said the tall white man in a southern drawl that was not heard much in the Bay Area. "We've been trying to get something on Giovani for years. I was almost ready to get a warrant for his arrest from the D.A. when someone else took care of the matter for me."

"So what's with him?" asked Smith with a nod toward the Latino on the couch.

"His name's Carlos Suarez. Head of Giovani's security detail. Looks like the boss didn't have the best protection money could buy after all."

"Fuck you," yelled Carlos, grimacing as the medic tightened the tape around his ribs. "An army couldn't have stopped her."

"Her?" asked Smith. "It was a woman?"

"I don't know if the bitch was human or not," said the man, shaking his head. "We couldn't stop her with bullets or brawn. She killed the boss, then went through us like a dose of salts. She was a demon, as far as I'm concerned."

Smith saw one of his men closing a pad as he turned from a crying woman. Jamal waved him over as he walked away from the couch.

"What's the story, Sanchez?"

"Sounds like something out of a movie, Lieutenant," said the detective sergeant, combing his fingers through his dark hair. "We're gonna be trying to sort this one out for days. Three dead, all bad people. Giovani's head was off and there was almost no blood in his body, same as the others."

"Taken off with a knife? I would guess the security was a little lax tonight, huh?"

"No knife, Lieutenant. Doc said from the tearing of the skin it looked as if someone twisted his head off."

"You know what kind of strength it would take to do that?" said Smith. "It had to be a big man to do that."

"All of the witnesses say it was a petite redhead," said Sanchez. "A real looker. Giovani took her into his room to dip his wick and she took his head off. Then she threw a two hundred pound man across the room. Shattered his skull and neck when he hit. And drove her knee through the face of another man, killing him instantly as his neck snapped."

"And what's the story with Carlos there?" asked Smith, waving at the man on the couch.

"He says that the killer lifted him into the air with a shoulder as she ran into him. Broke his ribs, and slammed him into the wall."

"She must have been on something pretty strong to do that," said Smith. "PCP?"

"She was a fucking demon, man," said Carlos, shrugging off the arm of the medic as he came off of the couch and walked up to the detectives, grimacing with each step. "I hosed her down with a fucking machine gun, and she kept coming at me like I threw spitballs at her."

"We have the gun he's talking about," said Sanchez. "A real sweat number, licensed to Giovani. It had been fired, and we found a bunch of 9mm casings in the hall."

"Body armor?" asked Smith. "She must have had body armor."

"She was fucking naked man," yelled Carlos as his face went red. "Titties flapping and everything."

"There were six pistols fired in the house and the yard," said Sanchez, looking over his pad. "Witnesses said she went through the glass door, busted right through, and then jumped clear over the ten foot security fence. While all kinds of people were putting lead in the air."

"OK," said Smith, shaking his head. "So she got some holes put in her and got cut up. Still doesn't rule out that she was on something. We'll probably find her dead out on the street in the morning."

"She didn't have a mark on her according to the witnesses," said Sanchez. "Everyone remembers her pale, flawless skin. And no one saw any kind of wound."

"So you saying that she was a fucking ghost?" said Smith, looking around the room.

"Not a fucking ghost," said DeFalco as he walked through the front door. "A fucking vampire."

Smith shook his head at the sight of the FBI Agent and felt the heartburn rise in his chest. *It's gonna be a long fucking night*, he thought, *before we get this one figured out.*

* * *

Marcus stood in the gathering crowd of onlookers outside of the house. Listening to the people out on this late night or early morning something very strange had happened here tonight. More than just a normal gangland murder. Listening in on the police and medics gathered around the front of the house confirmed his worst fears.

The whelp has gone wild this night, he thought. *Showing too many of her abilities, before too many witnesses. She is giving the game away, and too many eyebrows had been raised. This will not just fade into the background as yet another set of ramblings of the lunatic fringe.*

And again she had taken to the air after fleeing the house. He had reconned the perimeter, keeping to the shadows, smelling her scent, the strong scent of a vampire fully aroused and at her most powerful. As well as a sexual scent that aroused the undead master's mind, if not his body. He had lost the trail as soon as she became airborne.

I must know where she is going to strike ahead of time, thought Marcus. His mind went back to his past, when he was a Tribune of a Legion of Rome, tracking the Gauls through the wooded terrain of their demesne. Always a step behind the barbarians. He could feel the frustration in the Legionnaires. It was his frustration too. And then the turncoat had come into his camp.

"For five hundred pieces of silver, Lord, I will show you where the Gauls will encamp on the morrow," said the fur clad peasant.

"You will have your silver," agreed Tribune Marcus. "But if you betray me you will suffer their fate."

Marcus had followed the traitor with a single cohort of foot troops, and all of his Equestria. They had waited on a nearby hilltop, using the forest as their cover. And the Gauls had come. He could still hear the sounds of their setting up camp. He could still hear their shouts and screams as he led his five hundred horsemen into the clear, striking down running men and torching tents. He could hear the cries of alarm over the swirling sounds of slings, as the fleeing Gauls ran into the shield wall of the Cohort he had run them into.

The traitor had received his five hundred pieces of silver. Marcus remembered looking up into the man's face as he was tied onto a cross with the surviving leaders of the Gauls, sharing their fate. He had no use for traitors beyond what they could do for him in the here and now. The man had delivered on his promise and outlived his usefulness. So he had become another casualty of the campaign. He looked down on his soldiers as they threw crude dice, gambling for the pieces of silver that had been cut from the man's belt pouch.

Marcus could smell the new whelp even as he heard the deep rumble of an engine as a car pulled slowly down the street. He turned to look into the eyes of a big black man sitting in the passenger seat of a new Lincoln. He saw the man sniff the air, as his eyes went wide and he whispered something to the driver. The car sped up a little as it continued down the street.

Marcus walked quickly into the shadows, completing the transformation as soon as he was sure no one could see him. His sense of smell heightened, and he could scent the hundreds of people out on the street and in the nearby houses. He could hear the conversations going on at the murder scene, as the people discussed the unusual nature of the assailant. He bared his teeth in anger, then ran out of the shadows, his four paws carrying him through yards, leaping over fences, as he raced to head off the Lincoln. *I will have my anvil*, he thought. *To flush my enemy toward and smash her upon.*

* * *

"Goddamn," screamed Marvin as he hit the brakes of the Lincoln. Tires squealed on the asphalt as the vehicle slowed to a halt.

Tashawn braced his arms against the dash as he turned his head to the front. He bared his fangs as he saw the massive wolf in the center of the road, white and black fur raised as it snarled at the car. He sniffed and bared his fangs again as he scented that which the wolf really was.

The wolf changed in front of them within seconds, shifting bones and muscles until a short man stood before the car. The man wore a faint smile as he brushed at his dark blue windbreaker.

"He's one of you, ain't he?" whispered Marvin, panic rising in his voice. "You can take that little dude, can't you man?"

"No," said Tashawn. "There's more to him than you see."

The man smiled again and walked toward the car, angling to come around to the passenger side window. He placed his strong hands on the side of the car and leaned into the window.

He's a soldier, thought Tashawn. The man moved with the inborn assurance that Tashawn associated with his dad, the ex-drill sergeant, ex-Ranger who had ruled young Tashawn's life. *Whatever you may be now, you started out as a soldier.*

"Good evening, gentlemen," said the man in a smooth, unaccented voice. "This neighborhood to your liking?"

"Yeah man," said Marvin in a nervous voice. "We like it here just fine."

"Shut up, motherfucker," said Tashawn, glaring at his friend. He looked back up at the man looking down at him and tried to compose himself. "Can I help you, master?"

"What the hell you calling him master for," hissed Marvin. "We ain't no slaves, man."

"Shut up, man," whispered Tashawn.

"Yes Marvin," said the man. "Do shut up before I decide you make better food than you do a minion."

Tashawn could feel his friend stiffen in the driver's seat, as he whispered to himself for Marvin to shut the fuck up.

"I have no love for you, mistake," said the man in a pleasant voice. "I would just as soon end you here as smell your stench."

Tashawn felt anger rise in him. The desire to get out of the car and break this man in the street. But he could feel the presence of the vampire lord, the strength radiating from the man. And realized that his existence depended on how he handled himself with this man.

"I see you have some control, whelp," said the man. "That is good in one so young and inexperienced. I think I may be able to use you, after all."

A general, thought Tashawn. *Whatever he is now, at one time he was a general.*

"I have led more men in more battles than you can imagine," said the man. "Yes, I can sense your thoughts, whelp. So do not try to deceive me, or you will die in a manner you cannot imagine. Hell will be a relief from your torment."

"What do you want with me, man?" asked Tashawn, feeling his voice crack with his unmanning fear.

"I know you too seek her," said the man. "And I know you too feel the frustration of always being two steps behind her. I think that maybe together we can achieve our mutual goal."

"I know what I have against her, Lord," said Tashawn. "But what could she possibly have done to you."

"She makes us too, visible, to the world at large," said the man, his eyes changing from green to red as his anger grew. "Soon she will unleash the hunters who will make our existence a hell. Who will soon end our existence altogether."

"Bring em on, man," said Tashawn, trying to cover the uncomfortable fear that was rising in his breast.

"The bravado of youth," said the man. "After you have lived for a time as one of us you will realize how strong they are in their numbers. I have seen tens of thousands of our kind destroyed through the millennia. Only a few actually make it to any kind of age. "Do you want to be one of those few, whelp?" asked the man, his hands clenching on the side of the car. Tashawn heard the crunching sound as the metal bent under the man's fingers.

"Yeah," said Tashawn, looking up at the man's eyes and seeing them grow colder. "I mean, yes master."

"Good," said the man, a smile touching his lips. "You may be able to survive for a decade or two. At least you have survived this night. We will meet again, to discuss our strategy."

"Wait," cried Tashawn, as the man released the car and turned to walk away. "What's your name? How do I find you?"

The man turned around and stared into Tashawn's eyes. Tashawn felt as if his soul were being drawn toward the man, and that the man would feed on the essence that was Tashawn.

"You can call me Marcus," said the man. "And do not fear. I will find you."

The man called Marcus raised his arms to his sides and transformed into a bat. The flying rodent flapped its wings and rose into the air, disappearing into the night.

"Goddamned," said Marvin, wiping the sweat from his forehead with the back of a hand.

"Yes," said Tashawn. "I think we are."

Tashawn continued to stare out the window into the night sky as the car pulled down the street, wondering what the future held for him now that he was no longer a free agent.

Chapter 4

"What the fuck?" said Detective Lieutenant Jamal Smith as the videotape ran in the office. Detective Sergeant Emile Sanchez, Detective Justine DeBarry and FBI Agent Jeffrey DeFalco sat in the chairs around the table of the smoke filled room, watching the same tape. Even though only Smith and DeBarry smoked there were enough burning or smoldering butts in the room for everyone.

"I told you," said DeFalco. "Now do you believe me?"

Smith shook his head in the negative, trying to deny with his eyes were telling him. *Tapes can be faked*, he thought. But this tape had been pulled from the security room of the Giovani house as soon as the police had arrived. *There was no way the tape could have been switched by one delusional FBI Agent, was there?*

"It can't be," mumbled Smith. "It just can't be."

DeFalco raised the remote and ran the few minutes of tape in question back. He stopped as the living form of Lucian Giovani moved on the bed, his hands moving in the air as if he were caressing some unseen person in the bed with him. His erection grew, and the men glanced nervously at Justine.

Lucian's neck was bent back, then holes appeared in the skin and blood ran out. The blood seemed to outline, something. Then the something went away and Lucian seemed to mumble some unheard words. The something appeared at his neck again, as blood flowed from the wound. Then he lay limp on the bed, until his dead head started to twist backwards, looking into the mattress, then beyond, until flesh started to rip. The head came free from the body, hovered in the air for a moment, then flew toward the camera. The image then went blank.

"It can't be," said Smith once again.

"Anyone else see a perp here?" asked DeFalco, his Brooklyn accent coming out in his excitement. "Or is our boy being killed and beheaded by his imagination? Vampire's do not produce an image. On mirrors or recording devices."

"But Carlos said he saw the woman in the screen of the security room," argued Sanchez. "Clear as day."

"He saw her live over the TV," said DeFalco, gesturing at the TV with the remote. "I'm not sure why that happened. But it's readily apparent to whoever has a bit of gray matter in his head that something killed Lucian Giovani in his own bedroom. And that someone did not turn up on the tape."

"Assuming this is some kind of undead monster," said Justine, "just what are we supposed to do to catch her. Go looking for her lair and pound wooden stakes in her heart?" The Detective looked around the room, making eye contact with all the men. "I mean, don't you think a judge is going to love us asking for a search warrant to go into a suspected vampire lair? Or that internal affairs might take a dim view on our staking a suspect without attempting to take her into custody first?"

"I'll take whatever heat comes from this," said DeFalco, staring at the TV screen while he played with the remote. "Everyone in my Agency thinks I'm crazy anyway."

"I know," said Smith, staring at the younger man. "I talked to the Charge of Office here in Tampa. She told me you're known in FBI circles as *The Fox*. As in the guy named Fox from the TV series."

"But they let me alone to work my cases however I want," said Jeffrey DeFalco in a voice loud with anger. "Because I get results."

"Yeah, she said that about you too. Unorthodox, but as good a prosecution record as anyone in the Agency.

"OK, Agent," said Smith, looking around the room at his team and seeing them nod toward him as he made eye contact with each. "We'll buy into this, I guess. But I'm not sure what you expect us to do about this woman?"

"Just follow my lead," said DeFalco, waving cigarette smoke away from his face. "I'm playing it by ear myself, though I might have some tips on how to trap and kill her."

"No chance of capture?" asked Sanchez.

"I don't know how," said DeFalco, shaking his head. "I can't think of any way to hold her, at night at least. No, we take her out."

"So far," said Debarry, pulling another cigarette from the pack on the table, "All we've seen of her is after the fact. To catch her we've got to be there when she goes after someone. Not clean up the pieces after she's left. And I'm still not sure if I buy this vampire shit."

"You don't have to buy it, Detective," said DeFalco. "All you have to do is follow instructions and cover your ass."

"So how'd you get involved in all this in the first place, DeFalco?" asked Smith after lighting up another smoke himself. "Why the interest in vampires?"

"We were doing surveillance on a major player in Philly," said the Agent with a faraway look in his eyes. His accent was all Ivy League, all the Brooklyn gone from it. "We heard screaming over the tap and decided to close in. We got there as she was going out the window. A window I might add that was twelve feet up the wall of the warehouse, and she jumped up to it."

DeFalco looked around the room, then down at his hands.

"Later, also in Philly, I interrupted her at a feeding. She didn't have time to finish her victim like we've seen her do before. I came in with a group of agents as she was completing her feeding, or enough of it at least to stop the heart of the victim, one Tashawn Kent. I think you've heard of him. He used to be a defensive end for the Eagles. And she had bent him back over like he was a child. We fired at her and she took off before she could take the head off his shoulders."

"Later I learned that Tashawn walked out of the morgue three days later, after killing two attendants."

"But you said our girl killed him?" said Justine, a puzzled look on her face. "And he was in the morgue?"

"Yes," said DeFalco. "He was dead. And he was lying in a chilled cabinet in the morgue because no one wanted his punk ass body. But she had fed on him, killed him with her bite. And three days later he rose from the dead to become undead himself."

"So you're saying she takes off the head so she won't create more vampires," said Emile with a frown. "Why would she do that? I thought vampires liked to make more of their kind, like some kind of plague carriers. Or at least didn't care how many they left behind them."

"Salem's Lot, Emile?" asked Smith with a chuckle. "David Soul taking on the horde of vamps. I think he fled to Mexico in the end, didn't he?"

"I don't know why she is so careful to not leave rising victims behind her," said DeFalco. "I do know that I've been down to your morgue to check out some bodies over the last couple of days. Bodies that were found drained of blood, with twin punctures in their necks."

"So they're going to rise as vampires?"

"No, Detective Sanchez. Because I put a blessed wafer of unleavened bread in their mouths. A host, from the Church."

"So that's one of her weaknesses?" asked Smith.

"She's susceptible to anything holy," said DeFalco. "Crosses, Stars of David, Holy Water, the works. Anything that is blessed or is a symbol of faith is anathema to her. So I would make sure you have one of these at least before you join the hunt."

DeFalco pulled a golden cross on a chain from under his shirt and showed it to each of the Homicide Detectives.

"Get one. And we'll meet back here a couple of hours before sunset," he said, stifling a yawn. "I know I need a little sleep, and I suspect everyone else does too."

DeFalco got up from his seat and walked to the door, opening it and leaving the room without looking back.

"What the fuck, Lieutenant," said Sanchez. "You don't really buy this vampire shit, do you?"

"What did you make of the tape?" said Smith, looking back and forth between Sanchez and DeBarry. "And the testimony of all the witnesses at Giovani's house. Fact: A naked woman killed three strong men, ran from a house with a half dozen men shooting at her, and leapt, not jumped up, grabbed the top and swung herself over, but leapt a ten foot fence. I don't know about you, but it seems pretty damn unlikely to me that a normal human being could do that."

"So does that make her a vampire?" asked Sanchez, rewinding the tape again to Giovani's murder.

"I don't know what it makes her," said Smith. "But a decorated law enforcement officer has a theory that seems to fit all the facts. And I don't think any of us can make that claim. So unless you have something better we'll go with the vampire theory."

Smith stood up and grabbed his pack of cigarettes from the table, glaring at Justine as she tried to snatch the pack herself. The big Lieutenant stretched as he groaned, then walked to the door.

"I've got some paperwork to do," he told his partners. "I suspect both of you do as well. And then I know I need some sleep if I'm going to wrap my head around this thing."

Smith closed the windowed door behind him as he walked out of the room, leaving the two detectives to look at each other in wordless confusion.

* * *

Lucinda sat in the chair of the second bedroom of the house she had rented. The computer was humming in front of her as it displayed web pages for her perusal. A loud roar of a departing plane came to her through the walls, a departing early morning flight from MacDill.

George Padillas, she thought as she looked at the man's picture on the net, looking out with a smile on his face from the Padillas Shipping Company website. She swore in frustration as she switched pages with a mouse click. She could find the address of the company offices down at the Port of Tampa. But there was no listing of Padillas' home phone or address.

As if a man like Mr. Padillas, billionaire shipping magnate, would post his address on the net. She has already looked through the online phone book, but his number had been unlisted. Other searches had resulted in no hits.

Lucinda felt the weariness come over her that portended the approach of dawn. She needed to sleep today, to replenish all of the energies she had used tonight in the pursuit of Lucian Giovani and the escape from his house.

Lucinda turned the computer off and walked from the room to the short hallway. She grabbed the cord hanging from the ceiling and pulled down the folding stairs. Walking up the stairs she crouched over as she entered the attic, her eyes adjusting to the darkness and bringing the wooden coffin into focus. She pulled the stairs back up with a creak of springs, then shot a bolt to hold it in place.

Too bad about the water table, she thought. *Then they could have proper cellars like the civilized states. But then again*, she thought as she climbed into the coffin and lay on the soil of her resting place, *it's probably safer here than in a cellar. The cellar is always the first place they look.*

Lucinda closed her eyes and faded into sleep as she felt the sun coming over the horizon.

*   *   *

Monsignor John O'Connor awoke with a start as the beam of light hit his face from the opening in the manhole cover above. He hadn't meant to sleep, but had been determined to keep his vigil through the night. His body had not cooperated. He jumped up with a start, switching the flashlight on as he noted that the Starlight goggles were flashing a low battery warning. Pulling the goggles up to his forehead he shined the flashlight around the room.

It looked as if nothing had been touched in the chamber. The priest walked to the coffin, feeling the kinks in his back from sleeping against a hard wall. The coffin had been undisturbed, and a quick shine of the light showed that the chest was closed and untouched. The spot of the flashlight showed the cover still over the manhole. O'Connor sniffed the air. The musty odor of death still permeated the air, but it had grown no stronger through the night.

She had to have come here, thought O'Connor. He knew that vampires could walk during the daylight, unlike the made up monsters of TV and movies. But they still had to rest in their coffins as the sun came over the horizon. So she had to be here, or...

"She has another lair," he said, and then went quiet as he heard his voice echo in the chamber. It wasn't unheard of for the undead to plan ahead, to have multiple hiding places, bolt holes, secret stashes. But she had not been one of the undead for very long. She should not have the wisdom to plan beyond the animal instinct stage. But obviously she had.

And now she's out there in a large urban area, he thought as he crouched back out through the entrance to the chamber and into the storm drain. *A million places she could be, in one of tens of thousands of houses, or buildings, warehouses, ships. Or she could be out of the Tampa Bay area altogether.*

O'Connor walked through the tunnel, heading back to the light that marked the far entrance. A hot shower awaited him, and a soft bed. He would catch a few hours of sleep, a hot meal, and then begin the search again. A search that must needs start with prayers to the God who sent him on this quest. He squinted as the sun hit his eyes, as he scrambled up the slope of the earth to the street beyond.

* * *

Jeffrey DeFalco tapped the pointer on the resilient surface of the screen, drawing everyone's attention to the face of a distinguished looking man of middle age. He could see from the expressions in the room that the figure was recognized by all.

"So you think she's going to go after Padillas?" asked Jamal Smith, doubt in his voice.

"Why not," said DeFalco. "Her normal pattern is to work her way up the food chain. Padillas is the next level up."

"We think he's the top of the food chain here," said Sanchez, looking into his coffee cup.

"Why not bring Vice or Narcotics in on this?" asked Justine, looking at her own boss. "I mean, they have more of a handle on these players than we do."

"I think having your team in on it is enough," said DeFalco, looking pointedly at the woman. "At least you people think I'm only a little bit crazy. I don't have time to convince a bunch of other people that my madness has a rhyme."

DeFalco took a sip of his own black coffee, and looked from face to face around the table at the half dozen detectives who occupied the room.

"And I think she is going to strike Padillas tonight," he said, thumping the pointer on the table. "We don't have time to go over this shit with more people."

"And the uniforms?" asked Smith, staring at DeFalco. "What about them? They may want to know what's going on, don't you think?"

"Then we tell them that a female assassin is thought to be hunting the crime lords of the Bay Area," said DeFalco, a smug look on his face. "Same as we tell you locals when we want your help and don't really want you to know what we're really doing."

"I don't like it," said Detective Lowrey, slamming his own beefy hand down on the table and scowling at DeFalco. "From what you're saying, those men will be in extreme danger if the perp decides they have gotten in her way. She'll go through them like an Army Ranger through Boy Scouts. Don't you think they ought to know what they're facing?"

"Look," said DeFalco, staring back into the big man's eyes. "We'll tell them that she is very dangerous, and they are not to try and take her without one of us on hand."

"They may still try and take her," growled Lowrey. "They're professional law enforcement officers. I don't think they're going to back down just because they're told the perp is extremely dangerous."

"So you want us to take her out ourselves?" said DeFalco. "That's great if she just happens to come out our way. Or we spread ourselves too thin to actually stop her."

"DeFalco's right," said Smith, putting a hand on his enraged detective's shoulder. "We need the backup. She's most likely to hit Padillas tonight. And we don't know where she strikes after that. So we need to make do with what we have and pray for the best. You understand?"

"Yes sir," agreed the detective, nodding his head with a frown. "I understand. But I don't have to like it."

"No you don't," growled DeFalco in a strong Brooklyn accent. "As long as you do as you're told I'll be satisfied."

DeFalco turned back to the screen as he hit a button on the remote. An image of a large house just outside of the City of Tampa came on the screen.

"Now that we've wasted enough of our precious time," said DeFalco, tapping his screen with the pointer, "I think it's time to get back to business. Now here we have the house of Mr. George Padillas…"

*   *   *

Marcus could tell the moment he walked into the bar that the men he was supposed to meet were waiting for him. And that they had no intention of dealing fairly. He walked past the several whores who tried to get his attention, a stare into the eyes of one turning her away with a shudder. He could see the rat faced little man he had made contact with last night standing up near a table and waving at him. A trio of big, beefy, tattooed men sat at the table, sipping from beer bottles and trying to look as menacing as they could, staring at Marcus as he weaved around a couple of tables to approach theirs.

"Welcome, sir," said the rat faced little man who Marcus knew as Frenchy. "I'm so glad you came."

"Me too," said one of the large men, a bald biker with a large belly, taking a quick pull from an imported beer between his mustache and goatee. "I didn't think you was gonna show. Frenchy said you had a wad of cash on you."

"Which I will give to you, Mr., ah."

"Call me Ironhead," said the man. "And my partners are Chainsaw and Hammer."

"They're the local representatives of the Satan's Disciples," said Frenchy, his own chest puffing out with the pride of association.

"Shut the fuck up, you little shit," growled Hammer, a man who looked like he spent as much time in the gym as the bar. "I'll stick a hand up your ass when I want you to be our puppet."

Fear flew across Frenchy's face as he looked to the other two for support. Seeing none, he closed his mouth and moved away from the table.

"Pleased to meet you, Mr. Ironhead," said Marcus with a smile on his face. "Mr. Hammer, Mr. Chainsaw."

"Now don't he sound like an educated man," said Chainsaw, a smaller but still muscular man who picked up his beer bottle with a fluid grace.

Marcus recognized him as the most dangerous of the bunch. But he had faced down the chieftains of barbarian nations, men who would have him tortured to death while they ate their breakfast and loved their women. These men did not frighten him, especially since they could only hurt him permanently if they pierced his heart or cut off his head. Not that he expected them to know that. In fact he was counting on them to not know that fact. Or to think that the sun was about to go down over the horizon.

"You have some cash for us, man?" asked Ironhead, leering up at Marcus. Marcus nodded his head as he looked down at the man, his crimson orbs boring into Ironhead's eyes. Ironhead kept eye contact for a few moments, then looked nervously down at the table.

"You try to stare me down and you'll regret it," growled Hammer, slamming his beer bottle on the table and sloshing suds onto the surface.

"Gentlemen," said Marcus in his best calming voice. "I'm not here to fight. I'm here for information."

"Information don't come cheap," said Chainsaw, speaking up when Ironhead continued to sit staring down at the table.

Marcus could feel the fear battling with anger in the man. The Vampire Lord knew that the man had lost face in front of his partners. And he knew that the man would now want to take his anger out on the object of that fear.

"I'm willing to pay for it," said Marcus in his smooth voice, pulling a wad of hundreds from his pocket folded into a heavy gold band. He could feel the greed in the men. And the willingness to commit violence against him to get more than he was willing to offer. He smiled again at the men.

"It's not a good idea to talk here," said Ironhead, glancing quickly up at Marcus, then turning to glance at his partners who both nodded their heads. "I think we could talk in the back, if you wanted your information right now."

Both the partners smiled as Marcus nodded his head. Chainsaw got to his feet and gestured toward a door at the back of the bar and started to walk toward it. Hammer and Ironhead picked up their beers and fell in behind Marcus as he followed the most dangerous of the bikers to the private area, a back room. Chainsaw walked across the room and opened the far door and swaggered into the alley behind the bar, as the other two crowded close to Marcus to keep him from changing his mind.

It was still twilight outside, though the sun had left the sky and Marcus could feel the strength that lived in his dead muscles. Ironhead walked around him and turned, putting his back against the concrete block wall of another building. Hammer and Chainsaw both took up positions slightly to the rear of Marcus, one to his left and one to his right.

Boxed in, thought the vampire. *Trapped by men used to using violence to get what they want.* But they had no idea what they had trapped.

"Let's see that money, pops," Ironhead growled, thrusting his beer breathe face into Marcus'.

"I have some questions to ask first," said Marcus, again backing the man up with his stare.

"What you want to know, little man?" asked Hammer over his shoulder. Marcus could feel the man's foul breathe on his cheek.

"I want to know who are the movers and shakers in the criminal world here?" said Marcus. "I want to know where they work, and where they live?"

"You ain't asking for much," said Chainsaw with a laugh. "We give you those names, what you gonna do with them?"

"That is for me to know," said Marcus, letting the veiled anger show in his voice. "But let me assure you," he continued, allowing his voice to switch to calming mode, "I mean them no harm."

"Let me assure you," said Hammer in a mocking voice, breaking out into a laugh. "What the hell are you?"

"I think he's a Narc," said Chainsaw, putting a hand on Marcus' shoulder and gripping tight. He pulled a switchblade from his pocket and clicked it open, holding menacingly behind the vampire.

"You will release me this instant," growled Marcus, tiring of the game.

"Or what, you faggot," grunted Chainsaw, putting the tip of the knife against the small of Marcus' back.

Marcus reached his right hand up casually, placing his fingers over Chainsaw's. He heard the man grunt as he applied a bit of pressure, then felt the cold blade slide painlessly into his back. A second grunt, this one filled with pain, followed, as Marcus felt the bones of the hand crack under the pressure he now applied.

"What the fuck," yelled Hammer, swinging a fist into the side of Marcus' head. The heavy fist smacked into Marcus' temple, and rocked the vampire a bit on his feet.

Marcus twisted the hand he gripped in his, hearing the cracking sounds of wrist bones breaking and the tearing of cartilage. Chainsaw screamed as he brought his knife back and stabbed into the back of his tormentor. With a swing of his arm Marcus twisted Chainsaw to the side and away, to smack into the concrete block wall. Chainsaw slid down the wall, his good hand gripping the other after dropping the knife.

Hammer grabbed Marcus by his jacket and tried to lift and push him at the same time. Ironhead came off the wall swinging a combination of blows toward the vampire's head, landing them without effect. Marcus grabbed the wrists of Hammer as he fell back, stopping the fall as he dug his sharp fingernails into the human flesh. The smell of blood hit his nostrils as he bared his fangs and felt the hunger begin to war with his rational mind. But he had been around long enough to always be in control.

Marcus pushed back, throwing Hammer into the air, the man flailing his arms as he fell onto his back with a huff of expelled air. Ironhead had stooped down and come up with a section of iron pipe. He raised it over his right shoulder and brought it down with all of his might. To Marcus it was as if the man moved in slow motion. He reached up his right hand as he twisted toward Ironhead, grabbing the pipe and pulling it from Ironhead's hand. Marcus brought the pipe back swiftly and struck at Ironhead's skull. He bared his fangs in satisfaction as he felt the bone of the man's forehead crack under the pipe, followed by spurting blood that sprayed over the alleyway.

Ironhead fell to the ground, his wide-open eyes blank as his frontal lobes were destroyed. Marcus threw the iron pipe at the quivering body, propelling the cylinder through the man's biker vest, blasting through ribs and into his chest. Grunting in satisfaction Marcus turned to the rising Hammer.

Hammer took one look at Marcus, another at the body of Ironhead lying on the ground with blood pouring from his head and chest, and turned to run. Marcus watched him run, feeling a smile creep across his face. A huge black man appeared then at that end of the alley, standing calmly in the way of the fleeing biker.

"Out of my way, nigger," yelled Hammer as he reached into his jacket and pulled out a short barreled revolver. The black man stood there, not a bit of emotion showing on his face. Hammer pulled the trigger, firing point blank into the body of the obstacle before him. He stopped and fired again, as the black man stood there as if nothing was happening.

"You may feed, Tashawn," said Marcus, as he caught Chainsaw out of the corner of his eye as the man struggled to get back to his feet.

Tashawn reached forward and slapped the pistol from Hammer's hand. He then reached and grabbed Hammer's shirt with the speed of a striking viper, jerking the man toward him. Hammer stared at Tashawn like a bird caught in the gaze of a serpent as Tashawn pulled him close. The giant opened his mouth, his jaws hinging wider than humanly possible. With a thrust of his head Tashawn pushed his sharp canines through the skin of the biker he was holding close.

Marcus could hear the slurping from Tashawn's feeding as he turned his attention to Chainsaw, who was now on his feet and stumbling toward the other exit from the alley, holding his shattered wrist and hand close to his body. Marcus could hear the sobs of the fleeing man, could feel the fear radiating from him.

With a rush of speed Marcus was past the man and in front of him. He turned to face the running Chainsaw, to his heightened speed looking as if he were creeping down the alley. Marcus slowed down his time acceleration and stood in front of the frightened biker, seeming to have just appeared there to the human's perception.

"What the fuck are you?" screamed Chainsaw as he skidded to a halt and almost fell to the ground.

"I would think that would be obvious by now," said Marcus, allowing his long canines to show, reaching toward the man.

"That's impossible," yelled Chainsaw, trying to turn and run, stopping as he saw the huge black man at the other end of the alley still bent over the standing form of Hammer.

Marcus grabbed the man by the shoulder and spun the biker back to face him. Marcus then grabbed the front of his shirt and lifted the bigger man into the air.

"Now," said Marcus, his fiery gaze boring into the man's eyes. "How about we talk about that information I wanted."

Ten minutes later Marcus was sure that he had drained all the information the man had. Minutes after he was sure he had drained all of the blood the man had. He dropped the body to the ground, looking down on the man as he decided what was to come next. He felt Tashawn over his shoulder, and turned to face the huge vampire.

"I don't want these rising, Tashawn," said Marcus, looking at the three bodies scattered around the alley. "Not that they wouldn't make useful minions. But I have no need for this area to become crowded with our kind."

"What's the deal with that," said Tashawn, a frown on his face. "Why do you care if they rise or not. What can the puny humans do to us?"

"Ah," said Marcus, laying a hand on the giant's shoulder as he looked up into his face. "The exuberance of youth. That is why so many of our kind meet their ends before they develop the wisdom to survive."

"Yeah, man," said Tashawn, towering over his master. "Why ain't the cops here yet? Someone had to hear the commotion. At least the gun shots?"

"I have a feeling that this is their home turf," said Marcus, nodding at the body of Chainsaw. "Things like this must happen often around here, and people are used to staying out of things and minding their own business.

"Or maybe things not quite like this," laughed Marcus. "I'm sure they had no idea what was to transpire tonight."

Marcus reached down and picked up the body of Chainsaw, holding him like he would a small woman. He walked the corpse to the center of the alley and laid him against the foot of the door. He turned to Tashawn as he stood over the dead man.

"Go and get the gas can from the car," he ordered his minion. "Bring it back here and we will take care of this trash."

He watched the back of the enormous man as Tashawn walked from the alley. *What I could do with such strength*, he thought. Unfortunately that strength was attached to a youth with no wisdom. *But if he survives he will become formidable. I wonder if she knows what she has unleashed upon the world.*

Marcus picked up the other two bodies and carried them to the door, then opened the door and looked into the back room. It was deserted. Crossing the room he grabbed the knob a twisted it out of shape, destroying the opening mechanism and insuring that no one would come into this room. He walked back to the door and tossed the first body into the room. He followed with the other two and Tashawn appeared with the gas can.

Marcus took the three gallon can from his minion and poured the gasoline over the bodies, then poured some more over the floor boards around the bodies. He motioned Tashawn out of the room. In the alley he pulled a Zippo out of his pocket, flicked it to life, and tossed it into the room. The gasoline flared to fiery life as flames engulfed the bodies.

"What if the building burns down?" asked Tashawn. "Be kind of rough on the whores if they can't get out."

"As you so eloquently say, my friend," said Marcus, looking into his minion's face. "Fuck em. Now we have a place where we need to be, and this is not it. So let us go and wait for our prey."

"You know where she's gonna be?"

"No, Tashawn," said Marcus as he gestured for the other vampire to lead the way. "But I have a good idea where she might strike next. I hope your human servant is good at reading maps."

* * *

Monsignor John O'Connor stood on the sidewalk looking across the street at the eight-bedroom house that was the Padillas manor. He cringed a little again as another unmarked police car cruised by, the man in the passenger seat staring at the man who had spent the last fifteen minutes on the corner.

I need to find a better vantage point, thought the priest. He was not doing anything illegal, and he had the permit for the gun he carried. But police were more likely to take him to the nearest station to clear him as not. And that would take him away from her hunting grounds when he most needed to be there.

The only problem was that this was a residential neighborhood. There were no bars, restaurants or convenience stores to cover behind, not even a church he could pray in. And he knew no one in the neighborhood, so he couldn't shelter in a nearby house.

This was where she was most likely to come this night. He could feel it in the air, as if God was telling him where to be to fulfill his destiny. So here he had to stay.

O'Connor tried to blend in with the landscape as he saw another car going slowly down the street, driven by a young white man with another in the passenger seat. The sure sign of an unmarked car on patrol, when just about every other car on the street either whizzed by a fifteen miles per hour over the speed limit, or crept along barely under the control of an elderly retiree who should have given up the license years before.

The car was just a hundred feet away now, one of the Fords that police departments around the country liked to use for cruisers. The passenger window was rolling down as O'Connor tried to look like he was buried in a book.

"And what brings you out on this fine Florida night, Padre?" said a familiar voice.

O'Connor looked up and into the eyes of the FBI agent he knew believed. The only one that he was sure did.

"You know what I am about Agent DeFalco," said O'Connor, drawing himself up to his full height. "Can I assume the same for you?"

"You sure can, Father O'Connor," said the agent with a smile. "I know how I ended up here. The police have solid intelligence on where our girl might strike next. But how did you end up on this quiet street?"

"Would you believe that God sent me to this spot?"

"As much as I believe in vampires?" said the agent, nodding his head. "But I think it might be a little too hazardous for a civilian to be hanging around here. Why don't you go home, or to the Mission, or where ever the hell you Holy types go when you're not working?"

"Who better to try and stop the spawn of the devil?" said O'Connor, staring the agent in the eye as he fingered his cross. "A soldier of God will have the best chance of stopping her, no matter what you might think."

"OK," said DeFalco, holding a large Greek Cross up for the priest to see. "You can stay. But stay out of our way." DeFalco then chuckled for a moment. "Unless you see her kicking our asses. Then come a running."

"Let's go," DeFalco said to the driver, as he pulled up a microphone to his lips.

"Bless you my son," said O'Connor, sketching out the sign of the cross.

DeFalco looked up from the microphone and grinned. "I'll take any help I can get from the Almighty."

O'Connor breathed a sigh of relief as the car moved down the street. It seemed he would be allowed to stay. And much as he liked the idea of the police being near when it hit the fan, he still felt that they didn't know what they were dealing with and were out of their league.

* * *

"I don't like the smells coming from down there," said Marcus, sitting in the back seat of the car five or six blocks

from the Padillas house. "The police are there in force.
And I smell the stench of a priest."

"You afraid that the police might get her before you
do?" asked Tashawn from the passenger seat, looking into
the back of the car.

"I have no fear that they will *get her* as you say. But I
am afraid that they might frighten her away. What I can
sense so can she. And she has shown uncommon wisdom
for one so young."

"Let's see how wise she looks when I tear her head
off," growled Tashawn, as Marvin pulled the car forward a
block and made a left turn, trying not to stand out too
much.

Poor youngling, thought Marcus LaMons, staring at the
back of Tashawn's head. *Yes, you are strong, stronger than one
should rightly be at your stage of development. But physical strength is
not everything, and I would bet on my dear Lucinda should you ever
meet her by yourself.*

* * *

Lucinda banked over the city, several blocks to the east
of the Padillas house. She sniffed the air, screeching in
anger as she picked up the multiple scents from below and
sorted them out. She could smell the priest down there, and
the FBI Agent. People who had been on her trail for
months. But innocents she could not harm, no matter that
they were trying to destroy her.

She could also pick up the faint scent of the vampire
lord, close to her own mistake. *Those two are now in league*,
she thought. She couldn't say that she could take either one
of them, much less the two of them together.

She felt the hunger deep in her breast at that moment.
The instinct that told her to take her victim, to feast on his
blood, no matter the risk. She knew this instinct was what
killed so many of her vile kind. And she wanted no part of
it.

Tonight is a bust, she thought, forcing the hunger back down so she could think. *But I still need to feed.* The image of her sinking her fangs into the skull of a baby came unbidden to her mind, as she shuddered in revulsion at the same time as she felt the hunger surge back again. Again she forced it back. *I will not be a slave to my instincts.*

With that thought a sense of calm came over her and she could think rationally again. Undead she may have been, but the exercises she performed daily to quiet her mind worked on the non-living as well. She banked back to the right as she released a sonar screech. She thought she knew where the secondary target might be. And that action would impact the primary as well.

*   *   *

Jacob Padillas had his dad's olive skin tone, and his mom's striking blonde hair. He moved toward the bar of the *Club Astropolis*, feeling the eyes of the many women in the club follow him. With his rugged good looks and athletic body, he knew he would have no trouble finding a bed warmer this night, as he didn't on any other night of the week.

Of course the Armani suit and the Rolex bought with daddy's money doesn't hurt either, he thought as he leaned over the bar and flashed Gregorio, the bartender, a smile.

"Your nose, Jake," said the bartender as he approached Padillas.

Jake rubbed the underside of his nose, dislodging the coke that had stuck there. He licked his fingers, tasting the almost pure Columbian crystal.

"Gimme a scotch on the rocks," he said the Gregorio.

"Yes sir," agreed the bartender, pulling a bottle from under the counter. The good stuff, reserved for those who could afford it.

Jake took the offered drink and turned his back to the bar, leaning against the bar's bumper as he let his eye roam around the club. He took in the dance floor, where a couple of dozen women danced with the losers who were trying to pick them up. He dismissed half the women out of hand. They did not meet his standards. Almost another dozen were past conquests. He would try for them again if he no luck otherwise. The rest were to his taste and strange, but he could see two of them would probably want nothing to do with him. Wearing expensive jewelry and original Paris dresses; his money wouldn't impress those bitches. Maybe by his looks, but again, seeing the pretty boys they were dancing with, maybe not.

Then she caught his eye. A stunning redhead he had never seen in the club. Her knee length blue dress set off her pale complexion and fiery hair perfectly. She had tastefully selected diamond earrings and a pearl necklace. *A professional lady*, thought Jake. Not a whore, but a businesswoman out for a little fun. Who might be impressed by Jake Padillas.

The woman met his eye and she squirted some breath spray into the mouth. Jake felt his heart beat faster, and not from the coke in his system. The woman radiated sexuality, and Jake found himself imagining how she would perform in bed. In his mind's eye he could see her straddling him as he lay on the silk sheets of his bedroom, lust in her gaze as she moved up and down on him.

"What," he said, as suddenly she was at his side, smiling at him with one of those half smiles that hide most of the teeth. As if she was laughing at him inside. He felt his face flush with anger. But a look into her wide blue eyes killed the anger with lust.

"I don't think I've ever seen you in here before," he said, trying to calm a voice that came out too high from his nervousness. *What the fuck*, he thought. He hadn't been nervous around a woman since taking Charlotte Harden's virginity in the storeroom of St. Agnes' Catholic School. But this one made him nervous, with a thrill of danger that had his blood pumping in his ears.

"I've never been here before," she said leaning toward him so he could smell the minty fresh breath from her mouth. "So I'd be surprised if you had."

I'm Jake," he said, putting out his hand. She took it in hers and he started for a second at how cool it felt.

"I'm Lucy," she said. "Lucy Tegano. Pleased to meet you."

She gave it a gentle shake, then lightly raked her fingernails over his palm as she withdrew her hand. Jake took in a sharp breath as he looked into the wide pupils of her eyes. Either a sign of interest, he knew. Or of drugs. But she didn't act like she was on any strong narcotics.

"Would you like a drink, Lucy?" he asked, nodding toward Gregorio.

"I don't drink, liquor," she said in a throaty voice. "But I would love to dance. Would you dance with me, Jake?"

"Sure," whispered Jake, feeling a little light headed. He reached out his hand and she put hers in it. He led the way from the bar to the dance floor, the psychedelic lighting scheme dazzling his eyes. He pushed his way through a couple of ecstasy heads, the man turning an angry gaze on him until he realized who it was. People moved out of his way as he led her to the center of the floor. Jake reveled in the power that he held in the nightlife of Tampa.

As they reached the center of the floor Lucy pulled her hand from his and started moving to the music. Jake stared at her in fascination for a moment, watching her graceful movements in perfect rhythm to the metal music that was playing over the expensive sound system. She smiled at him and he felt embarrassed to be acting like such a schoolboy. He started moving himself, arms and legs attempting to find her rhythm. But she moved like a professional dancer, and he did his best just to keep up.

Looking at the slender curves of her perfect body under her tight fitting dress, he felt himself becoming aroused. She flashed him another bemused smile, and moved toward him, falling into his arms. He flinched for a moment as she molded her body to his and began moving in a rhythm that had nothing to do with the music. His arms went around her, feeling the taunt muscles of her back moving as she swayed. Her soft breasts pressed against his chest, as he ground his hard manhood into her hip and groin.

There was a musky scent about her that pulled Jake even further into her spell. He frowned for a second as he smelled something else under the perfume and natural scent. Something that reminded him of the corruption of death. But then her mouth nuzzled his ear and all thought that dealt with anything but lust fled his mind.

"I want you so badly," he whispered into her ear. "I want you now."

"I think the dance floor may be a little too public," she said with a chuckle.

"No," he said with an answering laugh. "I think I can wait till we get in private."

"I want you too," she said in a husky voice that dripped with sexuality. "I want you so bad."

"Then let's get out of here," he said, pulling out of the embrace and grasping her hand. He led her from the dance floor, nodding at a smiling Gregorio, while he wondered who had won the pool on him tonight.

They walked toward his car hand in hand, and Jake waited in anticipation as they approached his car. He knew that the silver Maserati Spyder normally sparked excitement in his women. He pulled his keys from his pocket and triggered the lock/alarm system. He felt a little bit of disappointment as she took her hand from his and walked to the passenger door, pulling it open and sliding her lean form into the seat.

Jake shrugged his shoulders. What did it matter if she was impressed or not by the car. *I'm gonna get that pussy*, he thought, and that was all that really mattered.

As he slid into the seat and put the key in the ignition she shifted over toward him and stroked his back through the suit. Her other hand went down his chest, sliding unerringly down to his groin, where it rested for a moment, then started kneading. Jake felt his erection spring to full life again.

"I really think it might be better to wait till we get back to my place," he said, a wide smile on his face. "Unless you want to give me a blow job, this place is just a little too crowded for comfort."

"It's spacious enough for my purposes," she said in a cold voice.

A chill ran down Jake's spine as the atmosphere in the car changed. The musky sensual odor went away, overpowered by the smell of death. He turned his head to look into red, glowing eyes, while the smile on her face revealed long canines. He felt the fear settle in his gut as he realized he was in deadly danger.

He jerked at the hand on his groin, while trying to shrug his shoulder out from under the other hand. She gripped tightly in both places. Jake hissed in agony at the pain that erupted from his testicles. He pulled with all of his strength, panic boosting the adrenaline flowing through his muscles. But Jake might as well have been pulling at a hydraulic press for all the good it did him. The slender arms didn't budge, telling of a strength many times his own.

Jake released the hand squeezing his balls and tried to reach under the front of the seat. There was a pistol there, and he needed it at this moment more than any other time in his life. But her hand moved like a striking rattlesnake, shifting from groin to moving hand in a blur. His hand froze in place, and he looked back at her face in a fascinated fear.

"What are you trying to do, little man?" she said with a smile that froze his heart. "You are all mine now, and I intend to enjoy you."

"Please," he croaked. "My father will give you anything you want if you let me go."

"Oh, I doubt that," she said. "Since I want the same thing from him as I do from you."

She moved her head to just off his neck, her cold breathe chilling his skin as it chilled his guts.

"I want your life, little man," she whispered. "Jacob Padillas. Raper of little girls. How'd your father get you off on all of those charges Jacob?"

She licked his neck, leaving a moist trail on the flesh.

"You will not get a reprieve this time Jacob. There is no clemency in this court."

Jake felt the sharp pain in his neck as she bit into him. He then felt her lips against his neck, sucking at the flesh. He struggled for a moment, but his strength could not free him from her grasp. The sucking continued, until he began to feel faint headed. Soon his vision began to go red, then black, until Jacob Padillas fell into a black hole from which there was no escape.

*   *   *

Lucinda stared at the corpse in the driver's seat for a moment, feeling the hunger abate as it was replaced by a feeling of satiation. She then looked up and around through the windows of the car. Nothing moved in the parking lot.

I still should have waited, she thought. Someone might have seen her. But the hunger had gotten too great, until she could not resist any longer. So she had fed and made her kill, and no one had seen.

Quickly she got out of the car and pulled the body over into the passenger seat. Lucinda then got into the driver's seat and started up the car. Her human memories were sparked by the rumbling purr of the high performance automobile. She shifted into gear and pressed the gas, moving the car out of the parking lot and onto the street.

A couple of blocks down she turned into the entrance to a towering parking garage. Stopping at the automatic gate she pushed the button and accepted the ticket, waiting a moment for the gate to swing up. The Maserati responded to a slight touch of the gas as she headed for the up ramp. She accelerated as the ramp sloped up.

Lucinda drove the car past the second floor, then the third, ignoring all of the open spaces that would be full when the business day started tomorrow. She pulled onto the tenth level, the rooftop of the garage. With a squeal of tires she brought the car to a sudden stop, got out, and walked to the concrete guardrail. She looked over the guardrail and down onto the street a hundred feet below. There was very little traffic on the street, only a couple of cars a minute. *Good enough*, she thought. A risk worth taking.

Lucinda got back into the car and backed it across the roof until the bumper tapped the far guardrail. She noted with satisfaction that the gas tank was three quarters full. She then got out of the car and pulled Jake's body back into the driver's seat, belting him in so he wouldn't go anywhere. Lucinda then got back into the passenger's seat and put her foot over the gas pedal. Shifting the car into gear, she grabbed the wheel and slammed her foot down on the gas. The car stood still for a moment as its tires squealed and sent up a cloud of smoke. Then it took off like a shot across the roof of the garage.

Lucinda shifted the gears twice as the car sped toward the far guardrail. She braced her arms against the wheel and the dash. The Maserati plowed into the concrete guardrail at seventy miles an hour. The front of the car crumpled in as it slowed to almost a stop in a fraction of a second. But it kept going forward as the momentum shattered the concrete and blasted through.

The vampire felt the concussion through her arms, watching as the airbags erupted from their compartments and race the shattering windshield into the car. Then the ruined automobile was hanging in space as it looped out and fell toward the street. Lucinda triggered the change at that moment, her corporal form turning to mist that streamed out of the car and into the air. She drifted down the street as the car struck its shattered front onto the hard asphalt. The car crushed under the momentum, then exploded in a ball of fire as the fuel system sparked and spread immediately to the gas tank.

That's one I don't have to worry about, she thought as she coalesced to human form. There would barely be enough left to bury, closed casket of course. He would not rise again.

Lucinda raised her arms to her side and changed again, soaring into the sky as a bat. She had accomplished much tonight, killing someone close to her primary target, a man who himself deserved death. And she had fed her hunger while not harming the innocent, either tonight or in the future when the monster would have awoken from the corpse she had left behind. Fire instead purged the body of her taint.

*   *   *

"I don't think she's gonna show," said Tashawn, looking back at Marcus as he leaned on the back of the seat. Marvin struggled in the driver's seat to stay awake in the early morning hour.

"Of course she won't show tonight," said Marcus, glaring back at the big man and making Tashawn lean back a little. "There were too many hunters here tonight. She was scared off and went for other prey."

"Then why the fuck are we here, man," cried Tashawn. "We could have been chilling back at the crib."

Marcus grabbed Tashawn's forearm in an iron grip, squeezing hard enough to bring a grimace to the big man's face.

"You are now a predator, my friend," said Marcus, bringing his face close to Tashawn's. "You need to develop the patience of a predator. Not all of your gifts are fully developed yet. As you age you will get stronger, swifter, and your other abilities will grow. That takes time. Time you may not have if you give me your version of attitude."

Marcus felt the bone crack under his hand as Tashawn gasped in pain. Marcus released the grip and Tashawn jerked his arm back, rubbing where the ancient vampire had crushed the bone.

"You didn't think you could be hurt," said Marcus, grinning like a feral wolf. Tashawn looked sheepishly back as he rubbed his arm, and then the look turned to surprise.

"Yes," said Marcus, nodding his head. "We can hurt each other. Even kill each other. I have killed many vampires in my day. But we also heal quickly from the few things that can injure us if they don't kill us."

Marvin was now fully awake in the driver's seat, staring from face to face with terrified eyes. Marcus gave Marvin a quick smile as he gazed into the minion's eyes, seeing the face slack as calm came over it.

"Drive us back to the, what did my friend call it? The crib. What a curious term. A home for babies."

Marvin started the car and pulled out into the empty street, while the vampire Lord laughed out loud in the back seat.

*   *   *

"I don't think she's going to show tonight people," said DeFalco over the radio.

"No shit," came back the voice of Jamal Smith. "What the fuck gave you that idea?"

"I knew this was a stupid fucking idea," said Sanchez, glaring at the FBI Agent from the patrol car's driver's seat. "A waste of fucking time."

"I could have been trying to make time with Justine," came Lowry over the radio.

"Fuck you, you Mick mother fucker," came DeBarry's reply.

"Can it people," ordered Lieutenant Smith. "What do you want to do now, Agent DeFalco?"

"I guess you could go work that burning over at the Club Astropolis," said DeFalco.

"Mother fucker," yelled Smith into the radio. "We needed to be there, instead of out here in nowhere land. Instead Wilson probably fucked it up."

"Water under the bridge, Lieutenant," said DeFalco. "People die every night. Especially drug dealing biker scumbags. She's much more important to us, to the country, and to the mother fucking world." DeFalco's Ivy League accent vanished as his temper rose, and he was now pure Brooklyn. He struggled for a moment to get himself under control before getting back on the radio.

"Cut the uniforms loose, Smith," he said in a calm voice. "We'll meet back at your office for a debrief. DeFalco out."

"Pull up to that asshole," ordered DeFalco to Sanchez, pointing to where O'Connor still kept his silent vigil. "I want to talk to him."

DeFalco leaned out the window as the car came up beside the priest. O'Connor looked up at the car, the beads of a Rosary in his hands. He finished mouthing the words of a prayer as the unmarked police car stopped.

"Kind of a wasted night, eh, father?" asked DeFalco, smiling at the priest.

"No night is wasted in the service of the lord," said the priest, shaking his head. "She may not have come tonight. But she will be drawn to this place. If not this night, then another."

"I think she was going to come here tonight, Father," said DeFalco. "I think all of the activity scared her off."

"My thought exactly, Agent DeFalco," agreed the priest. "Perhaps if there was not so much police activity here tonight she would have come."

"I'm thinking more likely that she sensed that you were here," said the FBI Agent. "You're the one carrying around the holy items. You're the one praying up a storm out here on the city street. She's the devil's spawn, and you know it. And the devil's spawn can feel when the holy is near."

O'Connor scowled back at the agent for a moment, pushing his rosary beads back into his pocket. He crossed his arms over his chest and thrust his chin out.

"You can act like a little child if you want," said the DeFalco, waving a hand of dismissal at the priest. "But I want you to be conspicuous in your absence tomorrow night. And every night after. Or I will arrest you ass and make sure you spend a few nights in the County Lockup."

"You don't have the right to arrest a citizen who is doing nothing wrong," argued O'Connor.

"Obstruction of Justice," said DeFalco, ticking off the points on his fingers. "Disobeying the orders of a Law Enforcement Officer. Destruction of evidence at a crime scene. And that's just the start."

"You cannot make any of those stick," said the red faced priest. "The Church…"

"Yeah," interrupted DeFalco, pointing his finger at the chest of the priest. "Mother Church will get you out of jail, even if the Papal Ambassador has to come to your rescue. But you will still spend time in lockup. And if you get out and come back here I will just lock you up again. Am I understood, Father."

O'Connor continued to glare back, his face red with anger.

"I'll take that as an affirmative," said DeFalco, turning away from the window and looking ahead. "Take us back to the station, Sanchez."

The car moved off down the road. DeFalco looked back in the side view mirror, staring at the priest, standing on the side of the road with his head down.

* * *

The station house was a buzz of activity as Jamal Smith walked in, heading for his office.

"I heard your stake out was a bust," said a young female detective, trying to catch him.

"Yeah," growled Smith. "Mother Fucker wasted my whole night." Smith stopped for a moment and looked down at the attractive black woman. "You're Tanesha Washington?"

"Yes sir," she admitted, offering her hand. "Captain Richards wanted me to fill you in on what happened tonight while you were off the scope."

"Off the scope," said Smith with a smile. "That sounds kind of military. And I know that asshole Richards was never in the military."

"Airforce," said Washington. "I was a radar tech for three years, before I took my degree in Forensics from FAMU."

"I was a Marine myself," said Smith. "Didn't have tech on my name. I was a grunt, plain and simple. And my school was the street."

"I know sir," said Washington. "But times have changed."

Smith grimaced as he opened the glass windowed door to his office and gestured the female detective in ahead of him. He closed the door behind him and indicated a chair for her as he walked behind his desk and plopped his butt into the comfort of his own well broken in seat.

"Shoot," he ordered. "Tell me what happened," he continued, seeing the confusion on her face. She opened a notepad and spent a couple of seconds going over what was written on it.

"Three bikers were found dead in the Club Astropolis," she said, running a finger across the page. "Half the club burned down before the Fire Department got it out. But all of the victims were badly burned. Almost incinerated."

"So we have an accidental fire set by some stoned out scumbags," said Smith.

"That would be the first take on it sir," said Washington. "But the Fire Marshal stated that the residue of gasoline was found on the clothing of the deceased, what little of it was left."

"So they got careless with the gas."

"And one of the deceased had a crushed skull. The blunt object used to commit the murder was found in the alley behind the bar. It had blood and brain matter on it."

"Damn," said Smith. "So we do have a homicide. Did the other stone heads also have trauma on them."

"No sir," said the detective. "But they were lying in a pile, with the brain smashed one in the center."

"So a triple homicide," said Smith, slapping his desk. He looked at the detective under hooded eyes, wondering how to put the next question.

"Were any of them found light some of their, well, blood?"

"No way to tell sir," said the detective. "They were too badly burned to make any kind of determination."

Washington looked down at her pad for a moment and looked back up with a frown.

"You really don't believe you're looking for a vampire, do you Lieutenant?"

"Jesus Christ," cried the Lieutenant. "Does everyone in the fucking world know about that?"

"Word gets around, sir," said the detective. "Most of the division thinks you're crazy."

"And what do you think, Detective Washington?" asked Smith, steepling his hands in front of him on the desk.

"I've seen some strange things myself," she said in a hushed voice. "My uncle down in Miami was into Santa Ria. Some other relatives were Voodoo Priestesses. So I'm a little more open minded them most."

"Just so you don't think I'm crazy, Washington," said Smith. "Even though sometimes I think I am sometimes, to go along with this shit."

"Well, you're going to love this one, Lieutenant," she said with a smile.

"Why do I always hate it when people say that," he said with a grimace.

"Because you know some strange shit is coming," said the Detective with a laugh. "Well, they found the Maserati of one Jacob Padillas on the street by a ten story parking garage. Jacob was in the car, dead."

"Missing blood?"

"Hard to tell, sir," said Washington. "The car fell from the top of the garage and impacted the street below, blowing up and almost completely incinerating the body. Remains were identified by the engraved Rolex on his wrist. First indications were of a suicide."

"And what are the indications for now?"

"Well, Jacob was seen leaving the Club Astropolis in the company of a stunning redhead," said Washington. "Maybe she broke his heart and he couldn't handle it. But from what I heard, Jacob was the heart breaker, not the breakie."

"Jacob Padillas," grunted Smith. "The son of George Padillas?"

"Yes sir," said Washington. "The only legitimate son of the man whose house you were at tonight."

"Stunning redhead," repeated Smith. "Son of a bitch. She couldn't get to the father, so she settled on the son."

"If I were to believe in vampires, Lieutenant," said the young detective. "And I'm not saying that I do. I think that would be a very good assumption."

"And who worked the son's death?" asked Smith.

"I did, sir," answered the detective with a smile. "I was the first investigator on the scene."

"How'd you like to join my team?" asked Smith with a smile. "And help us track down things that go bump in the night?"

"I'd love to Lieutenant," said the young detective. "If you can use a crazy woman on your team."

"No crazier than the rest of us," said Smith, frowning as he watched DeFalco walked toward his door. "You're on the team.   I have a talk with Richards to get you transferred."

"Thank you, sir," beamed the young woman. "I've always wanted to work with you."

"Don't thank me," said Smith in a quiet voice as DeFlaco reached for the doorknob. "Wait till you meet the head mother fucker before you make that decision."

Chapter 5

"Monsignor O'Connor?"

O'Connor looked up from the magazine he had been looking at in the waiting room of the Padillas Shipping office. He saw a man with haunted eyes standing before him, a man whose face had been on the cover of the magazine the priest put down as he came to his feet.

"John O'Connor," answered the priest as he reached a hand out to the man. He looked down on the much shorter man as they clasped hands. George Padillas was a stocky man, a man who looked like he spent considerable time each week in the gym, and even more time on one of his yachts

"George Padillas. I'm glad you came, Father," said Padillas, leading the priest back through the door to a hallway.

"I hope this isn't a bad time, Mr. Padillas," said O'Connor. "You have my condolences on your son's death."

Padillas remained silent as he led the priest to a heavy, carved wood door and opened it onto a plush office. He gestured toward a comfortable chair set around a low round table.

"Drink, Father?" asked the man, moving to a large bar set against the wall.

"I'll take coffee if you have it," said the Priest. "I was up most of the night, and am a little off my feet."

"Trying to find a vampire," said Padillas as he poured coffee into a cup. "I talked with the Bishop, who thinks you are insane. But you also have the blessings of the Pope." Padillas made the sign of the cross as he mentioned the papal authority, then handed the cup of coffee to the Priest.

"I'll reserve judgment on your sanity myself," said Padillas, pouring a triple shot of bourbon into a glass. Padillas looked the priest over for a moment, then took one of the other seats around the table.

"I'll get straight to the point, Monsignor," said Padillas after taking a large swallow of the drink. "Jacob was a waste of body mass. But I loved him anyway. He was my son. And he will be buried tomorrow in a closed casket ceremony at St. Agnes'. His mother is devastated."

"I think your son was killed by a vampire," said O'Connor, putting his cup back on the table. "I think the vampire was after you, but was scared off."

"By all the police activity around my house," said Padillas. "Yeah, I knew they were out there, but I wasn't sure why. So the police believed someone was trying to get me."

Padillas took another large swallow of bourbon before looking at the priest. "But why would she want to kill me? I'm just a simple businessman. And there are so many easier targets out on the streets."

"This vampire is kind of picky about her victims," said the Priest. "And I don't think you are quite the simple businessman you try to portray. But that is between you and the almighty. Her destruction is my goal. My only goal at this time in my life."

"So you think she will still be coming to get me?" Asked Padillas, getting up to walk back to the bar and pour another drink. "I want her to come and get me, Father. Lord help me I want to cut her heart out and feed it to her as I watch the life leave her eyes."

Padillas up ended the second drink and chugged it down. He slammed the glass on the bar, breaking it, then came back to the table. He showed no effects of the alcohol.

Running on adrenaline, thought O'Connor. *And still not realizing what he is dealing with.*

"I'm here to help, Mr. Padillas," said the priest, looking into the man's eyes as tears welled up in them. "I'm here to destroy the one who has brought you so much pain."

"I'm sure I can handle myself, Monsignor," said the man, choking back his tears as he shook his head. "I have the firepower to take her out if she dares to come against me."

"That's what Mr. Giovani thought," said O'Connor, shaking his head. "And she killed him, then went through his security like it didn't exist. Are you sure you don't want my help? She is Satan's Spawn, Mr. Padillas. And who better to confront the spawn of Satan than a servant of God?"

"And what can I do to help you get her, Monsignor?"

"You can go about your business, in your own house."

"Like a goat staked out for the tiger?" said Padillas with a grunting laugh.

"Very much like that, Mr. Padillas," said the priest, nodding his head. "And I will be the hunter, waiting in the blind to kill her."

"Before or after she takes the goat from the stake?" said George Padillas.

"I won't lie to you, Mr. Padillas," said the priest, looking the man in the eye. "Hopefully before. Assuredly after. But I will do my best to make it before."

"OK, Monsignor," said Padillas, standing and offering his hand to O'Connor. "You're welcome in my house. Just as long as you get her for me. Or save enough of her for me to get my own satisfaction."

O'Connor stood and took the offered hand, smiling back as he shook it. But wondering if maybe he had made a deal with a different devil to kill the one he was after.

* * *

Lucinda opened her eyes as she was screaming into the heated darkness of the attic. Her instincts told her that it was early afternoon, the hottest part of the day, and the strongest sunlight. But safe enough for her to walk in the light of day, though she would be as weak as any mortal.

The baby dream, she thought with a shudder. Of course it was time for that sequence to play itself back in her head. *But I wish that particular dream would just go away.* Years of wishing had had no impact on the sequence. That dream had always left her drained, while renting space in her brain for the following entire day.

She had only been a vampire for a couple of days, living in a crypt, sleeping in the coffin that had been her resting place for the three days before her awakening, feeding on whoever happened to wander past the graveyard. Once she had woken as the sun had just crested the horizon, feeling danger in the air. She had fled to one of the large crypts at the graveyard, feeling the weak sunlight through the clouds burning her skin. She had listened to men talking about grave robbers. Glancing out of the crypts she saw a couple of Sheriff's cars sitting on the access road through the cemetery.

She knew she would have to move or they would catch her. And she knew that she would be destroyed if caught. But where to go? All of the vampires she had read about or seen in movies had been filthy rich, able to rent large manor houses off the beaten path. She had been flat broke before her death. And the little bit of money she had gotten from the wallets of those she had fed on might pay for a night in a Motel Six.

She continued to hide the day through the crypt, hiding under a desiccated body in a stone sarcophagus at one point while armed men searched through the building with flashlights. When night came she felt relief as her strength came back. She would at least be able to fight if found. Whether that would be enough she did not know. But in the night she was the predator, and the humans the prey.

He came for her that night. She could sense his presence before he entered the crypt. She could smell his scent as he walked through the doorway into the dark chambers. She could feel his power as moved toward her.

"So you have survived, youngling," said the man in a smooth voice. She could see with her dark vision that he was a short man, no more than five foot six, and slender. He had the swarthy skin of a Spaniard or Italian, with the hook nose of an aristocrat. At the time he was the most ancient thing she had ever been around. Later she would find that his six centuries of existence paled beside that of the true Vampire Lords that he had crossed paths with.

"I have something for you," he said, flinging a small object at Lucinda. She snatched it from the air, feeling the life pulsing through it as she looked down at the small form in her hands. The one year old began to cry, a sharp piercing wail that called for the mother who was no longer there. Lucinda felt the hunger rise in her, and the disgust at the thoughts that were racing through her head.

"Feed," ordered the vampire. "And we will talk."

Lucinda felt the compulsion grow stronger at his command. She tried to fight it, but she could not stop her fangs from piercing the soft skull of the child. She could not stop her lips from planting a tight kiss on the wound, nor could she stop her mouth from sucking the sweet life's blood from the child.

"I am Don Diego Comacho Garcia-Mendez," said the vampire, bowing at the waist. "I am the one who made you. But you were not a mistake, as many of our kind are. No, I was captivated by your beauty, senorita, and wanted you to join me in eternal darkness."

"Why?" asked Lucinda, looking at the lifeless form in her arms. "Why did you bring me to this hellish existence?"

Don Diego reached over and pulled the baby from her unresisting arms. He looked at the child, then raised it over his head by the feet and smashed the head onto the edge of a stone sarcophagus. Lucinda cried out and started to move to stop him. The man looked at her with glowing red eyes and she felt all of the willpower leave her body, freezing her in place. Don Diego raised the small body again and swung it into the hard stone, as the baby's head exploded this time into a ruin of bone and brains. He then flung it to the end of the crypt to strike the far wall with a splatting sound.

"I did not want that one to rise, you see," he said, putting his arms on her shoulders and gazing into her eyes. "Of what use would be one who would spend eternity so small? Unlike you, who will be of great benefit to me in opening doors that are barred to strange men."

He turned away and started to walk from the crypt, turning around at the entrance when Lucinda made no move to follow.

"You are mine, you know," he said in a quiet voice. "To do with as I please. I could order you to walk into the rising sun and destroy yourself, and you would have no choice. You are my slave."

Don Diego smiled a wolfish smile, baring his fangs.

"You will now follow me, woman. And do as I tell you."

Lucinda did not want to go with the cruel monster before her. She tried to resist, telling herself that there was no way she would follow him. But her legs moved with a will of their own, and she found herself walking smoothly toward Don Diego. The man raised his head to look at the ceiling and emitted a deep resonant laugh that seemed to still echo in Lucinda's head.

* * *

"Hi. I was wondering when I was going to meet you."

Lucinda looked over at the elderly woman who was standing in the front yard of the neighboring house, holding a leash as a small dog squatted near her. She smiled back at the woman as the dog came out of the crouch and started growling at her.

"Dante," cautioned the elderly woman, pulling on the leash. "You behave. Don't you bark at the nice lady."

He knows something you don't, thought Lucinda.

"I'm sorry ma'am," said Lucinda, looking at the dog which whimpered and backed up to the end of the leash. "I'm allergic to dogs."

"I'm sorry too, young lady," said the woman, pulling her dog forward, bending over and scooping the pet into her arms. "I don't know what I'd do without Dante."

Lucinda looked over the lined face of the white haired, frail woman. *I will never be as her*, she thought with regret. *I will be forever young. Unless I am destroyed. I wonder what she would do if she was told she could regain her youth. And the only price would be the taking of a human life on a daily basis.*

"I'm Mrs. Flannery," said the old lady, starting to come forward, then stopping as the dog began to bark furiously. "Rose Flannery. And I'm sorry again about Dante."

"No problem Mrs. Flannery," said Lucinda, flashing another smile at the dog. The dog took the smile for what it was, the baring of teeth of a dominant predator, and stopped barking. "He's just doing his job. Protecting you from strangers."

Lucinda bent down and picked up the paper that was lying on her walkway. She unfolded it to get a look at the front page.

"I don't get the paper," said Mrs. Flannery. "There's nothing but bad news in there. At my age you want to hear all the good news you can."

"I'm sure that's true, ma'am," said Lucinda, glancing at the story about the death of Jacob Padillas, right next to an article about three bikers dying in a bar fire.

"This is the first time I've seen you in the day," said Mrs. Flannery. "Do you work at nights?"

You might say that, thought Lucinda, hiding a smile. "I work at Tampa General," she said, nodding her head. "Night shift."

"A nurse? Or a doctor?"

"Not quite enough education to be a physician," said Lucinda. "I'm a nurse."

"Well as far as I'm concerned the nurses do the real work in the Hospital, miss?"

"I'm sorry Mrs. Flannery," said Lucinda with a smile. "Lucy Tate. Nice to meet you."

"I was a nurse myself," said Mrs. Flannery. "On the night shift myself for fifteen years. People must have thought I was a vampire."

Lucinda felt a constriction in her throat at the double threat of what the woman had just said. *She might be able to pin me down*, thought Lucinda, *if she asks too many questions about nursing. And the vampire remark.* Lucinda calmed herself down after a moment of panic. She thought that she had seen enough hospital shows to fake the nurse persona, even to a retired nurse. And vampire images were plentiful on TV and in movies.

"I have to get ready to run some errands," said Lucinda, folding the paper back up. "Nice meeting you."

"Nice meeting you, dear," said Mrs. Flannery, putting Dante back on the ground and tugging on his leash. "Don't make yourself a stranger. Maybe you could come over to dinner some night before you go to work."

Lucinda nodded her head as she walked back to her front door. *And what would you think when I didn't eat anything? When I was incapable of ingesting the food you put in front of me? And when I was not able to join you in prayer?*

Lucinda closed her door behind her and walked to the kitchen. At least one of the neighbors had seen her during the day. Gossip would spread, until everyone in the neighborhood would be sure that the nice young nurse couldn't possibly be a vampire, such as the papers were saying had invaded the city. Because she had been seen in the daylight.

Lucinda spread the paper out on the kitchen table as she sat in one of the hard wooden seats. First she read over the story about Jacob's death. The police thought it might be a murder, but there was no mention of there being little or no blood in the body. No mention of a vampire. *So the burning technique works well*, she thought. There was no way they could link the death to her. Except for the mention of a suspect being sought. There had been many people to see her in the club. But she had to make a quick strike with little planning since the primary target was too well protected.

She then looked over the second story, which on the surface looked like either a gang killing or a cover-up gone badly. But something about the story made her shudder. *I'll bet this was a killing by another vampire*, she thought.   *Or vampires*. Someone else had made a kill and had covered it up with burning the bodies.   She felt and smelled the presence of the ones who were looking for her, both the Ancient Master and her own mistake. This killing would fit perfectly with one or both of them making a kill.   And maybe trying to get some information on Tampa's crime network at the same time.

"Well," she said to herself as she headed toward the bedroom, "nothing I can do about it now, but watch my back."

Lucinda had her clothes laid out. She let the bathrobe fall from her naked form and started to dress. The problem was to not show so much skin that the burning sensation caused her too much discomfort. But in Florida she would be looked on with suspicion if she covered herself from head to foot. She had settled on jeans, tennis shoes and a top that bared her shoulders. After pulling on the clothes she smeared some sunscreen on her shoulders, arms and face. The last touch was the mirrored sunglasses and she was ready to go.

Have to remember to buy some scrubs, she thought as she left the house. If she was going to tell people she was a nurse on the night shift she might have to play the part for nosey neighbors. Dressing the part would probably satisfy the casual observer.

Lucinda waved at the taxi that was cruising down the road, looking for her address. The cabbie pulled the taxi into her driveway as she walked up and pulled the door open, sliding into the front seat.

"The company prefers for the fares to ride in the back," said the cabbie, a middle aged man in a Hawaiian shirt. Lucinda looked up at his license and picture over the sunshade as she thought, *can't have you looking at me in the rear view mirror and seeing nothing, now can I?*

"I promise you I don't bite, much," she said to the cab driver with a laugh. "And I get car sick riding in the back."

"OK," agreed the cabbie. "You don't look too dangerous to me."

Lucinda could feel how the man's eyes undressed her, and she knew what was going through his mind. *I hate to disappoint you, Fred*, she thought, looking up again at his license, *but you wouldn't enjoy the experience*. While she could exude sex, and stimulate the senses of any man she wanted to make her prey, she could only simulate the sex act to a certain degree. And that degree did not include the lubrication of her vagina. And the thought of sex itself was not something that brought any excitement to her.

Drat the luck, she thought. It would have made her feel more alive to have actually made love to a man, to feel the feelings that went with a man's touch on certain areas of her body. *But I'm not alive, am I*, she thought with a snort.

"Something funny?" asked Fred the cabbie, looking over at her with a frown.

"Just a private thought," she said. "How about you take me to city hall."

"You're the boss," said Fred. "Traffic's kind of rough in that part of town this time of day."

"There's a very nice tip in it if you get me there quickly," she said with a smile, as Fred backed the car up onto the street and the started to accelerate forward.

*   *   *

This was the fifth real estate agency that Marcus had visited today. The first four had turned up nothing. He had thought about having Tashawn do this leg work for him, but decide that a well-dressed white man would have more luck that a huge black man that looked, to say the least, like a gansta out of the rap videos that Marcus despised.

"I'm Ms. Martin. And what can I do for you, Mr. LaMont?" said the slightly plump woman behind the desk of the office he had been shown to.

Marcus looked her over with interest. The women of his day had been of her build, unlike the skinny women of today, or conversely the extremely obese women that seemed to be growing in numbers. *I would love to have real sex*, thought the vampire lord, thinking of the woman lying under him as they sweated together in bed. But that part of him didn't function. He assumed it was because one needed a beating heart to provide the blood pressure needed for an erection. Marcus shook himself out of his thoughts as he felt the woman's eyes on him.

"I was wondering if you might have rented a property to this young woman?" he asked, producing a picture and placing it on her desk.

The woman picked up the picture and glanced at it, giving a slight grunt as she did. She placed it back on the desk, then she looked up at LaMont with her fingers steepled in front of her.

"It's not the policy of this Agency to pry into the personal affairs of our clients," said the woman. "As long as they're not involved in illegal activities and pay their rent on time. And what would your interest be in this particular woman, Mr. LaMont?"

"Nothing sinister, I assure you," LaMont said with a smile, feeling the woman's heart race faster. "Her family is worried about her is all. And I was hired to find her and let her know that all is forgiven."

"A private investigator," she said, returning his smile. "You do have credentials, don't you?"

"You don't need to see those," he said in a calm voice. "You trust that everything is as I said."

"You look like the trustworthy type," said Ms. Martin after a moment's hesitation. "I think you're legit."

"Thank you Ms. Martin."

"Call me Jane," she said with another smile. "And I think you're in luck. I rented a house to this woman, showed it to her just the other day. She paid cash in advance for three months' rent, plus the security deposit."

"Could you tell me where she is Jane?" said Marcus, keeping his voice at the purr that melted women's hearts.

"Of course," said the woman, her heart continuing to race. "Or better yet I could show you where she lives."

This one is showing a little too much interest, thought Marcus. But he smiled just the same as he nodded his head. "I would like that Jane. When could we go look?"

"I'm watching the office for the next couple of hours," she answered, breaking into a big smile. "I figure if you could meet me here after six, we might could go over to her house and surprise her. I mean, you don't want her taking off before you give her the news, do you?"

"No, Jane," agreed Marcus, nodding his head. "I don't want her taking off. And thank you."

"You're not from Tampa, are you?"

"Why do you ask?" said Marcus, a frown coming to his face.

"I don't know," she said, run her hand through her long hair. "Just a feeling."

"No. I'm not from around here. I'm just in town to find this poor child and let her know that she can come home."

"First time in Tampa?"

"Yes, Jane. I've never been here before. But I have to admit I like what I've seen so far."

"Well, maybe I can show you around the town after you've taken care of business."

"I would enjoy that Jane," said Marcus, standing up from his seat and reaching a hand forward. The woman grasped his hand in a shake, sliding her nails gently along his palm as she retracted her hand.

"The pleasure is all mine," she said with a smile, as Marcus got up from the seat. He flashed her a last smile before walking from the office and back onto the street.

The late afternoon sun stung his eyes as he walked from the building. He waved his hand and the car pulled off of the curb down the street and headed his way. He opened the back door and slid into the seat. Tashawn turned around and gave him a predatory smile.

"Any luck?" the big man asked. "You find the whore?"

"I think I've found her," answered Marcus, patting the big man on the shoulder. "And I've arranged for the delivery of dinner as well."

"Marvin," he said to the driver in his commanding voice. "We have a couple of hours to kill. Why don't you drive us to another place where the scum hangs out. We might learn something interesting."

Marvin nodded his head as he pulled away from the curb.

"Hey," said Tashawn. "He's my friend. So you don't need to do that mind control crap on him."

"Mortals are never our friends," said Marcus, staring into Tashawn's eyes. "They can be our servants, or our food. But never our friends. Remember that vampire, or you will come to regret it."

* * *

Monsignor O'Connor woke when the alarm clock went off hours before sunset, not feeling particularly rested.

What did you think at your age? That you could stay up all night and a few hours in the day would make you feel fresh as a puppy. O'Connor staggered into the small bathroom attached to the guest room and splashed some cold water on his face. He studied his visage in the mirror and grunted. *You look like hell. You're going to kill yourself if you keep going like this.*

O'Connor said a quick prayer in his head, asking God to just keep him going long enough to fulfill his mission. But he also knew that God helped those who helped themselves, and taking care of himself was the best way to make sure he kept going long enough.

O'Connor took a shower, reveling in the feel of the hot water flowing over his skin. He toweled off and climbed into a set of black clothing, making sure that he looked the part of the priest in this Godless house. Then he went to the door and put his ear against the hollow core barrier.

"Sounds like he's up," said a rough voice outside the door.

"How'd you come up with that deduction, Sherlock," said a deeper voice. "He could of woken the whole house if anyone had been asleep."

"A fuckin priest," said the first voice. "What'll the boss want next, a damn Voodoo Witch Doctor?"

"Don't you get sacrilegious on me," said the second voice. "You show some respect for the good Padre, or I'll have to beat some respect into you."

"I didn't mean nothing by it Manny," said the first voice. "Boss tells me to bow down to the bastard, I'll bow down. He tells me to cut his throat…"

O'Connor shuddered as he pulled away from the door. *A Godless house indeed,* he thought. *Maybe I should let her do her work, then come after her. At least this pack of scum would not be a bother to this town. But then another would just rise in its place. And at least they're human.*

O'Connor fumbled with the door knob for a moment, making sure that the men in the hall knew he was coming out, and hoping they didn't think he had overheard them. As he walked through the door the man named Manny, a big brute of a man who looked like a steroid freak, turned and gave him a shark like smile.

"Like something to eat, Padre?" he asked. "Mr. Padillas told us to take care of your every need."

"I'd like some coffee," said O'Connor. *And he probably told you to keep a constant eye on me as well. So I don't stumble onto something I shouldn't.*

"Right this way, Padre," said Manny, leading the way down the long hall, the other man, his crazy eyes looking this way and that, falling in at O'Connor's back.

O'Connor took in the good paintings on the wall as he followed the big man. They walked through a doorway and into the large kitchen, where a Latina woman was stirring a pot while something that smelled delicious cooked in the large oven.

"Cream and sugar, Padre," said Manny, pulling a large cup from a cupboard and putting it on the counter next to a large brewing machine.

"Cream will be fine," said O'Connor. "And some sweetener if you have it. Sugar's not good for me."

"Diabetic, Padre?" asked the crazy little guy with the rough voice. O'Connor nodded. "That sucks. My dad had diabetes and it was a bitch."

"How is your father now?" asked O'Connor, accepting the cup from Manny and taking a sip. He nodded in appreciation at the very good coffee he had been given.

"Dad's not doing so well," said the little guy. "He had an accident when I was in high school."

O'Connor shuddered to think what kind of accident dear old dad had with the little psychopath in the family.

"Vinny is pulling your chain, Padre," said the big man. "What kind of priest are you anyway?"

"I'm a Jesuit," said O'Connor, taking another sip of coffee and feeling the wonderful caffeine entering his system.

"An educated priest, huh?"

"PhD in Clinical Psychology," answered O'Connor. "BS in Psychology and Biology."

"So what made you want to be a vampire hunter?" asked Vinny with a chuckle.

"God, Vinny," said the bigger man. "Excuse the little shit Padre."

"That's OK, Manny," said John O'Connor with a smile. "I didn't choose to be a vampire hunter, Vinny. I was called to it by the Lord."

"Whatever you say, Father," said Vinny, shaking his head.

Just as I was called by the Lord to enter a den of vipers, he thought. *And protect them from the Devil that will claim them in the end no matter what I do.*

* * *

Lucinda felt that her time spent in the public records section of City Hall was fruitful, if not as enlightening as she had hoped. The Padillas Empire stretched throughout Hillsborough, Pinellas, Polk and Pasco Counties. At least the legitimate aspects of the empire. She had a pretty good rundown of what properties he owned, business and residential, and what bolt holes he might use if he felt threatened.

Some of the other aspects of his life might require a little more in the way of interrogation. But she was sure that she would get the information, one way or another. It would have been nice if she had been able to get to Padillas the night before. Then she could have been out of this town and on her way to another trouble spot. Now she could see no way to get into his house. Not with everyone in the town alerted and looking for her. She didn't think she could talk her way into the house, which meant she had to get Padillas when he was out of the house.

After stopping at an ATM to get some money out of her account she had gone by a medical supply store near Tampa General to pick up some scrubs. Waiting for the taxi to come, ensuring that she had gotten the same driver that would let her sit up front, she thought again about the benefits of having a car of her own. But that would entail getting a driver's license, or a fake, which came with problems of its own, like what to do if a cop ran it. And a car could also cause other problems if she left it in a place where it was found after a killing.

Now Lucinda spent some time getting into her stalking clothes, making herself up to look like a streetwalker. She worried for a moment that the heat might be too great on the street. That the dealers and pimps might be spending the evening in hiding, knowing that death stalked the night. A smile crossed her face at that thought. The pimps and dealers were for the most part greedy and stupid. They would stay on the streets selling their wares if Satan himself were walking by.

The sun was still up when she left the house, feeling like Superman, with her whore's clothing worn under her new scrubs, her heels in the large bag hanging from her shoulder. She walked away from the house and down the street, to the City Transit stop and the bus that would take her back to one of the high crime areas of the city.

* * *

O'Connor thought for a moment that he had been transported into a bad gangster movie. Big, beefy men surrounded him wherever he went on the estate. Men with names like Vinnie, Rocko and Mannie. He had asked one of them about it while he was working on his special project.

"My real name's Fred Sander," said the big man with the arms of a body builder. "But the boss likes to think of himself like the Godfather. You know, like that movie. So we all got Italian nicknames."

"Even though you're not Italian?" asked the priest, taking the paint and brushes the man had brought him.

"Hell," laughed Fred *Rocko* Sander. "The boss, he ain't even Italian. His parents came from Greece. His dad was a sponge diver while the boss was growing up."

O'Connor shook his head as he carried the paint into the room he had chosen, Fred following him like a very large shadow. O'Connor put the paint on the top of a drop cloth and started working on the lid with the little opening tool that was sent with the can. The top came off as easy as such things ever did, meaning with great difficulty. O'Connor started stirring the paint with the wooden stick that came with the paint, while Fred sat on the floor and pulled out a book. O'Connor grunted in surprise when he saw the title.

"Yeah," said Fred, looking at the cover himself. "Mark Twain is my favorite. Not all of us here are illiterate goons, even though we were hired for our strength of limb, so to speak. But the boss likes his bodyguards to have something in the head as well."

"I noticed that there are no blacks or Latinos here," said O'Connor, stirring away at the paint. He stopped for a moment to crumble some white wafers into the paint, then continued to stir.

"The boss will use the niggers and the spics," said Fred, his easy speech showing that he didn't think there was anything wrong with the labels. "But he says that he won't trust his life to them."

It tells much of him, thought O'Connor, *that he needs many men to guard his life in the first place.* After crumbling some more wafer in the paint and stirring for a while longer, O'Connor looked at his mixture with satisfaction. He tore the brush from its wrapping plastic and dipped it into the paint. Pulling the sopping brush from the can he started to work on one of the walls while Fred looked on.

"You really think this is going to work?" asked Fred, his brow furrowing as he watched the priest at work.

"I don't see why not," said the priest. "I've never tried this before, but I see no reason that it wouldn't."

"Why not just stake her when she shows up?" asked Fred. "That's what Buffee does after all."

"She isn't like a vampire that you see on TV or in the movies," said O'Connor, shaking his head. *No wonder they are able to move around us so easy, when most people are completely clueless about their true powers.*

"So staking her don't work?"

"Staking her works just fine, Fred," said the priest. "In the daytime it works quite fine. But at night they are very hard to harm, much less kill."

"So they're invulnerable at night?" asked Fred.

"No," said the priest. "They are definitely not invulnerable. But they are extremely hard to handle. I've heard of vampires being destroyed at night as well. Which is one reason I wish you would have let me keep my gun."

"The boss don't want anyone he hasn't known for quite a while to carry heat around him," said Fred. "Nothing personal, you understand."

"The only thing I want is to rid the Earth of this monster," said the priest. "I mean none of the living any harm."

"It's up to the boss," said Fred. "If he says give you back your piece, we give it back to you. If not, then you depend on us to watch your back. Besides, the boss has your gun on his person. If it needs to be used, he can use it."

O'Connor snorted at the obstinacy of the people he was forced to work with. But they were his best chance of getting to her, so they were the tools he needed to use. The priest continued to paint on one wall, then dragged the drop cloth and paint bucket to another. When finished with that wall he was feeling a little light headed from the fumes.

"I need some air," he told Fred. "Could we go out for a moment?"

"Sure," agreed Fred. "The boss is entertaining some people out in the back yard, and I don't think he wants you to listen in. But the front porch is free. Just make sure you don't get out of my sight."

The way the man looked at him O'Connor was sure there would be real trouble if he got out of the sight of his watchers. Therefore he had no intention of getting out of sight or trying to be secretive in his preparations. Yet.

* * *

Jane Martin pulled her car against the curb and got out, walking jauntily toward the front door as Marcus came out of the passenger door and followed. The woman was moving her hips in a sexy manner. Marcus smiled. He knew he had that effect on women, and had used it to advantage against her.

Marcus looked around as he followed up the walkway. He could see Marvin's car parked up the street. Then his attention was brought back to the real estate agent as she started knocking on the door.

Wait till I signal for you, he thought. An answering ascent came into his mind, as Tashawn, hiding in the bushes at the side of the house, thought back at him.

"I don't think she's home," said the agent. "Too bad she doesn't have a phone. We could have saved a trip out here."

"That's OK," said Marcus, staring into the woman's eyes. "Could we have a look inside?"

"I don't think so," said Jane Martin, shaking her head. "I don't intrude on the lives of the tenants. It's nosey and it's against the law. But now that you know where the place is at you can come back anytime you want."

Marcus stared into the woman's blue green eyes, probing deep into her soul. He could feel her will fleeing before his, as a blank look came over her face.

"You will open the door for me," he said in a calm voice.

"Why don't I just let you in," said Jane, pulling a set of keys from her purse, selecting the right one, and sliding it into the deadbolt lock.

"I'm sure she won't mind if we go inside," continued Jane as she opened the lower handle lock, then turned the handle and pushed the knob in.

Marcus could smell the faint scent of his kind in the air coming from the house. He gestured the woman in before him as he made ready to enter the house. *Now will be the test*, he thought. If it was the home of a living person he would not be able to cross the threshold without the invitation of the resident, and he would not be able to follow Jane Martin into the house. But if it were the dwelling of the already dead.

Marcus crossed the threshold easily, feeling no resistance whatsoever. The scent was slightly stronger inside, but still not strong enough to alert him to the presence of a vampire. *She is not here*, he thought. Did that mean that she was out for the night? Or that this was a secondary lair, one she had set up but not used.

"What are we doing in here?" said Jane Martin, coming somewhat out of her trance.

You may come, Tashawn, thought Marcus to the lesser vampire. He felt no need to feed himself this night, but knew that a youngling like Tashawn would soon be feeling the hunger. And he didn't want the youngling's instincts working against him this night.

"You opened the door and let us in," said Marcus to the woman, as she looked at the key she was holding in her thumb and forefinger like she had never seen it before.

"Why would I do that?" she asked, shaking her head as if to clear it. "I could lose my license for breaking into this house."

The door opened behind Marcus and Jane hissed in a breath. Marcus looked back at Tashawn. *He is an intimidating sight*, thought Marcus. *Even as a mortal he must have been intimidating.*

Tashawn stretched to his full six-foot five-inch height as he flexed his massive arm muscles. His eyes locked with those of the woman, driving the will from her with the force of his personality.

He learns quickly, thought Marcus. *Quickly enough? We will see.*

"Are you hungry, Tashawn?" Marcus asked of the towering giant.

"Just a little, Master," said Tashawn, showing a canine dominant smile.

"You will be ravenous in a little while," said Marcus, looking at the woman. "You may feed."

Tashawn nodded as he moved forward, keeping the woman locked into his eyes. He raised his hands, reaching for the woman. At that moment Jane Martin must have felt the total threat to her existence that the man represented. She opened her mouth to scream. Tashawn's hands shot forward, one grasping the woman's left shoulder while the other went over her mouth, stifling the nascent scream.

Jane tried to fight away as Tashawn brought his mouth toward the right side of her neck. She swung her hands to his face, then tried to push him away. The sun was not yet down and Tashawn had yet to gain his supernatural strength. But for a man who weighed two hundred and seventy pounds and had bench pressed over five hundred when he had been alive, the struggles of a woman of average strength were nothing.

Tashawn pierced the neck with his fangs, ripping into the flesh. The woman bit his hand, her eyes wide with fear.

Tashawn ignored the pinprick of the bite and started sucking the fluid that gushed from the wound in the neck.

Marcus could see the pure pleasure in Tashawn's eyes as the big vampire drained the life force from the woman. Jane Martin's struggles became weaker and weaker, her eyes shown with a pleasure matching that of her slayer. Then she was not struggling at all as her body no longer had enough blood for the heart to pump. With a final couple of sucks at the neck, Tashawn brought his head away from the woman. There was blood trickling down the vampire's lips and dribbling off of his chin.

Tashawn dropped the body of the woman. It fell limply to the floor, the head that would never feel again cracking on the hardwood floor. The corpse sprawled like a rag doll, wide eyes staring at nothing.

"Clean up your mess, Tashawn," ordered Marcus, nodding at the body. Tashawn looked blankly for a moment at the older vampire, still in the throes of the ecstasy of feeding.

"You are a guest in the house of another," explained Marcus is a slow voice that was sure to break through the younger vampire's cloud of pleasure. "You do not throw garbage on the floor of another's house and leave it. Put the body in a closet in one of the rooms."

Marcus wandered the house while Tashawn hid the body. The elder vampire looked from room to room. There were some clothes in one of the closets, no food in the refrigerator or cabinets. There was no coffin or other resting place where her soil was stored.

Walking back into the hallway he noted there was a set of retractable stairs in the ceiling. He grabbed the hanging cord and pulled the stairs down to full extension. The vampire could smell the scent of his prey, stronger than it was at the entrance of the house, but still not strong enough to indicate that she was actually up there. He climbed the steps and bent over in the cramped attic space.

"Don't bother coming up here," he called down as he heard Tashawn moving in the hallway. "It would be too tight a fit for you."

The coffin was in front of the vampire, only a dozen feet from the hatchway to the attic. He moved to it and lifted the lid. There was a thin layer of soil on the bottom of the coffin, but no imprint of a laying body. *Not that it matters*, he thought. Many vampires cleared the imprints in their coffins each morning.

"What we going to do now?" said Tashawn from below.

"Why we wait, of course," said Marcus, "and hope she returns this night."

Marcus climbed down the steps, looking into Tashawn's eyes and noting that the youngling was over the feeding ecstasy.

"Go tell Marvin to come in here and wait with us," said Marcus. "He'll look too suspicious sitting in that car for hours on the street."

"Wait," he said as Tashawn started to move, stopping the big man in his tracks. "You stay here. I will go and retrieve Marvin. You stand out too much yourself."

Tashawn nodded as Marcus walked toward the door. *I have to drive some culture into the minds of these savages*, he thought. *Before I find myself becoming a savage as well.*

* * *

"Isn't that the son-of-a-bitch you chased off last night?" said Sanchez, pointing toward the long porch of the big house.

DeFalco looked to where the homicide detective was pointing, to where a gray haired man stood talking to a big blond haired man who was smoking a cigarette. It took the FBI agent a moment to figure out who the gray haired man was, since he was wearing a white T-shirt instead of the black shirt and white collar that DeFalco was used to seeing on him.

"Goddammit," swore the agent, shoving the door open and climbing out of the car. "I told that SOB to stay clear of this place. What the hell is he doing here?"

Sanchez got out of the car as the FBI agent came around to his side and stood with his face turning red with fury. He put his hand on the FBI Agent's shoulder and shook the man.

"Get a grip, DeFalco," said Sanchez, as the agent turned to look at him. "He must have a good reason for being here. He's in the house, after all."

DeFalco shrugged off the detective's hand and stormed toward the house, staring straight ahead at the people on the porch. He stopped at the chest high chain linked fence, as a pair of Rottweilers came running up, barking at the potential intruder.

"You bastard," yelled DeFalco toward the porch.

"You talking about me," said the big blond haired man, turning an angry scowl toward the agent.

"No, scumbag," said DeFalco, "I'm talking to him." The Agent slammed his hand on the top of the fence, then pulled it back quickly as one of the dogs tried to jump up and take it off.

"Who you calling scumbag, dickweed," yelled the blond man, striding off the porch and heading for the fence.

"You better stop there Fred," called Sanchez, coming up to stand beside DeFalco. "Unless you want to catch some charges. Starting with threatening a Federal Agent."

"He wants me, Fred," said O'Connor, walking toward the fence. "What can I do for you Agent DeFalco?"

"You can tell me what the hell you are doing here," yelled DeFalco in the Brooklyn accent that came out in his fury. "I told you to stay away from this house. Now I'm going to take you in and you can spend a night or two in jail."

"I'm afraid that Mr. Padillas wouldn't like that," said Fred, glaring at the Agent. "Father O'Connor is his personal guest, invited to stay at Mr. Padillas' house as long as he wants. And he is not an unwelcome intrusion."

"I told him to stay away from here," yelled DeFalco, his face growing even more strained.

"Tell that to Mr. Padillas' lawyers," said Fred, thrusting his face over the fence as the dogs went into a frenzy. "I'm sure they will be happy to explain to you about the rights of a citizen in this country. In case you've forgotten Mr. Federal Agent."

"Let it go DeFalco," said Sanchez, putting a hand on the FBI man's arm. "All we're doing here is attracting the attention of the neighborhood."

DeFalco looked at Sanchez, then at the hand the detective still had on his arm. He shrugged the arm off and turned away from the fence, walking back toward the car. He turned after a couple of steps and walked back to the fence.

"I hope you enjoy your little vampire hunt, Father," he said, pointing a finger at the priest. "I'll not be responsible for whatever happens to you when you get in the line of fire."

DeFalco turned away again and stormed back to the car, flinging the passenger door open and climbing into the car, then slamming the door with a sound that rattled the windows of nearby houses. "You coming?" he yelled out to Sanchez.

"Sorry about that outburst there, Father," said Sanchez. "I'm afraid Agent DeFalco has been under a lot of stress."

"The man's a nut," said Fred, shaking his head. "You better keep him on a leash." The big man turned around as he growled something at the dogs, and headed back to the porch, the two guard dogs following at his heals.

"I understand that Mr. DeFalco wants to get her himself," said the priest, nodding toward the car. "What he doesn't understand is that this is something more in my area of expertise than his. Watch yourself, detective. You just might find yourself in a situation that you can't get out of."

O'Connor turned away and walked back toward the house, one of the dogs running up to sniff him, then running back after the hired muscle.

"Motherfucker," said Sanchez as he walked back to the car under the stare of DeFalco. "This is becoming a real freak show."

Chapter 6

Lucinda felt the normal satisfaction of a feeding, just like any other time. But the feeling battled with the frustration of not being able to get to her primary target. As the body went limp in her grasp she locked her fingers in the hair and released her other hand, holding the small man's corpse up by his long locks. She pulled the long knife from her back sheath and swung it at the neck, slicing through the flesh, bone and cartilage. The limp body fell bonelessly to the asphalt as she held the dripping head in her hand.

Lucinda pulled the manhole cover up from its berth with her free hand and looked down into the flowing waters from the night's thunderstorm. She tossed the head into the fast moving waters below. Then she set the cover down and picked up the body, tossing it into the water as well. *And out into the bay with luck*, she thought. Replacing the cover on the hole she moved back out of the alley and starting walking down the sidewalk, trying to blend in with the other streetwalkers.

A blue and white came down the street from the other way, shining its light into her face. She put her hand up to shield her eyes and continued to walk. The car slowed for a moment, then flashed its light. Lucinda got ready to run as the siren came on. But the car accelerated down the street and away, gaining speed as it responded to the distant call.

Lucinda wanted to breathe a sigh of relief, but remembered at the last moment that she didn't breathe. That act would have called for a forceful filling of her lungs with air. She could wipe her brow, but without the ability to sweat it would merely be a gesture. At least she could still smile, and she did as she thought that the night had been perfect as far as the stalk and kill had gone. One more scumbag off of the street, even if he was just a minor player.

The vampiress looked quickly to her front and rear. All she saw was a whore wrangling a price with a John in a car and a couple of addicts lounging on the steps of their building, their minds in the other place where dwelt those whose lives were too hopeless for reality. She ducked into the nearby alley, straining her ears to locate anything that might be waiting. All she could locate were a couple of rats rummaging in some garbage cans, and the quiet breathing of a cat lying in wait for one of the rats to come out of cover.

Good luck with your hunt, she thought. *Such a simple life you lead. Just like my so-called brethren. Sometimes I wish that I could hunt like them, just locate any sufficient prey and feed. But that would make me as evil as they are.*

Lucinda stopped in her tracks as the last thought hit her. *As evil as they are*, she thought. The image of the dying drug dealer came to mind, the feel of his flesh as her fangs broke through, the taste of the blood that flowed into her mouth. *As evil as they are. I am a very special kind of evil.*

Lucinda raised her face to the sky and laughed, a cry of manic mirth. The rats stopped scurrying as they quivered in fear, as the cat left its watch and darted from the alley, causing a car to swerve as it crossed the street. Lucinda laughed for minutes, then gathered her wits about her.

I'm going to attract attention I don't need, she thought. She looked at the entrance of the alley as she strained her hearing. Nothing that she could find. Shaking her head at her own stupidity, Lucinda raised her arms to the sky and started the transformation. Soon she was soaring over the city as her leathery wings flapped through the night air.

Below she could hear the sounds of the city. The cough and growl of engines, the screams of women as men beat them within their dwellings, the cries of frightened children. Men groaned in the agony of their injuries, while junkies called out for help as they sweated and tossed from the throes of their addictions. Lucinda wished that she could cry the tears for them that they deserved, but she couldn't. The heart that no longer beat in her seemed to ache at the realization that she could do nothing to comfort them in their suffering.

All she could do was try and remove some of that which caused the pain and suffering. *And I am like this flying rodent whose form I now inhabit, she thought. I can fly the night and kill some few of the vermin which inhabit it. But when the new day dawns there are still as many of them as there were the night before.*

For a moment she had the urge to fly into the night until the coming dawn, to let the rising sun burn her from the sky. Or to go to the priest and allow him to send her to the hell that she deserved. But she knew that was a useless thought. Her instincts would prevent it. The instincts of the hunter that worked according to a single principle; survival at all costs.

With a screech of sonar Lucinda wheeled in flight, banishing her depression with the relish of her powers at work. *There are compensations, she thought. And if I can't make much of a dent in the world's problems, at least I made what dent I could. Which is more than most beings can say.*

The giant bat bared its teeth to the night, heading for home. *And there is the personal satisfaction, she thought, of a job well done.*

* * *

"Well father," said George Padillas, looking into the room the priest had been working on through the night. "How's the project going?"

"Very well, Mr. Padillas," said O'Connor. "I'm almost finished."

"Call me George," said the crime boss. "After all, you are a man of God, much higher in his standing than this plain old sinner. So you deserve the respect, not I."

"OK, George," agreed the priest. "But it is not too late to turn your life around."

The older man laughed deeply as his eyes looked around the room. Within a moment he stopped with a wheeze, tears in his eyes.

"It may be too late," said Padillas, catching his breath. He stopped chuckling as a serious look came over his face and he studied the layout of the room.

"So you think this is going to work?" said Padillis, walking to one of the walls for a closer look.

"I think so, yes," said O'Connor, glancing at the floor, ceiling and walls. "At least it will disorient her. At most it will do exactly what I want it to do."

"And then you will send her to the hell where she belongs," said Padillas in a hushed voice. "The hell she sent my only boy to."

"I hope so," said the priest, patting the man on the shoulder. "For all of our sakes I really hope so."

"She's not going to come tonight," said Padillas, putting his arm around the priest and steering him out of the room. "It's almost dawn. Why don't you get some sleep?"

"We need to get her here in the first place," said O'Connor, shaking his head. "It will be kind of hard to do with a police cordon outside the house."

"I'll talk to my attorneys," said Padillas. "Maybe we can talk to the city about harassment. Make them go away for a few days. Then we can do things your way."

The devil's way, you mean, thought O'Connor. *But sometimes one must make a deal with the devil in order to destroy the greater evil.*

*   *   *

Marcus could tell that Tashawn was panicking by the way the big vampire kept clenching and unclenching his hands and looking at the windows, as if expecting to see the sun at any minute.

"There is still over an hour to dawn, Tashawn," said the elder vampire, trying to sound soothing. "When it hits a half hour and she hasn't shown you can fly back to your lair."

"If I make it back in time," said the huge man, his eyes wide. "If I don't get hit by the fucking Sun and turn into a pile of ashes."

"I will give you plenty of time," said Marcus, trying to keep his voice under control. "If you use it wisely you will be under cover and in your resting place well before the first rays of morning light come over the horizon."

"I still don't like it, man," complained the youngling.

Marcus came to his feet and moved in a blur to where the big man sat. Looking down on him, he could see Tashawn trying to sink into the chair under the elder's overpowering gaze.

"You are a worthless piece of crap," yelled Marcus in Latin, the force of his words beating down the other vampire, even if Tashawn didn't know the meaning. "If you had been in my Legion I would have put you on the cross as an example to others."

"Heah man," said Marvin, struggling to stay awake on the couch. "Could you please speak English where we can understand it?"

In the blink of an eye Marcus was standing over Marvin. His clawed hand reached down in a flash and grabbed the front of the man's shirt. With an ease of movement that was similar to a normal man lifting a cat, the vampire pulled Marvin up by his shirt and overhead.

"I will brook no back talk from one such as you," said Marcus, showing his fangs in a horrid grin. "One more word from that sewer you call a mouth will be your last."

With a contemptuous shrug Marcus slammed Marvin back into the couch and walked away. Coming to the only other chair in the room the ancient vampire dropped into it with a heavy thump. He looked from Tashawn to Marvin's face, back and forth, daring either to say a word. He could feel his own frustration building up within him. Using the discipline that the centuries had instilled within him, he used a calming inner speech to battle the anger. Marcus knew he still needed these two for his plans, for now at least. Later he could see about disposing of them if that suited his purposes. The problem solved for now he released his feelings over it and felt a wave of calm sweep through him.

"Go," he finally told Tashawn, nodding his head. "Get yourself back to your lair before you piss yourself. And take this worthless hunk of worm bait with you."

Tashawn nodded as he got up from the chair, motioning for Marvin to follow him. He looked sheepishly at the elder vampire as he moved to the front door.

"You had best fly," said Marcus to the youngster. "Your minion can follow you."

"What about you?" asked Tashawn, hesitating at the door.

"I'll be fine as long as I stay out of the direct rays," said Marcus, nodding toward the window. "Two thousand years gives on a bit of resiliency."

"So someday I'll be able to nix the dawn sleep," asked Tashawn hopefully.

Marcus glared at Tashawn, shaking his head. Tashawn frowned and looked to Marvin. Marvin shrugged his shoulders and opened the door, walking out into the night air. Tashawn followed.

Marcus could feel the power in the air as Tashawn changed form. He heard the hypersonic screech of sonar and the flap of leathery wings. *If you get to live two thousand years you might add a bit of resiliency to your repertoire*, thought Marcus, shaking his head. *But I would have bet the Empire that you wouldn't.*

* * *

Lucinda floated out of the sky and down toward the grassy surface of her back yard, her eyes darting up to the sky, looking at how the clouds were beginning to lighten with the approaching dawn. Soon that beautiful light would be flooding the world and her life would become a vision of flames and pain, if she didn't get inside.

She transformed back to her human form in the darkest shadows of the backyard, under the cover of a Norfolk Pine. Listening for a moment until she was sure that there was nothing moving nearby, expanding her nostrils as she brought in samples of the night air to gather the scent of anyone in hiding, Lucinda shook her head in satisfaction that no one was nearby.

Lucinda pushed open the wooden gate to the backyard and moved around the side of the house, keeping to the shadows and being very alert to any motion or scents. *No use stirring up the neighbors,* she thought with a smile. It was not her purpose to be the object of gossip among the good retirees of her community. Or to cause them stress related health problems. So she stayed close to the house as she came around the corner and into the streetlight exposed front yard.

The feeling of something wrong came over her as her feet hit the concrete of the front walk. She could not place what it was, just that a feeling of something horribly wrong was settling over her. Lucinda crouched down, all thoughts of the nosy neighbors fled from her mind.

Lucinda looked intently at the door, not more than a dozen feet away. *That has to be it,* she thought. *Something or someone is waiting for me. But who?* She sniffed at the air, trying to pick up the scent of her foes. But nothing would come to her senses; nothing that would tell her what might be waiting on the other side of the entrance to her home.

The vampire looked again to the sky. She really couldn't tell if the clouds were any lighter, but the contrails of a jet shown pink higher up in the atmosphere. *No time,* she thought, looking back at the door as she reached her hand toward it. The nearest alternate lair was at least fifteen minutes flight away, and she could feel the sun closer to the horizon than that. She tried to quell the panic as she felt trapped between the intruders in the house and the burning death outside.

That death would almost be welcome, she thought, looking again at the door. *Whereas I might be fighting for my life within the house, and taking the lives of the mortals within, if they are mortals.* She placed the key within the deadbolt's hole and turned it over, still trying to sense what might be within the house.

But as she struggled with the dilemma in her mind, her senses again focused on the sun, which was just over the horizon. The clouds were very pink now, and her hand reached for the knob of its own volition, to place the key in the lock and turn it. Her instincts were driving her toward the path of greatest survival, and she had no choice as she turned the knob and pulled the door open.

Her instincts forced her to hold for a moment as her eyes scanned the inside of the living room and she brought the air into her nostrils. *No one here*, she thought, feeling the tension flow out of her muscles.

A ray of light struck the top of the house, blindingly bright to her supernatural eyes. She jumped inside the house and pulled the door closed behind her, thumbing the dead bolt back to the locked position, then turning the door lock.

Faint light was now coming through the cracks between the heavy drapes. Lucinda moved as fast as she could, now limited to the speed of a mere mortal, into the hallway, pulling down the stairway to the attic. Up the stairs she went, sensing the rising light outside, and the plywood and shingles overhead that separated it from her and her true death.

Pulling open the coffin, Lucinda climbed in a fast as humanly possible, hitting her head on a rafter in her haste. As she lay down she thanked the God she normally cursed for the unyielding nature of her undead flesh. There was no pain, and she knew there would be no bruise when she awoke later in the day.

Lucinda felt her eyes grow heavier as the drowsiness came over her. The last thought she had before sleep claimed her was that the feeling of dread she had might be a precursor to an invasion that would come this day, while she was helpless in the coffin. Then she lost consciousness and became like a sleeping infant in her coffin.

* * *

Marcus could feel her presence just before the coming dawn. But it was distant, as if the coffin was calling to her and her link to it. *But not here*, he thought. She was going to another lair, one he didn't know about, yet.

The curtains lightened as the sun came up over the horizon and flooded the outside. Marcus walked to the curtain as he gripped one of the panels, slightly opening the curtain and moving his other hand into the beam of light. The ray burned as it touched the flesh, a pain such as the elder vampire hadn't felt in ages. He focused his will power onto his own flesh, as smoke began to wisp away from his hand. It threatened to burst into flames with the killing power of the day star.

The smoke stopped as pain began to fade. *I am in control*, he thought. *I will be the day walker. The one who brings the terror of the darkness to the light.*

The pain roared back as the smoke reappeared. Marcus dropped the curtain back into place just as the hand burst into flame. Roaring his agony he backed away from the window, waving the flames out. He looked in horror at his hand, at the seared flesh and scar tissue that it had become. He clutched his hand to his chest as he fought against the pain with his mind. He felt the agony turned to pain, then to ache, then to nothing. He looked at his hand, to see the scar tissue had faded back to vibrant looking flesh.

"One day," he said to the empty room. "One day I will be old enough and powerful enough to keep anything from harming me."

One day, he thought, *I will become the Emperor. And the world will be mine, to do with as I please.*

*   *   *

"No killings last night," said Smith, waving his report in the face of DeFalco. "I thought you said she had to feed, every single night."

"She does," said DeFalco, looking the Detective Lieutenant in the eyes without flinching from the anger revealed. "Just because your department has yet to find the body doesn't mean there isn't one. After all, she seems to be getting smarter."

"And I thought she was some kind of beast," said Lowrey, scowling at the FBI Agent as well. "Unreasoning, unthinking, operating only on instinct."

"She will be nothing like that," said Tanesha Washington, looking from DeFalco to Lowrey's face. "She is the spawn of the dark lord, and will have his cunning within her."

Washington nodded her head at Lieutenant Smith. "She will be pure evil, with the strength and intelligence that only the purely evil possess. A gift of the dark lord Satan."

"I don't see it," said Justine DeBarry, looking at Washington. "I mean, wouldn't a totally evil creature be out there killing the good of the world? And she goes and kills the scumbags we are trying to get off the street. Wouldn't she at least be taking out the innocents of the world, and turning them into her kind? Swelling the ranks so to speak."

"Vampires aren't like that," said DeFalco, looking at the disbelieving faces of the people around the table, and the oh too believing face of Tanesha Washington. "They kill at random, whoever happens to get in their way. They are pure but unreasoning evil."

"Then again," said DeBarry, "how do you explain the fact that in a number of cities across the east coast this one vampire you have chased after has never killed anyone who at least didn't deserve it?"

"So you're defending her?" asked DeFalco, shaking his head. "You're for allowing a criminal to walk the streets, a vigilante killer who takes the law into her own hands?"

"No," said DeBarry in a loud voice that startled the tired people in the room. "I'm not defending her. And I think we need to take her off the streets. But maybe killing her isn't the way. Maybe we should try to apprehend her, and bring her to trial. We are, after all, the police, and it is our job to catch people suspected of crimes alive if at all possible."

"But she's not alive in the first place," yelled DeFalco, slamming his hand on the table. "She was pronounced dead by a Philadelphia Coroner, for Christ's sake. I don't think the writers of the Constitution were thinking about the undead when they wrote that document. And she would burst into flames while she was sitting in the courtroom, so a trial really wouldn't help at all."

"If she really is a vampire," said Smith, glaring back at DeFalco, "And not just some crazy murdering bitch on PCP or something?"

"I didn't think we had to go over this again," said DeFalco, lowering his voice. "You saw the video. You saw how she did not appear on the tape of Giovani's murder. How do you explain that, huh?"

"Something Giovani's men faked," said Lowrey, nodding his own head toward DeFalco. "Maybe one of them killed him, to take his place, and planted this special effects sci-fi masterpiece in the hope that a crazy fool like you would believe it."

"This is nonsense," said DeFalco, slamming his own hand hard onto the surface of the table. "Don't tell me you believe a crazy story like that?"

"No crazier than a fucking vampire," said Smith. "Besides, it's a moot point. Padillas' lawyers filed a motion with the judge, stating that we were harassing their client. The Commissioner doesn't want us anywhere near his house unless we have some kind of verifiable proof that something is going on there. Something that warrants the attention of homicide."

"I still say that's crazy," said Washington, looking around the table. "We're trying to protect him. So why does he want to get rid of us?"

"Because he's a crime boss," said Sanchez, speaking up for the first time. "Because he's uncomfortable with having lots of police, and the FBI," Sanchez nodded at DeFalco, "watching his house and possibly listening in on him."

"Maybe he trusts his own security more than he trusts the police," added DeBarry. "After all, we haven't brought her to justice after Giovani's killing. So why would he think we could protect him. Instead we're hanging around his neighborhood, making the neighbors nervous, making him nervous."

"Sure," said Washington. "That all makes sense. But I think a man like Padillas has something else in mind. Like making his own deal with the devil and all."

"Now what would he want with another stone cold killer?" asked Lowrey.

"As I was saying," said DeFalco, "she's not just an ordinary killer. He might see something in her that he thinks he can use. But believe me, she's not going to let anyone use her, and he doesn't know what he's messing with."

"Well, he'll have to deal with her without our interference," said Smith. "The commissioner was very plain in what he ordered. And I, for one, want to make it to retirement without having to write parking tickets or go on patrol in Podunk."

"His order means nothing to me," said DeFalco, jutting his jaw out in defiance. "As far as I'm concerned he can go straight to hell, or to Podunk, or to writing his own tickets out on Dale Mabry. I will do what I feel I need to do to get her."

"I'm sure the Commissioner will be glad to talk with your boss as well," said Smith, looking at the Agent. "If you push him. But if you want to go off on your own and be the Fearless Vampire Hunter, that's up to you. Just don't get any of my people involved."

"If you think for a moment," said DeFalco, standing up from his chair.

The door flew open to the conference room and a uniformed sergeant poked his head in.

"If you detective types don't have anything better to do," said the rough voiced veteran, "they have an actual killing for you to consider."

"What?" said Smith, getting out of his own stair as everyone in the room started to move. "Where? What happened?"

"An anonymous call came in," said the sergeant, "so we sent a blue and white to the house in question. They found a body there, and called for homicide. So I guess that means you, Lieutenant."

"Let's go people," said Smith, walking toward the door as the sergeant moved out of the way.

"Can I still come, Smith?" asked DeFalco, following after the Homicide Detective. "Or am I barred by the Commissioner and Padillas' lawyers from investigating something not in his neighborhood?"

"You can come, DeFalco," said Smith, as he headed toward his office to grab what he needed for the road. "But just remember that this is our bailiwick. And you can ride with Sanchez."

DeFalco nodded his head as he turned to follow the Latino detective, listening to Sanchez mumble in Spanish about Gringos and their crazy ways.

*   *   *

Lucinda flew toward the third safe house lair, after having checked out one other and finding nothing. But she remembered the feel that something was wrong with her dwelling, that intruders had entered her space. And she knew she had to find out what it was that had triggered that feeling before it came to call at the house where she was staying.

The giant bat passed over Bush Boulevard as she headed north, looking down at the heavy flow of traffic on the thoroughfare. She could see the beginning of the lower scale retirement neighborhood ahead, while the thunder of a jet coming into Tampa International drowned out her hearing for a couple of moments. Sending her senses ahead she could feel the presence of intruders in the house in the middle of the neighborhood. Who they were she could not feel, but the aura of trouble surrounded the house.

Lucinda knew who they were as she came within blocks of the house. The flashing blue and red lights lit up the street, as a couple of more blue and whites pulled onto the street, followed by the boxy shape of an ambulance flashing its red lights. The siren of the ambulance was piercing to her animal hearing, and she flew around the block in confusion. She kept circling the house as a trio of unmarked cars with blue lights flashing on the dashes pulled onto the street and raced for the house.

The doors to the unmarked cars opened and men and women in suits got out and headed for the house. Lucinda brought their scent into her nostrils, as the short fur on her body stood up in recognition. *The people*, she thought. Those from the police department who had been dogging her trail over the last several days. Those who had been standing watch around the house of her primary target. Which meant the primary target was unwatched, unguarded.

Letting out a screech of triumph as all thought of what was going on below fled her mind, Lucinda wheeled in the sky and headed to the east. Toward the target she had been stalking for the last three days. The target that was at the head of the heap of scum who preyed upon the city. The reason for her being here, and the reason she could leave, once he was taken care of.

*   *   *

"What do we have here?" asked Smith as he got out of the car and approached a pair of uniformed officers in the front lawn who were keeping the curious at bay.

"What the fuck," said Lowrey, stopping in his tracks and looking up to the sky.

"What the fuck what?" said Smith, turning around before either of the uniforms could speak.

"That was the biggest fucking bat I ever saw," said the detective, pointing to the sky.

Smith followed the finger, but could see nothing in the sky that was obscured by the bright lights of the city.

"Come on," said Smith, turning his attention back to the people on the ground. "This isn't the nature channel."

Smith walked toward the house as the rest of his people fell in behind him. A black man in uniform with lieutenant bars in his collar tabs came out of the house and intercepted the homicide detectives, holding his hand out to Smith.

"Hey Johnson," said Smith, grabbing the man's hand and shaking it quickly. "Haven't seen you in a dog's age."

"Yeah," agreed the shift chief for North Tampa in a rumbling voice. "I wish we could meet somewhere a little more savory, like in church."

"Just haven't had the time," said Smith, shaking his head. "Not that brother Johnson is not a dynamic minister and all," he said, talking over his shoulder to his people.

"Well," said Johnson, "God still loves you, whether you have time for him or not."

"What we got inside?" said Smith in an uncomfortable voice.

"A dead woman," said Johnson, leading the detectives into the small house. "Doc says she's a little light in the blood department. Sound familiar?"

"Yeah," said Smith. "Too familiar. Must be the same psycho we've been trailing across the town."

"I heard she was more than a psycho," said Johnson, as they walked into the living room and to the hall.

Smith looked at the body that was lying half out of the hall closet, and the forensics people who were taking samples of everything. The head pathologist looked up as Smith stopped in the hallway and hurried over to the detective lieutenant.

"What do you have so far, Doc?" asked Smith, pointing at the body.

"We have a forty-three year old white female by the name of Jane Martin," said the Forensics Chief. "We're estimating the time of death as somewhere between seven and ten PM last night."

"Cause of death?" asked Smith, looking into the wide, staring eyes of the dead woman.

"The only wounds on her body are two puncture marks on the left side of her throat," said the Doc, moving toward the body as he leaned over and pointed at the dried and crusted blood on the neck. "She appears to have bled to death. At least that's the preliminary finding. We'll have to wait for the autopsy to be sure she didn't expire from other causes."

"It had to be her," said DeFalco, coming up behind Smith and looking over his shoulder.

Smith turned to one of the uniformed officers and wriggled a finger at her. The small blond haired woman came over to him, looking down at a legal pad that she had been taking notes on.

Doesn't want to look at the body, thought Smith, glancing again at the corpse half crumpled into the closet. *Can't really blame her there.*

"Officer," Smith said, looking at her nametag, "Garcia. Kind of a strange name for someone so fair skinned."

"Married name, sir," said the petite woman as she found herself drawn to looking at the body, a look of revulsion on her face.

"What do we have on the woman, Officer Garcia?" said Smith, drawing her attention back to him.

"She is, or was, a real estate agent working out of an office on the south side," said Garcia.

"Any known criminal involvement?"

"No sir," said the officer. "A couple of political rallies that got kind of out of hand. One arrest for refusing to leave the scene of a protest. But otherwise as clean as could be expected."

Smith turned to DeBarry and looked her in the eyes.

"Kind of ruins the avenging angel angle, doesn't it?" he said to her, then pointed back at the woman. "Here's one that was a productive member of society. No involvement with organized crime."

"I can't believe it," said Debarry. "I've looked over all of the files on her, and she's never done anything like this."

"Remember," said Washington. "If she is a vampire then she is a destructive force of nature. Random in her killings. And she needed a victim, and this one just came along at the right time. Or the wrong time for the victim, if you look at it that way."

"Or she's just some psycho," said Sanchez, looking directly at Washington. "She wants to look like an avenging angel, but she's only human. So she made a very human mistake, and killed the wrong person this time. It had to have happened eventually."

"But it happened in my city," growled Jamal Smith, staring down at the body of a citizen that he had sworn an oath to protect from this kind of tragedy. "Now I really fucking want this bitch."

*   *   *

"So why the hell did you call the police?" asked Tashawn, sitting in the passenger seat of the car, listening to the police scanner that Marvin had purchased that day.

"I wanted to tarnish the image that she had created," said Marcus, looking out of the window and to the sky. "And it takes the police away from the person she really wants."

"And all this shit about protecting our <u>kind</u> from the world," said Tashawn, shaking his head.

"I consider it a minor divulgence of information," said Marcus, looking back at the huge vampire. "She is already going about her business, giving away our existence to the world at large. If it helps to drive her into our hands, it actually minimizes the damage to us, in the long run."

"And what about leaving her head on her body?" asked Tashawn. "She normally takes their heads off. Don't you think the police might notice that?"

So the youngling is not as stupid as he looks, thought Marcus. *The four years he spent in an institution of higher learning playing ball must have inoculated him with a bit of knowledge and reasoning ability after all.*

"That was my mistake," confessed Marcus, looking down sheepishly at the floor of the car. He looked up and into Tashawn's eyes, challenging the big man to gloat at him.

"I thought she might make a good minion," continued Marcus, looking again to the outside of the car as if he were looking into forever. "I prefer women to serve me. And she had a pleasant appearance about her."

"Goddam," said Tashawn with a chuckle. "Thinking with the little head, were you. And I thought Mr. Superior never let emotion intrude on his logical mind."

Turning from the window Marcus stared Tashawn straight in eyes, boring into the vampire's soul with his will. Tashawn recoiled back before the gaze of the elder vampire.

"Remember who is master here," said Marcus, feeling the minion's will collapse before his. "I do still have emotions, youngling. Hate and anger among the most noticeable. Take care that you do not arouse those emotions toward yourself. You might regret it, in the short time that you still exist."

Marcus moved his gaze away, seeing Tashawn relax as the onslaught was discontinued. Catching the eyes of Marvin, Marcus beat down the man's will in an instant.

"Drive us to the Padillas manor," ordered Marcus, using the same tone of voice he would have used to order a legionnaire to face the enemy. "And drive within the limits of the law. I would hate to be stopped and have to explain our presence to the police. Or to have to kill one of them, and bring notice to ourselves."

Marvin turned the key in the ignition and the V8 engine roared to life. Still listening to the scanner, telling that the police were engaged elsewhere, Marcus grinned a mirthless smile to the night.

* * *

"I'm sorry," said DeFalco to Smith as the detective was jotting down notes on his pad. "I don't believe that this killing was done by our girl."

"Why not?" asked Smith, looking up with a sour face at the FBI man.

"Her head," said DeFalco, nodding toward the body that the forensics men were carefully picking up and placing in a black plastic body bag.

"What about her fucking head, DeFalco?" growled Smith.

"It's still attached to her body, for one thing," said the Agent. "She has always made sure the head was off the body. Or destroyed in some other way, so that the victim would not rise from the dead."

"Fucking vampire shit," Smith spit out. "Maybe she was rushed and had to go."

"Maybe she forgot," offered Sanchez.

"How could she be rushed?" asked DeFalco. "The woman was killed last night and we didn't find her till tonight. And I really don't think she would forget something that was a part of her MO for so long."

"He's right," said Tamesha Washington, coming up behind the arguing men. "She should have done that she has always done."

"So now you're on his side?" accused Smith, glancing back at the woman.

"This isn't about sides," said Washington, laying a hand on Smith's shoulder. "You know it isn't. It's about the truth, and bringing the murderer to justice. And I believe that we have another vampire in town, taking his own prey and trying to blame it on her."

"Jesus Christ," exclaimed Smith in anger, turning on the woman. "One crazy bastard chasing after one vampire wasn't enough. Now we have to have you join him, and bring another undead creature into the mix. Goddammit."

"You know you have to sterilize this body," said Washington, nodding at the now filled body bag that a forensic tech was zipping up.

"What do you mean, sterilize?" asked Lowrey, moving over to stand looking down at Washington.

"She means that the woman was killed by a vampire," said DeFalco, moving aside as the gurney was wheeled into the hall. "The woman will rise again in three days as a vampire, and the situation down here will grow even more complicated."

"Like fucking Jesus Christ," said Lowrey with a sneer.

"Like a parody of Jesus," answered Washington. "The devil's own rises into unlife after three days in the grave. So she must be prevented from coming back to unlife, or more people will suffer."

"Sure, Washington," said Smith, giving her a short smile. "We'll get right on that."

The other detectives and police in the house gave out a variety of laughs. Even the techs that were placing the body on the gurney joined in. Washington looked from face to face, tears welling up in her eyes.

"It's OK," said DeFalco, putting his hands on her shoulders and kneading the muscles. "I believe. You believe. And we can set matters straight ourselves."

"I'm going over to watch the Padillas house," said DeFalco, dropping his hands from the detective's shoulders. "Anyone else coming with me?"

"You know we're not allowed over there," said Smith. "You saw the court order."

"Which didn't mention anything about the FBI," said DeFalco, moving up chest to chest with Smith. "And if it did, I have a Federal Judge who would be willing to write an order overruling your little Circuit Judge. So anyone?"

"I'll go with you," said Washington, walking toward the door. "There's nothing for me here."

"You walk out that door with that man, Tanesha," growled Smith, "and you can kiss your job goodbye."

Tanesha Washington stopped for a moment, her shoulders slumping. Then, with a shake of her head, she walked through the door and out into the night.

"You just fucked her career in the ass," said Smith, turning his anger on DeFalco.

"I think I can fix that problem as well, Smith," said DeFalco, returning Smith's stare. "You don't know what you're messing with, either with Lucinda Taylor, or with me."

DeFalco turned on his heel and stormed toward the door, as all of the eyes in the house followed his back.

"Son of a bitch," hissed Smith under his breath. He continued to stare at the door for a moment before getting control of himself.

"OK, people," he growled, looking around at the officers all standing staring at him or the door. "We have an investigation to conduct. So let's get a move on."

* * *

Lucinda over flew the house a dozen times, scanning the night with all of her senses. She could not feel the presence of the police. Or the scent of the FBI man. There were some men around the house, but she could feel the taint on them. They were bought men. Padillas' men.

She bared her teeth as another scent came to her. A faint scent, but one very recognizable to her from its intrusion into her life.

The priest, she thought, flapping to get higher into the air. But the scent was very faint. As if he had been there earlier but was no longer there. She flew over the house a couple of more times, noting the men walking the fence line. A pair of large dogs ran through the yard, barking up at her in their frustration.

The giant bat descended toward the shadows of a power substation a couple of blocks from the house. The city had placed lights on high poles to illuminate the important structure. But the lights on one of the poles had burned out, and the other poles cast dark shadows on one side of the complex.

She landed there and again changed, a plan forming in her mind. The dogs were something that needed taking care of first, if she was to have a chance of getting into the house without an alarm being raised. But taking the dogs out would in itself raise an alarm. It couldn't be helped, and might provide the impetus to flush her prey from cover.

The large red wolf sprang from the cover of the substation and ran across the street. Through one yard it hurried, leaping the fence into another. A dog barked at her, then backed up with a squeal as she turned baleful red eyes on it. Another leap and she cleared another fence. She ran along the back fence of the Padillas house, hearing the large dogs barking at her as they ran along the other side of the fence, paralleling her moves.

"What the fuck's wrong with them?" called out a voice in the yard. "What's driving them so crazy?"

"Hell, I don't know," said another voice.

Lucinda ran to the corner of the property, under a large tree that provided shadow on both sides of the fence. She ran away from the fence and into the adjoining yard, turned one hundred and eighty degrees, and rushed the fence. With a leap she was in the air, flying toward the fence to smack three feet up on its ten-foot height. Boards splintered as her forepaws struck, then caved inward under her one hundred forty pounds of weight. But she had timed the speed and momentum of the jump perfectly, and did not completely smash in the fence.

"What the fuck was that?" yelled the first voice she had heard outside the fence. Something hit the broken boards hard as she backed up. She let out a low growl as the large body hit the boards again. Then again, as the boards splintered out and the head of the Rottweiler growled out at her, its paws scrambling to propel it through the hole in the fence.

The large dog landed heavily on the ground and scrambled to its feet as the second dog appeared at the fence and started to push through. Dog one moved in a crouch to the side of Lucinda while number two fell through the fence and came back to its feet. It took one look at Lucinda, another at its partner, and then moved to the opposite side of the giant wolf. Both dogs growled as they moved forward, and cursing and yelling voices approached the hole in the fence on the other side.

Lucinda turned and leapt into the night, her long legs propelling her at great speed along the grassy lawn. The two dogs yelped, looked at each other, and took off after her. Lucinda ran tirelessly across a street, then through other yards, howling into the darkness. It sounded to Lucinda's canine ears as if every dog for a mile started to barking or howling. But she could also hear the breathing of the two she was interested in following far behind her. She slowed for a moment, allowing them to close the distance. She wanted them to continue to follow, until they reached the place of her choosing.

The vacant lot came into view. Lucinda moved across the last asphalt street and into the weeds, the dogs within twenty yards of her heels. As she reached the center of the yard she spun around and launched herself at the lead dog, jaws wide. She clamped down as she struck the eighty-pound Rottweiler, pushing the dog back on its heels as she felt its windpipe give under her fangs. Planting her feet, she shook her massive neck and shoulders and felt the snap of the Rottweiler's vertebrae through her jaws.

The second dog hit her in the flank, its teeth ripping through her fur and into the flesh beneath. Lucinda tensed her neck muscles and flung the dying dog up and to the side, releasing her grip and sending the dog into the air, to hit hard on its side in the weedy yard. She turned on the other dog, which was standing there snarling at her with the hair on the back of its neck standing on end. Lucinda growled back, baring her large teeth as she moved toward it.

The other dog whimpered and yelped, and then turned and ran from the yard. Lucinda took off after it like she had been shot from a rocket launcher. She could feel the flesh healing on her flank as she ran, a bit of stiffness that slowed her slightly. But not enough to save the dog. She leapt through the air and landed heavily on its back, knocking it to the ground. The dog struggled to throw her off, but she clamped down on the back of its neck with her strong jaws and sank her teeth into its flesh.

Lucinda bit down hard, her teeth chomping through muscle, then bone, as the vertebrae cracked in her strong jaws. The Rottweiler went into a frenzy of motion, trying to get its killer off of it before it was too late. Then its muscles went limp as Lucinda severed its spine with her more than canine jaws.

Lucinda released her grip on the dead beast, standing over it for a second as she fought the regret that threatened to overwhelm her. She shook the feelings from her as she raised her muzzle into the air and let out a mournful howl. Answering howls erupted in the night air.

It had to be done, she thought. The dogs had been the best early warning system Padillas had. And now they were gone. But there was no way she was going to penetrate the yard and into the house tonight. Not with the uproar that reigned in that neighborhood.

She sniffed at the dead dog, and then trotted over to the other. It too was dead, and therefore of no use to her. And she felt the hunger coming over her again, as her body after its exertions and metamorphosis's demanded sustenance. Without a backward look she loped into the night, keeping to the shadows as she headed toward a seedier section of town and the prey she knew abounded there.

* * *

"What the hell was going on out here?" called George Padillas to his men from the back door of the house.

"Something got to the dogs, sir," said one of the men looking at the hole in the fence. "It opened a goddamn hole here from the outside and the dogs got out."

Flashlight beams moved on the other side of the fence as some of his men looked over the hole from the other side. And whatever evidence they could find of what had caused it.

"Fucking big paw print here," yelled a man from the other side of the fence. "Looks like a big ass dog was over here."

"Or a massive wolf," said Father O'Connor from behind Padillas. "That is one of their powers. The ability to take the form of several animals."

"You shouldn't be out here, sir," said one of the smaller men, walking back toward the house.

"I'm quite alright, Dominic," said George Padillas, stepping out into the yard.

"He's right you know," said O'Connor, following the boss out of the house. "She can get to you out here. You're safe in the house, as long as she isn't invited in."

"Then how the fuck we gonna get her into the house?" said Padillas, turning on the priest. "I want the bitch. Even if it takes putting my own life at risk to take her."

"I told you, Mr. Padillas," said the priest. "We will find a way to lure her into the house. But we may have to let the commotion the police caused die down a little."

"Well, we can tell that she's still interested, can't we?" said Padillas with a chuckle. "Why don't we go back into the house and plan how we're going to get the spider to come into our lair. Since she's so interested in getting to me I wouldn't want to disappoint her."

O'Connor stood outside for a moment after the boss went into the house, searching the sky with his tired eyes. *I hadn't thought about how we get her to come into the house*, he thought. *I knew Padillas would be the bait. But I never thought about the opening to the trap.*

* * *

"Dammit," cried Marcus, as he walked back and forth outside of the car. He glared at Tashawn and Marvin as they sat in the car, looking at him with worried expressions of their faces.

"She was here," he said, looking over at the lit up yard of the Padillas house. "She was here, mere minutes before we got here. We could have had her."

"And who was the one who wanted to see for himself if the police would swarm to the decoy?" asked Tashawn.

Marcus brought his fist down on the top of the car, denting the metal of the door frame above the driver's seat. Marvin jumped as he tried to retreat backwards, coming to a stop against Tashawn. Marcus stood quivering, looking back at the house. He closed his eyes and looked down at the roadway, thinking back to his Stoic training, gaining control of himself.

Turning back to the car with a slight smile on his face, Marcus transfixed the two in the car with his gaze.

"I was in error, yes," said Marcus, nodding his head at them. "It was my fault that we missed her, and my impatience is unbecoming a being of my age."

Looking down at the large dent on the roof of the car he chuckled. *Temper, temper*, he thought. *Here you go and throw a tantrum out in public, with all of your talk of not drawing attention to your kind.*

"I am sorry that a frightened you, Marvin," he said, looking at the man with his best calming look. "I think it might be a good idea for you to go back to the, crib. Since you will have to be up in the morning to get the dent taken out of the car."

"I'm starting to get hungry," complained Tashawn. Marvin seemed to notice that he was up against the big vampire, and scrambled back to the driver's seat.

"Then we had better take care of your appetite, my big friend," said Marcus with a smile. "We can't have you eating the hired help after all."

Marcus started walking down the street, moving toward the shadows under a tree, in a lawn far from a street light. He heard the door to the car open, then close, and knew that the big youngling was following him. The car started up behind him and pulled away with a squeal of tires.

Moments later a pair of bats lifted from out of the shadows. Turning in the air above the block they headed toward the bay and the docks. To where people prowled the night who would not be missed in polite society.

*   *   *

"I've seen that car before," said Tanesha Washington as they drove down Padillas's street, about five blocks from the house.

"That blue Monte Carlo?" said DeFalco, turning to follow the car as it passed, noting the black man in the driver's seat. "With the Pennsylvania license plates. That drove through this very neighborhood a couple of nights a ago with three men on board."

"That's the one," said Washington, trying to look over his shoulder as she drove the unmarked Impala interceptor.

"Why don't we have a talk with the driver," suggested DeFalco. "But let's follow him first and see where he's going."

Tanesha Washington pulled the car quickly into a driveway and back out on the street, accelerating after the Monte Carlo. When she got within a hundred yards of it she slowed and stayed on its tail, using her skills as an ex-patrolman to keep it in sight without getting close enough for the driver to notice her.

"Why don't you run his tag for me," asked Washington, flipping her badge holder at the FBI Agent. "Use my ID if you would."

DeFalco got on the radio and called dispatch while Washington followed the car. As DeFalco put the radio handset back on the dash the compact printer on the passenger's side started spitting out some paper. As the first sheet was finished DeFalco ripped it out of the machine and started to read. He grunted once as his eyes followed the page.

"What's so interesting?" said Washington, keeping her eyes locked onto the car to her front, looking around the vehicle that had pulled between them. The Monte Carlo pulled onto the broad, six-lane expanse of Kennedy Boulevard, heading toward East to the downtown section of town.

"Our boy definitely has a record," said DeFalco, glancing over at Washington. "Says here that Mr. Marvin Jackson, thirty-one year old black male, has a record as long as my arm."

"Lovely," said Washington, pulling around a slow moving car to keep the chevy in sight. "What are we talking about?"

"Possession and sale of narcotics," said DeFalco, staring intently at the paper. "Grand theft. Nothing violent except for the beating of a couple of prostitutes he ran."

The FBI agent pulled the next sheet of paper off the machine after he tossed the first into the back seat.

"Hum," he grunted as he looked at the fresh sheet. "Says here he was the running boy of one Tashawn Kent."

"That name sounds familiar," said Tanesha, glancing from the FBI agent to the road and back. "Where have I heard it before?"

"Boy led the NFL in sacks his second season in," said DeFalco. "He had strength, speed and instincts. Until he tore his ACL and lost his position on the team in his fourth season."

"I thought they could fix those things," said Washington.

"Most times they can," agreed DeFalco. "But in his case it was too much for them to totally repair, and he was on his butt the next year. That's when his trouble started."

"And what are we talking about here?"

"He became the head man on the west side of Philly," said DeFalco. "Drugs, prostitution, you name it. Was his own leg breaker as well. A five hundred and seventy pound bench press can break a lot of legs. He was the terror of the city."

"All that on Mr. Jackson's rap sheet?" asked Washington, accelerating to get around a bus. "Or you reciting that from rote memory."

"Guilty," said DeFalco with a chuckle. "Tashawn was the case that started it all. We were on a surveillance of his turf when our girl took him out. Fangs in the neck, blood sucked out of his body, the whole mess."

"And Marvin's trying to get revenge for his friend," guessed Washington. "That's pretty noble for drug dealing scum of the Earth."

"Tashawn's not dead," said DeFalco, looking over at Washington.

"I thought you said the man's blood was drained from his body," she asked. "What part did I miss?"

"I was on close surveillance that night," said DeFalco, his voice distant. "I saw him go into an alley with a gorgeous redhead. Figured he was going to get his dick sucked for some kind of consideration. Excuse the language."

"I'm a big girl," said Washington with a laugh. "Heard all the dirty words and everything. Even participated in a few of them."

"OK," said DeFalco. "Point taken. Well, I heard yelling and cursing, followed by a man roaring in pain. So I grabbed a flashlight and high tailed it into the alley."

DeFalco looked back out the window, his voice going cold again.

"I'll never forget that sight till the day I die," he said. "Maybe even after I die. There was this huge hulk of a man lying on the hard concrete of the alley, one of his legs bent at an unnatural angle. And this redhead was leaning over him, holding him down while he struggled to get up. But he couldn't get up. This five hundred bench pressing monster could not move this petite woman off of him."

"So what'd you do?"

"I shined the flashlight on her and screamed for her to stop and move away from Tashawn," said DeFalco, looking back at Washington with haunted eyes. "She ignored me for a moment, as Tashawn stopped struggling. Then she stood up and turned toward me. Her red eyes glared in the light I was shining on her. There was blood dripping down her chin. And I felt those eyes boring into me, sapping my will. I never felt so helpless in my entire life."

DaFalco stopped for a moment, putting his face in his hands. He looked up as the car turned a corner and Washington followed the Monte Carlo. He saw the woman glance over at him, a concerned look on her face.

"Are you OK?" she asked in a quiet voice, turning her attention back to the highway and the pursuit.

"As OK as anyone could be," he replied, shaking his head. "After seeing what I've seen."

"What happened?"

"I broke her spell," he said in a hushed voice. "I don't know how I did it. It was the hardest thing I ever did. I wanted to fall into those eyes and do whatever she wanted me to do. But somehow I summoned the strength to break away."

DeFalco took a deep breath as he steadied himself, pulling a flask from his jacket pocket, twisting off the top and taking a large swig. He capped the flask and thrust it back into his jacket.

"I pulled my gun out," he continued. "I really don't know why I didn't have it out in the first place. She turned back to Tashawn and pulled a large knife from somewhere. So I raised my pistol in a two handed grip, just like I had been taught at Quantico. And I fired; over and over again, center mass. And I heard the bullets hit the brick wall behind her, saw the sparks fly as they struck. And it didn't faze her in the least. She didn't even bleed where the bullets had hit her. Then I heard the sirens, as the rest of the team responded to the shots."

DeFalco's face turned white for a moment, as he drew in breath.

"She looked at me for a moment, and then was in my face, her eyes boring into mine. I'd never even seen her move, she was so fast. I thought I was dead. But she shook her head and released me. Then scrambled up a wall like a spider."

"So she didn't take Tashawn's head?" asked Washington. "And she didn't hurt you? Why?"

"I really don't know," answered DeFalco. "I've asked myself that question over and over again, and can't really come up with a good answer."

"And Tashawn rose again," said Washington, "three days later."

"I didn't know," cried DeFalco, smacking one hand into the other. "I couldn't have known. I found his empty grave some days after he dug his way out. And he was back on the street, as an undead killer."

"Like you said," agreed Washington as she made another turn after the car she was following. "You didn't know. So you can't blame yourself."

"I have blamed myself every day since I let it happen," he said in a quiet voice. "And I have blamed her. And chased her across the Eastern Seaboard."

"And what if we run into Tashawn tonight?" asked Washington. "He'll be even stronger now. And bulletproof."

"Don't you worry about that, ma'am," said DeFalco, patting his jacket and the gun underneath. "I'm much better prepared now. If he gets in our way he will be going down. Permanently."

"He's turning into a hotel," said Washington, turning the wheel to follow. "What do you want me to do?"

"Wait until he pulls into a parking space in front of his room," ordered DeFalco. "Then run the siren and lights."

"OK," said Washington, closing behind the Monte Carlo as it turned between the rows of rooms. The Monte Carlo pulled into an empty space among empty spaces. The engine cut off and the lights of the car went out. Washington hit the alert switch as she pulled the unmarked car to block the Chevy. The blue dash strobe flashed as the siren howled.

The man in the car struggled with the driver's side door for a moment. When it didn't move he slid over to the passenger side and threw open the door.

Washington had run from the unmarked car, pulling her gun from her waist holster and pointing it at the driver's side of the car. DeFalco had his gun out and in Jackson's face as the black man staggered to a stop in a crouch, coming out of the seat with one hand still on the door frame.

"Going somewhere, Jackson?" said DeFalco, waving his .40 cal auto in the man's face.

"What you want, man?" whined Marvin Jackson, his eyes darting around as he looked for a way out.

Tanesha walked around the front of the car, aiming her 9mm at the suspect. Seeing Jackson was covered, DeFalco slipped his own pistol back into the shoulder holster and grabbed the man by one of his shoulders.

"You know the drill," yelled DeFalco, as he pulled the man out of the car, spun him around, and slammed him back into the car. Jackson got his arms out barely in time to keep his face from striking the metal. DeFalco kicked the suspect's feet apart, then started to frisk him from the shoulders down.

"What have we here," said DeFalco as he felt the large metal object in Jackson's waistband. The FBI Agent pulled a Glock out from under Jackson's shirt, and held it up beside the man's head.

"And I bet you don't have a concealed carry permit either, huh Jackson?"

"I got one," said Jackson, nodding his head.

"State of Pennsylvania?" asked DeFalco.   Jackson nodded his head again.   "I'm not sure Florida has a reciprocal agreement with Pennsylvania."

"They sure do," said Jackson. "You can look it up on the net."

"Maybe later."

DeFalco pulled one of Marvin Jackson's hands down behind his back and slapped a handcuff on it. It was a little bit more of a struggle to get the second one down, but a clop on the side of the head convinced Marvin to let DeFalco pull the other hand down and link it into the cuffs.

"Who the fuck are you?" whined Jackson, as strong hands spun him around and pushed his back against the car.

"Oh yeah," said DeFalco, staring into the man's eyes. "I forgot that bit of the drill."   Reaching into his jacket pocket he pulled out his credential holder and flipped it open in Jackson's face.   "Agent Jeffrey DeFalco of the Federal Bureau of Investigation. And you are under arrest."

"What for?" asked Jackson, looking over at the black woman who had lowered her pistol. But she still held it at the ready pointed toward the ground.

"Possession of a concealed weapon to start with," said DeFalco, as he brought his face up close to the man's. "I don't think Florida gives reciprocals to convicted felons. And a warrant for questioning concerning a murder or two up in Philadelphia. Let's say we go to your room and you can answer a couple of questions."

"I want my lawyer," whined the man as DeFalco removed the hotel room key from Jackson's pocket.

"I really don't have time for you to speak to an attorney," said DeFalco, grabbing the man's jacket and steering him away from the car. Washington moved to stand in his way.

"What are you doing?" she asked. "He asked for an attorney and we have to provide one. And you didn't read him his rights."

"Detective Washington," said DeFalco through clenched teeth. "I don't have time for this nonsense. You know what we're dealing with. I couldn't give a fuck less if what he says is admissible in court or not. As long as he tells me what I need to know to catch a vampire."

Washington looked at the two for a moment, then stepped aside, pushing her gun back into her waistband holster.

"Vampires," said Jackson, on the verge of a hysterical laugh. "Are you fucking crazy?"

"I just may be," whispered DeFalco into Jackson's ear. "So maybe you better go ahead and tell me everything you know."

DeFalco pushed the man along, toward the room number that was on the key.

"What do you want me to do?" asked Washington.

"Park the car and come over here to the room door," said DeFalco. "I'll wait for your before we go in."

Washington got into the unmarked car, flipped off the strobe light, and started it up. DeFalco pushed Marvin Jackson up against the wall and held him there while he waited for the detective to park. Within a few moments Washington was hurrying toward him.

"You take charge of the suspect," ordered DeFalco, releasing his hold on Jackson and pulling his gun out of its holster. "I'll go in first and cover the room."

Washington gave him a quizzical look as she grabbed the back of Jackson's jacket.

"I have something special in here," said DeFalco, waving his gun. "It'll make Tashawn sorry he showed his ugly face."

"Tashawn's dead, motherfucker," said Marvin Jackson, as Detective Washington pulled him away from the wall.

DeFalco put the key in the door and turned the lock. Holding his gun at the ready he pushed the door open hard as he brought the pistol down into a two handed hold to cover the room.

DeFalco coughed as the stench of the room hit him in the face. It smelled of Earth, decay and death. The iron smell of dried blood competed with the stronger odors. DeFalco moved cautiously into the room, tracking with his gun as he moved his eyes. There was an unmade bed close to the door, and a dresser with a TV sitting on it. A small table and some chairs were placed close to the heavily curtained window.

DeFalco walked past the bed, his gun moving to cover the other side. His eyes grew wide as he saw the make shift coffin on the floor. Made from a pair of refrigerator boxes stapled and taped together, it had a cardboard lid that was fitted over the top. DeFalco kept the gun trained on the box as he kicked at the top, lifting it enough to see inside. When nothing appeared to be in the box he pushed the top completely off and found himself staring down into a thin layer of soil.

"He's been here," said DeFalco over his shoulder. "But he's not here now. Bring him in."

Washington pushed Jackson into the room and closed the door behind her as DeFalco checked out the bathroom. He came out a moment later, pushing his gun back into its holster.

"It's clear," he said to Washington, pointing at one of the chairs. "Take a seat Mr. Jackson. I think we have some business to discuss."

Tanesha pushed Marvin Jackson into one of the chairs, then walked around the bed to look at the homemade cardboard coffin. She put her hand over her mouth as the odor hit her.

"Yeah," said DeFalco, sitting on the bed. "It had that effect on me too."

"Now Marvin," said the Agent, turning toward the man in the chair. "What do you say we discuss Tashawn, or whatever he calls himself these days?"

"I want to talk to a lawyer," yelled the man, pulling at the handcuffs behind his back.

"I don't really think a trial is in your immediate future," said DeFalco, moving over so Washington could have sitting room on the same side of the bed. "You think I'm going before a judge with you to talk about a vampire?"

"Then let me go," said Marvin, a pleading look on his face. As DeFalco shook his head the man's face took on the appearance of a wild animal's as he jerked the cuffs and started to stand.

DeFalco was off the bed in an instant, pushing the man back into the chair.

"You don't know what he's capable of," said Marvin, glaring up at the FBI Agent.

"What if I tell you I'll get you Government protection?" said DeFalco, looking down on the man.

"You think you can protect me from him?" said Jackson, his voice frantic. "Or that other bastard who's leading him around?"

"Now that's the stuff I want to hear, Marvin," said DeFalco, leaning over the man to go nose to nose. "Tell me about Tashawn. And this other bastard you're talking about."

"Fuck you, man," yelled Jackson, "and your fucking bitch too."

DeFalco stood straight as he pulled his pistol back out of his holster. He raised it into the air, then swung it down hard on Jackson's left shoulder. He controlled the force he struck with, not wanting to break anything, just to cause pain. The grunt from the man told him that he had achieved his goal.

"It's going to be a long fucking night, Marvin," said DeFalco, looking at his watch. "It's only eleven right now. We have a long time till dawn."

"He's going to kill you, man," shouted Jackson, tears in his eyes. "He's going to kill you, her and probably me."

"I'm counting on him coming to try," said DeFalco, moving back to the bed and sitting down. "I'm counting on it."

Chapter 7

Lucinda approached her house from the shadows, having walked in human form the four blocks from her landing spot. She moved slowly and quietly, all of her senses testing the night for traces of an enemy, human or otherwise. There were still hours to go before the dawn, so she felt no need to hurry. If the house wasn't safe she would move to another.

Only one more spare, she thought, thinking of the overflight of the one the police were swarming over. She could rent some more, and move in a couple of coffins (which was always the tricky part) and set up the necessary safe houses to guard her existence. Or she could go ahead and take out her primary target, her reason for being in this city, and move on to another place.

But danger will always follow me, she thought, straining her hearing and sense of smell as she came within sight of her house. *If it isn't already in front of me, or beside me.*

She shook her head. The house appeared to be clear. She moved to the front door and inserted her key, opening the lock.

But does it really matter, she thought again. *Would it be so awful if I were destroyed, and end of this hellish existence?* She thought again of the night, of the killing of a couple of dogs, followed by the death of a small time pimp down a scummy street. Again she had gotten rid of the body in the storm drains, though there was no flood this time to whisk it away. But rainstorms were a daily fact of life in this area, and she had no doubt that today's showers would take the body to a place where it would be difficult to find.

She opened the door and moved into the house, opening the panel near the door and punching in the seven-digit code. The alarm system flashed off and reset itself to its secondary mode. Now it would no longer track motion within the house, but would still trigger if the doors or windows were opened. Lucinda locked the door, making sure that the deadbolt was secure. She then moved to all of the windows and doors, checking that they were secure.

Satisfied that everything was as it should be she plugged her laptop into the cable line and logged onto her Internet account. First she clicked onto the news link on her homepage, then on the headline that interested her most. As the page opened almost instantly she started scanning the print.

"Dammit," she hissed as the words scrolled before her. She was being blamed for the murder of an innocent. She looked up again at the smiling picture of the plump-faced woman whose body had been found in the house Lucinda had been renting. *I'm so glad I rented each and every location through a separate agency, so there's nothing at her agency to trace me to somewhere I'm still using.*

Lucinda thought for a moment about returning to the storm drains, or some other decrepit location where the normally curious would keep their noses clear. But going there made her feel even dirtier than she must. It was the habit of her real life to live in a nice house with all the trappings. And she still hoped to get out of this town within the next couple of days.

But how to get into the Padillas house, she thought, *since he doesn't seem to want to come out. At least at night.*

She flipped through page after page of Internet files, looking for something that might get her into the house. The hour passed, then another half hour, as she strained her mind to come up with an answer. She could feel the dawn approaching, and with it her time to solve the problem.

Now this looks interesting, she thought as she scrolled to yet another site. *This just might work.* She filed the information away in her head as she disconnected from the Internet and shut the computer down.

She set up her primary means of defense, rigging the tear gas grenades to the doors and windows with the wire she had emplaced earlier. They would stop anyone who was human from coming into the house, and the noise and smoke might make a vampire back up for an instant. Beyond that, there was nothing much she could do to awaken herself in the early hours of the morning. Anyone who entered would do so while she slept the sleep of the dead. And she might awaken to the searing pain of a wooden stake plunging into her heart.

A human minion would solve that problem, she thought as she pulled down the attic stairs. *But then I would be just like those I despise.* She shook her head as she climbed the stairs. She quickly climbed into the coffin and triggered the remote for the alarm system, turning the motion sensors back on. Pulling the lid closed, she shut her eyes as she felt the sun peek over the horizon. The waves of weariness swept over her as she felt consciousness fade away.

* * *

Tashawn changed back to his human form in the shadows of the motel pool, reveling again in the power that his state of unlife gave him. Then his awareness of sunrise came over him, and he realized that he had less than twenty minutes to get into his resting place.

I actually thought I might have had her there for a moment, he thought, moving into the light and orienting himself to his room. He had soared over the downtown section of the city for hours, then headed out to the Bay front, where he had picked up a faint trace of her scent. Tashawn had even found the spot where she had fed this night, focusing in on the overpowering smell of human blood that filled the alley.

But she was long gone, and he couldn't pick up a trail from that point, since she had taken to the sky as well. *I'll get you yet, bitch*, he thought, raising a fist to the sky. He stopped for a second as he thought about the anger that still surged through him.

Hell, he thought, *I'm ten times stronger than I was as a mortal. And I'll live forever if nothing takes me out. So why am I so angry at her, when she did me a favor.*

Tashawn saw the figure of a woman walk down the street at that moment, clear to his night vision as if it were day. He watched her ass move as she walked, and felt the lust come over him.

"God Dammit," he said softly to himself as nothing stirred in his groin. He had loved sex. As much as he could get, with as many different women as he could get. And since he had become undead he had not had the merest physical stirring of desire.

That's why I hate her, he thought, slamming a big hand into the other. *She took so much away from me. And it's not like she turned me out of the goodness of her heart. She was out to kill me, permanently. If she had her way I would have been a piece of dead meat on a slab. Then rotting away in the ground.*

The awareness of the sun about to come over the horizon broke his thoughts. He hurried along, relief coming over him as he saw the Monte Carlo parked in front of the room. He was home, and would soon be at rest.

The voices alerted him to the intruders in the room. He stopped for a couple of seconds, honing in on the speech coming out of the chamber. Marvin, and two others.

"He has to be here soon," said the female stranger. Tashawn looked again at the sky, where the high clouds were beginning to lighten.

"Unless he has someplace else to hold up during the dawn," said the male stranger. *Not likely*, thought Tashawn, planning his next move. He could shelter in another room if he broke in quickly. But he would lose strength during the day because he had not slept in the soil of his own resting place.

"He's going to fuck you up," said Marvin, his voice cracking.

If it's the priest there will be hell to pay, thought Tashawn, weighing his options. *If it's the police I go through them like shit through a goose.*

"Oh shut up Marvin," said the male voice. "I'm tired of hearing how Tashawn is going to destroy us."

"It's got to be close to dawn," said the female voice. Tashawn saw that the high clouds were turning pink. He had to move soon or be destroyed.

His eyes landed on the compact car in a parking place across the narrow lot as he was searching for an out. Tashawn ran in speed mode toward the car, to his own perception running normally, though to the world at large it would appear as if he just popped into existence next to the vehicle.

Tashawn bent down to the side of the car and placed his hands underneath the side. The Rio weighed about a ton, and to his supernatural strength it was nothing to flip it over on its side. He cringed for a moment as some of the windows cracked and metal bent, sounding like an explosion to his sensitive ears. He didn't have time to waste, so he grabbed at the beams on the undercarriage and clamped his hands down hard.

Setting his powerful legs wide, Tashawn strained with his arms while pulling back. With a jerk of his arms he pulled the car off the ground, raising it to his chest and overhead so quickly that the weight of the car didn't have a chance to pull him off balance. As a Defensive End Tashawn had jerked and pressed four hundred pounds during strength trails. As a vampire Tashawn could lift ten times that weight, and the car went easily overhead.

Making sure he had his balance, Tashawn started walking across the lot toward his room. People had come out of other rooms at the noise of the car being flipped and manhandled, and several people shouted or gasped as they saw the huge man with a car held over his head move across the parking lot. The noise quieted as people realized that they did not want to attract the attention of someone doing the impossible task they saw.

The door to his room opened and a white man looked out, shouting as he saw the man and car coming at him. He started to reach into his jacket, grasping the butt of pistol and trying to get it out of his holster.

Tashawn exploded into action, speeding up until he was running quickly at the room. He saw the gun coming out and the man raised it in the vampire's direction. Tashawn moved his arms forward and released, sending the car flying through the air at the room.

The man fell back into the room as the car hit to the door side of the big front window of the room. With a crash of metal and cracking concrete block the car broke through the window and the section of wall between window and door. Meeting less resistance at the window than the wall, the car started to turn to its side as it flew through.

Tashawn heard the screams and the yells in the room, then a choking gurgle. The sound of breaking furniture and smashing glass came out of the room as the car continued on to hit the far wall. It had lost enough momentum to only crack the concrete block, then fall to the floor.

Damn, thought Tashawn as he moved toward the door in a quick run. *Now what the fuck do I do?* He had to get under cover and into the makeshift coffin. But now the police would come here to his resting place, while he was asleep. Tashawn cursed himself again, and his tendency to act without thinking.

What choice did I have, he thought as he hit the door with both fists, knocking it off of its hinges and into the room. *Have to play dead and hope the police that come don't know anything about vampires.* They might think he was truly dead, and transport him in a body bag to the morgue, after he had spent the necessary hours in resting on the soil. Then he could wake in the morgue and go from there.

Tashawn looked into the room, his sight falling on what was left of Marvin, sitting in a chair, his head gone where the passing car had taken it off. Marvin had been his friend, and his daytime helper. And because of the interference of the pigs he was dead.

"Motherfucker," said Tashawn, as he balled his fists and walked into the motel room. He would kill the motherfuckers who had forced him to do this. He would kill them in a way that would horrify the police that would come later. First he looked down on the white man in the suit, lying unmoving on the floor by the bed. Then he saw the black bitch with blood on her scalp, struggling to her knees, pulling a pistol from her waistband.

"Fucking nigger bitch," growled Tashawn, stepping over the rubble of broken concrete blocks. She had the pistol pointing at him and it started barking, flame shooting from the muzzle. To Tashawn it felt as if something unreal passed through his body, almost an illusion. But he heard the bullets striking concrete and ricocheting off. "I'm gonna stick that pistol up your ass and see if you like it."

The woman's mouth opened in a scream as the big man towered over her, reaching his hands down to grasp her wrists and jerk her to her feet. As he squeezed the gun fell out of her hand and clatter to the floor. Tashawn bared his fangs and lunged toward her throat.

* * *

DeFalco felt the shock start to overwhelm him as the giant of a man came toward him, holding an entire car over his head. To the credit of his training he did not succumb to the shock, and tried to get his pistol out and to bear before the creature could throw the car. It wasn't his fault that the thing sped up and flung the ton of metal through the wall of the motel room.

DeFalco had back stepped into the room before the vampire had released the car. He ducked down by the bed, hoping that the car would miss him, and knowing that he had no control over where it was going to hit. He could be crushed in a second.

The thoughts were thrust from his mind as the window smashed in and the block wall between the window and door shattered into pieces of concrete and dust. The rear of the car spun around in the window. Marvin tried to move back, but the handcuffs restricted the motion and he couldn't push the chair back in time. A rear tire struck his head from below his chin on up, and carried his head away with it. The body jerked in the chair, blood spurting from the severed neck.

DeFalco closed his eyes for a second to keep the dust from blinding him. The noise beat down on his ears and deafened him for a moment. He lay on the floor, trying to will his body to get up, as he faintly heard the car hitting the far wall and fall to the floor. The bed he was laying against collapsed under the weight of the car, and the bed frame pushed into his back. Pain shot up from his lumbar region.

The FBI Agent could feel the footsteps of the huge man through the floor. He knew the man was standing over him, but he was unable to rise and defend himself. His system was in shock, and his limbs felt leaden. The footsteps moved on and he knew that he was safe, for the moment.

DeFalco cursed himself for his cowardly immobility, even as he realized that the vampire was having a supernatural effect on him that no mortal could ignore. But he could resist, and he fought to will his limbs to move. His head rose off the ground as the shots rang out. The supersonic crack of bullets sounded above him, followed quickly by the whine of their ricochet off the wall. One round smacked into the bed behind him, another into the carpeted floor by his side.

The vampire was standing over Washington as she tried to stop him with her useless pistol. DeFalco rose to his hands as knees as the vampire reached out and grabbed her wrists. As her gun fell to the floor he picked his up and rose to a kneeling position on the floor. He brought the pistol full extension in a two handed grip as the vampire's head shot toward Washington's neck.

I can't miss, he thought, as he aimed carefully, holding half a breath as he squeezed the trigger. The gun bucked in his hand as he sent the .40 caliber round toward Tashawn's left shoulder, the one that cleared the form of Tanesha Washington. Tashawn jerked as the bullet struck his shoulder, splattering blood over his shirt and the ceiling. The bullet sprung from the front of his shoulder and smacked into the wall beyond.

The vampire threw Washington to the floor as he spun around, pain, fear and anger on his face. His red eyes burned into the eyes of DeFalco, trying to push his will aside and make him lower the gun. DeFalco squeezed off another round, his aim off slightly, fighting to keep his focus. The bullet smacked into Tashawn's lower right ribs, and not the heart as DeFalco had intended. The big vampire staggered, then looked at DeFalco as the Agent came to his feet. Confusion was written on the giant's face as his hand went to his side and came away bloody.

"Special bullets," said DeFalco, grinning at the vampire. "Silver, with crosses worked into their points. Soaked in Holy Water overnight and blessed by a priest. I know it sounds like overkill, but I wasn't about to take chances."

"Motherfucker," yelled the vampire. He started to move toward the agent, a lunging reach across the room.

DeFalco squeezed off a pair of shots, one hitting Tashawn in the right thigh, another higher up near the groin. The vampire staggered to a halt, his face showing his shock.

"I guess the sun is up, Tashawn," said DeFalco calmly, feeling the weakness in the creature before him. "None of that super speed shit now." DeFalco waved the gun, bringing it to point at the vampire's face. "Why don't you tell me about this master you're serving?"

"What the fuck you talking about?" said Tashawn, his eyes darting to the window where the parking lot was brightly lit.

"Come on Tashawn," said DeFalco. "Marvin told us all about him. So you can come clean and I might let you survive."

"You're full of shit, pig," said the giant, shaking his head. "You ain't gonna let me survive, knowing what I am. What you gonna do? Bring me victims every night in jail? Or let me pick out my own from the inmates?"

"You got me there, Tashawn," said the FBI Agent, steadying his gun. "Yeah, I can't let you take more life."

The vampire went into a crouch, and DeFalco knew that in an instant the big man would be flying toward him in a tackle. He brought the gun down quickly and squeezed off three shots. The first hit the vampire in the upper right chest, the second in the side of the neck, and the third just below his nose.

The vampire reeled back, a roaring scream coming from his lips through the blood pouring from his face. His face took on the look of a panicked animal, looking for a way out of an impossible situation. And like some animals he moved without thinking, out the window, to escape the death in front of him.

DeFalco ran to the window in a couple of steps as the roar turned to a high-pitched squeal. His eyes went wide as he stared at the horrible sight of Tashawn kneeling on the asphalt of the parking lot, smoke streaming from his body as the dawn light shone down on him. The screaming continued as the vampire burst into flame. The limbs moved spasmodically as the face screamed to the sky. Skin blackened and then turned to ash, and the man writhed in agony.

DeFalco raised his gun one more time, taking careful aim, then squeezing off the shot. The bullet blasted through the back of Tashawn's skull, exited through the forehead in a spray of smoking brains. The vampire went limp with the destruction of his brain, falling flat on his face on the asphalt. The skin continued to burn as DeFalco looked on, coughing at the odor of burning human flesh. Within moments the skin and muscle were completely ashed, the bones exposed to the brightening sunlight.

DeFalco turned as he heard the groan behind him. Tanesha was struggling up to her knees, her right hand holding the side of her head. A trickle of blood ran down the side of her face and dripped from her chin. Her eyes were still trying to focus as DeFalco knelt at her side and put a hand on her shoulder.

"Easy now," said DeFalco to the detective. "Don't try to stand up too fast."

Washington stared into DeFalco's eyes as the intelligence started to come back into them. She groaned again as she took her hand away from the side of her head. DeFalco turned her head gently and looked at the wound.

"It doesn't look too bad," said the FBI Agent, running his fingers over the superficial scalp laceration. "But you'll need to let the paramedics look you over when they get here."

"You call them?" she asked, as sirens appeared in the distance.

"No need really," he answered, turning his head to look at the wreckage of the window. "I think everybody and their brother must have called 911 after this ruckus started."

Washington reached over and pulled his head back to look in his eyes.

"He really was a vampire, wasn't he?"

"Yes," replied DeFalco. "He really was."

He saw the doubt in her eyes and smiled.

"How else would you explain the hurling a car through a wall?" he asked. "Or the fact that you put multiple rounds into him with no effect. Hell, he didn't even bleed."

"You seemed to do better than me," said Washington. "What are you packing in that pistol anyway?"

"I came prepared," said the FBI Agent. "We need to get you equipped too, if you're going to work with me."

"He's not the one you're after, is he?"

"No," said DeFalco. "The one I'm after is much more cunning than that one. Which makes her much more powerful in her own way."

"God," said Washington, as the sirens got closer, sounding like they were just a block away. "My Uncles and Aunties would tell me stories about the supernatural. People rising from the grave, demon possession. I believed, a little bit. But not completely. Not deep in my heart. And to confront, this…"

"Yeah," agreed DeFalco, putting an arm around her and helping her to her feet as a pair of police cars squealed to a halt in the parking lot. "I felt the same way when I first saw her, feeding. But I came to terms with it and started hunting her, learning as I went along. And you can have my hard earned experience for free. It might just keep you alive."

DeFalco walked through the doorway, supporting Washington with one arm while he held his ID out with the other. The police officers lowered their guns, turning their heads back and forth from the skeletal remains to the Agent, their eyes asking the question of what had happened here.

* * *

Marcus was just lying down in his coffin when the premonition that something was wrong hit him. He lay there in the darkness, straining his ears, listening for an intruder. Nothing moved in the large empty house but some mice in the cupboards and some rats in the attic. He sniffed the air, bringing in the scent molecules across his supernatural olfactory receptors. Nothing except for the body of his last night's victim, the streetwalker he had brought home, starting to decay in one of the back bedrooms.

If the sun hadn't just risen, he thought, *my senses would be sharper.* Of course one of the advantages of being so ancient in his power was that some of his nighttime ability stayed with him during the day. And his hearing and sense of smell were still superior to that of any mortal. But he could detect nothing in the house, though he strained to his limits.

Which means something else is wrong, with someone I am connected to. And the only one he was connected to in this place and time was Tashawn Kent. Marcus closed his eyes and tried to concentrate on the youngling vampire. *If I had created him I could look through his eyes. Hear through his ears. Even listen in on his thoughts.* But he hadn't created Tashawn, and his newly obtained over-lordship was only enough to make a very tenuous connection.

Suddenly pain and fear exploded across that tenuous connection. The image of a man, aiming a pistol and firing it toward the point of view. Suddenly there was heat and agony coming in loud and clear. Marcus clenched his teeth against the pain that seemed to live in his own nerves. And then it was gone, along with any awareness of Tashawn Kent.

DeFalco, thought Marcus, closing his eyes and trying to compose himself. *I knew Tashawn would probably not make it. And if he tried to confront DeFalco, he was sure to lose.* And the broken connection meant that Tashawn had indeed lost, and was removed from the board.

I may need to move my resting place, thought Marcus, *in case Tashawn let any information slip about me.* Then Marcus opened his eyes and his mouth and laughed, a sound that caused the mice and rats to scurry for cover. *I'm not that senile yet*, thought the ancient vampire. He had not let the youngling know the locations of any of the lairs. There was nothing Tashawn could have let slip, besides the fact that Marcus LaMons, AKA Marcus of Alexandria, was in town. A very large town, with millions of possible hiding places.

Marcus closed his eyes again and allowed the fatigue to wash over him. Sleep would come easy now that he felt that his safety was assured. And maybe, just maybe, DeFalco would take care of his problem for him, and he could go back to environs that met his taste more than the city by the Tampa Bay.

*   *   *

The FedEx truck pulled up to the curb in front of the large house. The delivery woman grabbed a box and climbed out of the vehicle, looking at the invoice on the clipboard she held in her other hand. Nodding her head she headed for the gate, stopping for a moment to look at the beware of dog sign posted on the front of the fence. She stopped and listened for a moment, then reached over the chain-linked gate to pull the latch open.

"Hey," yelled a loud voice as the woman walked into the yard, closed the gate behind her, and started up the walk. "Didn't you read the sign?"

"Dog's love me," she replied, continuing up the walk as the big man came down the steps. "I'm not afraid of them."

"They're meant to keep people out," said the man, coming down the walk to stand in front of her. He crossed his hands over his chest and stared down at her from his height. She looked up at him and batted her eyes, noting on the way up that there was a bulge under his shirt at the waist.

Either he's really glad to see me or he's got a gun in there, she thought.

"The dogs are temporarily gone," he said, giving her a smile.

"Nothing happened to them, I hope?" she asked, licking her lips.

"No," he said after a hesitation that might have indicated lying, or might indicate severe lust. "We just sent them out for a little bit of vet care. They'll be back soon enough."

"I'm glad to hear that they're all right," she said, looking down at his groin area, and noting that there was some activity there.

"What can I do for you sweetie," said the man. "My name is Manny by the way."

"Laurie, Manny," answered the woman, smiling again. "I have a package for a Mr. George Padillas."

"I can sign for that," said Manny, holding out his hands.

"Sorry," said the woman, shaking her head. "It requires Mr. Padillas' signature. If you could just get him for me, it won't take a moment."

"Mr. Padillas is a busy man, sweetie," said Manny, a frown on his face.

"Is he home, or do I need to leave a note for him to come down to the dispatch station tomorrow. If he's such a busy man that might be even more of an inconvenience."

"We also check everything that goes to Mr. Padillas," said Manny, nodding toward the house. "I can't bring him a package without looking inside."

"Look, stud," said the woman, again licking her lips, "I don't care if you throw the box away or set it on fire. I don't need to know that Mr. Padillas actually got the box. But I do need to have his signature."

"OK," said Manny, turning back to the house, "follow me."

The woman followed the big man up to the porch. Manny opened the door and turned back to her.

"I can't bring you back to see Mr. Padillas," said the man, looking her up and down, his eyes freezing for a moment on her breasts. "But I can bring you invoice back to Mr. Padillas and let him sign it. If that's OK with you?"

"Sure. As long as you guarantee that it's signed by Mr. Padillas that's fine with me."

"Would you like to come in for a second?" asked Manny, taking the clipboard with the signature slip from her. "It's hot out here, I know."

"I thought you'd never ask," she replied in a silky smooth voice. She noted how the man's pupils dilated as she spoke. *He's interested, sure enough*, she thought, following him into the house. He gestured her to an antique chair as he closed the door.

She sat down, trying to cover the nervousness, crossing her long legs. The man looked at her for a second with a quizzical expression.

"You don't get much sun, do you?" he asked, nodding toward her legs. "I thought you'd be out in the sun a lot?"

"I burn too easily," she replied, looking back into his eyes. "No way I can tan. So its lots of high powered sun block for me."

"OK," said the man, a look of lust coming back over his face. "You wait right here for a moment and I'll be right back."

The woman let her eyes roam the room as Manny walked out of the foyer and back into the house. She noticed that another big man moved into the doorway and stood there, staring at her. She smiled back at him but got no reply other than a frown. Moments later Manny came back with the clipboard in his hand. He handed it back to her with a wide smile on his face.

"Signed, sealed and delivered," said Manny as she took the clipboard from him. She handed him the box in return as she got up from the seat.

"You are one lovely lady," said Manny, lightly touching her hand with his as he took the box. "What are you doing later? I have some free time tonight."

"I get off at nine," she replied, smiling at him as she stared into his eyes. "I might could swing by a little bit after that."

"Why don't you," he said. "I'll keep an eye out for you, but any of the boys can let you in."

"Thanks," she said, as he held the door open for her. "So I can take that as an open invitation?"

"You got it, sweetie," he agreed with another smile. "You're welcome in this house anytime as far as I'm concerned."

"Thank you again," she said as she walked out on the porch. The man followed and closed the door behind him. The woman sauntered down the walkway, wiggling her ass as she walked. She could feel his eyes on her as she opened the gate and closed it behind her.

Lucinda climbed into the delivery van and cranked the engine. Waving to her new friend Manny, she pulled away from the curb and into the street. An angry driver she cut off held his horn down hard. She gave him the bird out the side of the van. The driver accelerated the car around to her side and rolled down his window.

"I have your license number, young lady," yelled the middle-aged businessman. "I'm going to report you."

"Whatever," she yelled back at him. He gave her an angry glare and pulled ahead of her, accelerating away in his rage.

A double invitation, she thought, a wide smile growing on her face. She had only needed one to get in the house, whenever she wanted to return. Two was not unheard of, but kind of rare.

Now I have to ditch this van, she thought, as she turned onto a main thoroughfare. *And untie the real deliver man.* She glanced into the back, where the blindfolded, gagged and restrained man sat still struggling against his bonds.

"Sorry buddy," she called back to him. "But you helped me immensely. Hope I don't get you in too much trouble, when the jerk reports the license number."

She laughed long and hard as she drove the van toward a spot where she could park it and call the police, so the poor schmo could get free. And she still had some hours to kill before sundown, when she could kill some other things as well.

*   *   *

"Why didn't you let me get her now?" yelled Monsignor John O'Connor, shaking a fist at the man seated behind the desk. "We had her, in the house, when she was at her weakest."

"I had my reasons," said George Padillas, looking over steepled fingers at the priest. "It will work out for the best."

"What possible reason could you have for delaying the inevitable?" yelled the priest, walking back and forth before the desk. "Why would you want to wait, until she has her powers, to come back for you?"

"I have you here to protect me, don't I?" said Padillas, picking up the drink on his desk. "And I really don't fear her, Monsignor."

"She can now enter this house, whenever she wants," answered the priest, putting his hands on the top of the desk and leaning over to look Padillas in the eyes. "She can come for you in any of her many forms, and there is nothing you can do to prevent her penetration of your defenses."

The priest turned away from Padillas and started his pacing again. George Padillas followed the priest with his eyes; reminded of a stalking panther he had seen at Bush Gardens. He felt another stab of pain from his gut as he swallowed more of the drink.

Pain killers not working too good, he thought, as he got up from his chair and walked to the sidebar. He glanced over at the priest while he mixed another drink.

"You sure you don't want a drink, Monsignor?" asked Padillas, gesturing to the open bar cabinet. "Might calm you down a bit."

O'Connor looked over with angry eyes, shaking his head in the negative. Padillas shrugged and walked back to the desk, taking a seat after placing the drink on the top. He reached into the top drawer and pulled out a bottle of pills. Taking a couple for the bottle he popped them in his mouth and swallowed, washing them down with more strong alcohol.

The priest stopped his pacing, turning to look at Padillas, a quizzical look on his face.

"You said you are not afraid of death," said the priest, looking down at Padillas. "Why are you not afraid of death, Mr. Padillas? You don't have much chance of entering heaven. At least not until you do some major penance. I would think the gates of hell would stretch wide for you. So why does death hold no fear for you? Is it because you are so single-mindedly focused on revenge? But you had your chance for revenge, earlier today."

The priest turned away from the desk and resumed pacing, his hands linked behind his back.

"If only you had alerted me that she was here," said the priest in a quiet voice. "I could have gotten her at her weakest and my job would be done. Here at least."

"You asked why I'm not afraid of death," said Padillas, grimacing again, then taking a strong pull on the drink. "I'll tell you why I don't fear death. I'm dying, Monsignor. Colon cancer."

"I'm sorry," said the priest, stopping his pacing and sitting back in one of the comfortable chairs in the room. "And I'm sorry about the remark about hell. Do you want to be absolved of your sins, my son?"

"Hell no, Monsignor," laughed the crime boss, swirling what was left of his drink in his hand as he looked into it. He looked up at the priest as he tried to control the pain. "I'll just fuck up again. I like this lifestyle. I have to admit that I love the power it gives me. The power of life and death over people.   That's a powerful addiction, Monsignor."

"Then I will pray for you," said the priest, bowing his head.

"Because I'm about to die?" asked the boss.   "Or because I'm addicted to something you cannot understand?" The priest looked up and started to open his mouth. But Padillas put up a hand to head him off. "Don't deny it, O'Connor," he said.   "You had the title of Archbishop, one step below Cardinal, a title you were bound to receive. And then from there you might have become the next Pope. But you gave that up, for what. To become an outcast in your own church."

"I seek other rewards," stated the priest, holdings his hands open in front of him. "Serving God is the only path I seek."

"See," said Padillas, gesturing toward the priest. "You gave up power to do something you thought was more important. Power was not an addiction to you. So you will never understand my viewpoint."

"But eternity?"

"I would rather rule in Hell than serve in Heaven," answered Padillas, staring at the wall. "I will go to whatever is in store for me with no complaint. So don't waste your time or your prayers on me."

"That is your choice, my son," said the priest, his sad eyes looking at the crime boss. "God allows free will, so that men may choose their own destiny. And the evil of this world is done by men. That concerns me the most about you Mr. Padillas. The evil that you do to others."

"What about the evil done by this bitch?" asked Padillas, his eyes turning cold. "That is not the evil done by men. She's sent by the devil to spread evil among us."

"She is the exception to the rule," admitted the priest.

"And she's the exception I need you to destroy," yelled Padillas. "She is the only reason you are in my house in the first place, Monsignor. So I want you to concentrate on her."

O'Connor nodded as he got up from his seat, turning to go to the door.

"One last thing, Monsignor," said Padillas. "What happens to those she kills? Do they rise up as vampires, like in the movies?"

"Yes," said the priest with a nod. "That part of the fiction is true. Those drained by a vampire rise again on the third day, in sinister parody of our Lord."

"And the vampires come back with all of her powers?"

"Yes," said the priest, "indeed they do. But she has been very careful to not allow any to rise after her."

"Isn't that kind of unusual, Monsignor?" asked Padillas. "I mean, isn't the Devil's work better served by spreading the plague? Making more vampires?"

"I am not sure why she doesn't spread the disease," said O'Connor, hunching his shoulders. "I'm also not sure why she only kills the evil of the world. That runs counter to everything I have ever learned about her kind. But she is the Devil's spawn after all, and must have reasons that are a mystery to us."

"Whatever you say, Monsignor," said Padillas. "And she would control the vampires she creates, wouldn't she? They would have to follow her orders?"

"Yes. I believe so."

"And if she were destroyed?"

"Then anyone she created would become a free agent," answered the priest. "They would act only on their own free will. Why are you so interested in this?"

"Just curious, Monsignor," said the crime boss, realizing that he might be giving the priest too much food for thought. "Just curious. Now why don't you get a little rest? The sun will be going down soon, won't it? And we'll need you at the height of your priestly powers."

The priest nodded his head as he reached for the doorknob. Pulling the door open the priest looked back at Padillas for a moment then walked out into the hall. Manny walked in after he left and stood in front of the boss's desk.

"I want you to watch the good Monsignor closely," Padillas said to his lieutenant. "You know what has to go down for everything to work the way I want it too?"

"Yeah, boss," said the thug, who had started his career collecting money owed Padillas in the Port of Tampa, and breaking the legs of those who wouldn't pay up. "Don't you worry. We'll make sure that everything goes just like you said. You can trust me on that."

"I know I can, Manny," said Padillas, standing up, coming around the desk and putting his arm around Manny's shoulder. "And then when I have what I want we will have a party the likes of Tampa has never seen. And you will have the power and responsibility you deserve as well."

Padillas laughed as he walked the lieutenant out of the office. Manny joined in as they both anticipated the night to come.

Chapter 8

"Are you sure you're up to this?" asked DeFalco of Washington, looking worriedly at her bandaged head.

"Wouldn't have missed it for the world," she said, then grimaced and put her hand to her head.

"Does it still hurt?"

"Let's see," said Washington, looking the man in the eye and ticking of her points on her fingers. "Just this morning I was hit in the head by an automobile thrown through a window at me. Then I was attacked by a two hundred and seventy pound vampire. And I saw my doubts about the supernatural destroyed with the rising of the Sun. Other than that, and the fact that my hard head hurts, I'm fine."

"You don't have to do this, you know?" said DeFalco. "The commissioner gave you to me for detached duty. But he left it entirely up to you if you actually wanted to be out here so soon after what happened."

"I'm ready," she said, patting the gun in the holster at her belt. "A lot more ready than I was this morning, thank you."

"And another thing," said DeFalco, trying to use his strongest argument to get her out of the line of danger he was putting himself in front of. But he also wanted the backup, and felt that she would be good at it. Because she believed. "Those bullets you have in there are not quite what I would want to trust. We could get you a .40 caliber, and you could use some of mine."

"I don't like that heavy a gun," she replied, patting his jacket where he kept his big automatic. "A 9mm is about all I can handle. And the bullets were sprayed with holy water and blessed by a priest. OK, not one who really believed what we're doing, and not a Catholic Priest. But he's an AME minister and that makes him as much of a Man of

God as I need. And I'll have the super duper handy dandy silver bullets with the crosses tomorrow. So don't worry."

"I'm sorry," he said, shaking his head. "But I do worry, about anyone who faces this evil down in the dead of night like I will."

"Well you have to admit I'm better prepared than Lieutenant Smith and the rest of the gang," she said with a smile. "After what I saw this morning they could have an Abrams tank and not hurt one of those things."

Tanesha pulled the silver cross from out of her blouse and waved it in front of the FBI man. "And I have my own backup just in case this time."

"OK," said DeFalco, nodding his head, then looking out into the night beyond the car windows. "But you follow my lead. You're my backup, which means I'm the point man here. So let me take point and you provide the cover I need to take her out. OK?"

"Yes sir," said the detective, sketching a sloppy salute to the FBI Agent. "Or is that aye aye sir."

"OK, detective," said DeFalco with a chuckle. "I'll depend on your professional abilities for you to do the right thing. I won't say another word."

"Agreed," said Washington, nodding her head, then grimacing again. She grabbed her purse and pulled the bottle of Tylenol from it.

"Sure you don't need something a little stronger?" suggested the FBI Man.

"I'm sure I do," she said, "but I wouldn't be that good a backup if I was stoned on narcotics, now would I?"

"Have it your way," said DeFalco, turning his attention to the front of the house as he looked through the darkened one-way windows of the unmarked cruiser.

* * *

Marcus flew through the skies above the mansion, straining his night vision for the first glimpse of anything inhabiting the night sky with him. He flew close to several bats before realizing that they were the harmless night flyers of the Florida night, on the hunt for insects. Another couple of contacts turned out to be birds of darkness, which flew screeching into the night at the sight of the giant bat heading their way.

Marcus headed lower over the house, skimming the rooftop as he turned his awareness to the structure below. He could feel the surging life forces within the building, scattered throughout the house, but a group clumped together in one of the ends. Focusing on the group he could feel the sense of wrongness in the room they gathered outside of. A wrongness that gave off a strong undercurrent of danger. Danger to his kind, if not to the mortals who stood near it.

She might not make it out of there intact, he thought. It would be nice if the priest destroyed her for him, easier on him that is. But maybe not easier on the race. It would be more evidence of their existence for the mortals who already believed to push into the faces of those who didn't. And there had already been enough of that this morning.

Damn Tashawn, he thought. *If he'd only thought ahead, had alternate lairs, and gave himself enough time to get there, he would still be here. And the mortals would not have the sun blackened bones of a man pronounced dead years ago to point their fingers at.* As long as only a few of them, the lunatic fringe, shouted to the world that vampires existed, and no one paid particular attention to them, the race was safe. But give them definitive proof, say the death of a vampire on CNN, and they might go to war with his kind. *And given their frightful technology they could wipe us from the face of the Earth. And I for one do not want to go the way of the dinosaur.*

In his mind's eye Marcus could see the future that might unfold. He could see unmanned drones populating the darkness, looking for his kind. Groups of specially outfitted soldiers with advance sensory and communications equipment, holding automatic weapons loaded with the bullets that could kill his kind.   He could see himself strapped to a table, while men in white coats scanned him, seeing if they could gain the secret of his abilities.

Marcus shook the image from his head as he headed out over the front of the house. He looked up and down the street, noticing the dark car parked across the street from the Padillas house, a couple of lots down.   Flying directly over the car he focused his awareness on the two sources of life force in the vehicle. He bared his fangs as he felt them, as the awareness of their identities entered his mind.

The Federal Bureau of Investigation man, he thought, *and a compatriot. I could kill them in an instant, and rid their stench from ever bothering me or any of my kind again.*

Marcus swore in his mind as he flapped his wings and gained altitude, moving himself away from the people he wanted so badly to destroy. It would draw more attention to his kind if they were found dead in their car, throats ripped out and covered in blood. And they still might prove to be useful. They were not tracking him, after all. They didn't even know of his existence. And they could always lead him to the one he sought.

Marcus turned back over the house and flew high into the sky, looking down at the toy like buildings and cars below. If only she would come. And if only she would fly into the airspace above the house. So he could pounce down on her like a fighter out of the Sun. Knock her to the ground and destroy her before she could cause any more trouble. But she had to cooperate, and she had a tendency to not do that where Marcus was concerned.

*   *   *

Lucinda stood by the waters of the bay, three quarters of a mile from the Padillas mansion. She looked over the always choppy waters, preparing herself for the task ahead of her. A task that she had tried in the past, but never to the degree she was trying tonight.

She looked down at the body on the ground before her, the iron smell of blood from the wound in the chest hitting her nostrils. She could feel the hunger growing inside her as she smelled the blood, but that blood was not to feed her. It was to feed the magic she must perform this night if she wanted to get into the Padillas house through all of the watchers who would try to stop her.

The vampiress dipped her hand into the blood and started tracing the pentagram on the concrete walkway a few feet back from the seawall. She took her time, making sure that all of the lines connected. Satisfied that it was a close to perfect as possible, she licked the last of the blood from her hands, cleaning them.

Lucinda dragged the body to the edge of the water, positioning it so that the head was over the seawall, dead eyes staring into the choppy waves. She drew the knife from her back sheath and raised it into the air above the neck. Closing her eyes she concentrated on the scene, as she wanted to see it, over this section of the bay area. Satisfied that the scene was as she wanted it she opened her eyes and concentrated on the neck, bringing the knife up to the height of her reach, then bringing it down with all of her substantial strength behind it.

The knife sliced through flesh, muscles and bone with a meaty thunk. The head fell the four feet into the waters of the bay, while blood streamed out from the body to stain the surface. Lucinda grabbed the dead man's ankles, lifting him and holding him over the water. She held the pimp's body over the water for several minutes, allowing all of the blood to drain. When she felt that enough had fallen into the waters below Lucinda dropped it after the blood. The body splashed into the waves as the vampire moved away from the seawall.

Lucinda closed her eyes again, concentrating on the changes she wanted to make to the local area. She brought her hands up into the air, palms inward in the ancient manner of prayer. In her mind she reached into the evil that inhabited her soul, feeding it with her body's energy, promising it souls to satisfy its hunger.

She could feel the connection forming, the connection with the dark lord who gave her the powers she possessed. She could feel its anger at her, the anger she had brought by her refusal to do his work on Earth. The anger brought on by her destruction of evil and the foiling of the dark lord's plans.

You will do my will, my child, came the thoughts of Satan to her mind. *You are an insect, a speck in the eternity that I am. You do not have the power to resist me. Do my will or you will be punished.*

Bring it on, she thought back at the anti-God, forcing all of her will to battle that of the arch demon. *I am my own creature. Not yours. And you will bow to my will as a child of God.*

She could feel the power of the demon battling her, as its will beat down upon her like storm waves upon a lone, struggling swimmer. And like the lone swimmer she fought to stay afloat, to resist the power of the waves that sought to drown her. She could feel the strength leeching from her body, as the demon lord of Hell pummeled her.

I defy you, she screamed in her mind. *I renounce you and all of your plans for the race of man. And I will use you as you sought to use man, for my purposes.*

She felt the presence of the demon as some of its essence was pulled into the circle of the pentagram. It fought her with all of its power. But once a part of it had entered the circle, more of it was pulled inexorably into the symbol. More and more flooded in, until Lucinda felt as if the power of a Sun was in the air before her.

Yes, weak one, said the demon's voice in her head. *Bow down before my might and worship your true God.*

Lucinda opened her eyes and looked skyward, her cruel laughter echoing into the night. She brought her gaze down, her red eyes burning into the shadowy form of the demon within the circle.

You are the weak one, she thought at it. *A liar and deceiver, who pretends to be his master.*

The demon seemed to shrink in on itself as she exerted her will upon it. It fought against her, trying to slash through the magical barrier that kept it imprisoned. It went into a frenzy, but the circle of blood was too much for it, and soon its struggles ceased.

"You will give me the power," Lucinda screamed into the night. "It is mine by right of magic, and you will give it to me."

Lucinda felt the power flowing into her as it was released by the demon that was now under her command. She could feel it struggle to escape back to its realm, but her hold was too strong. When the energy finally reached its peak, all that she could hold, she clenched her hands before her.

"Back to Hell, demon. Back to the slime pits from which you came. Obey me now and leave this realm."

She could feel the demon's power wane as it was sucked into the void that birthed it. A final laugh resounded through her mind before it disappeared.

One day you will be brought to Hell, came the last thoughts of the monster. *And I will be waiting for your arrival. Oh yes, I shall. And you will know torment through eternity.*

And then it was gone, and Lucinda let out a mental sigh of relief. The energy she had leeched from the creature was trying to explode from her body, and she must put it to its use quickly.

Come mist, she thought with her entire focus, raising her hands again into the sky as she walked toward the seawall, carefully skirting the pentagram that still had a residual trace of the evil it had contained. Lucinda looked down into the water, repeating the call in her head over and over, visualizing what she wanted from the water.

At first there were only a few wisps of mist, curling from the choppy water. Then the wisps grew in number, as the atmosphere over the water became a thickening curtain of moisture. It rose into the air, until a region of hundreds of yards in every direction was blotted out by the thick white covering.

Lucinda smiled as the mist did as she commanded, growing thicker and thicker. She turned from the sea wall and started walking across the grass of the small park, willing the mist to follow. Within several feet of the road the fog had enfolded her, as it reached tendrils ahead, flowing toward the target. The Padillas Manor, and the evil it contained.

She walked along the sidewalk of the street that the mansion was on, keeping a tight reign on the fog, while allowing it to cover a wide area so that it would seem a natural phenomenon to the world around her. She felt the fatigue start coming over her again as the last of the demon energy faded from her body. And with the fatigue came the hunger that was a constant part of her existence.

I have work to do, she thought as she came within a block of the house. *I don't have time to feel tired right now.* She could feel how the fog shielded her, and from more that sight. It was a magical shield as well, one that her enemies could not penetrate. And it would shield her from the next spell she must enact.

Mist, she thought, focusing on becoming to the exclusion of all else. She could feel her body begin to spread, as she became as one with the suspended drops of water surrounding her. She moved with the fog as it rolled down the street. She moved her own substance against the current as she came near to the wooden privacy fence of the Padillas property, going through the slats and over the top, recombining her substance on the other side. Rolling across the lawn encased in the covering mist, she veered toward the cupola vents on the top of the house.

Lucinda's substance spread through the vents, coming together into the attic of the house. She searched for the way down, rolling along the low roofed attic until she found what she was looking for. The juncture of a wall leading down to a bathroom below, the pipe bringing up its odors giving it away. Sensing nothing in the room and a closed door, she forced her substance through the small opening of the power outlet and the cracks between the duct and vent of the air conditioning.

The mist that was Lucinda started to thicken in the small bathroom, as she poured more of the beads of moisture that made up her corporeal form through the openings. The mist swirled in the room, thickening into a vortex that tightened, until her human form stood in the center of the bathroom.

I'm here, she thought, as she took in her surroundings, listening through the walls of the house, tagging where people were, and where they weren't. She felt excitement at finally being in the home of her primary target. And a little trepidation at being in her enemy's lair. *But I'm finally here. And for better or worse it will soon be over.*

* * *

Marcus could feel the power building over the Bay. The magnitude of the energy itself, and its leakage from the source, prevented him from pinpointing the origin. He was sure he knew what the source was, if not its location. Then he swore as he felt another source of power materialize in the area.

She's more knowledgeable than I thought. I had thought that only an adept could have such skill, and she has only been here for what? Less than a decade. Marcus thought back on his own life for just a moment. He had been centuries in the grave before he had learned to control weather like that. And even more centuries before he had tried to call up a demon on his own. Even while he was thinking about it the second, more powerful, more evil source was gone, its screams of rage following it into the abyss.

Marcus wheeled in the sky, but he could only get a general sense of direction on the power source. From the height he gained he could see that there was a fog rising from the Bay. And it had already spread far enough to obscure whatever had created it. It spread quickly before his eyes, covering square blocks within seconds as it forged into the city, topping off at about twenty feet above the ground.

The elder vampire flapped his leathery wings as he headed for a radio tower above a yacht club. As soon as his claws were heading for the service deck, a metal mesh platform a hundred feet above the ground, he triggered the transformation. His feet hit hard on the metal, and he turned toward the Bay, his arms reaching into the sky.

Marcus concentrated on the weather, using the innate power that was a natural to an ancient vampire like himself as breathing was to a mortal. He pulled the power from his core, the same power that the demon had used before at the call of the youngling. For in his centuries he had grown into a demon of Satan, and possessed some of their powers.

Lightning flashed over the bay, as dark clouds gathered into a concentrated mass. A breeze came off of the water, then strengthened into a gale force wind. Thunder followed lightning, then more thunder, as the storm clouds streamed toward the city. A rain started to fall, lightly at first, then in heavy streams that blew almost sideways in the winds.

Marcus looked down on the city as the storm blew in. Trash was blowing through the streets, and traffic on the main thoroughfares slowed from the obscuring rain. The fog dissipated as the wind blew it away and the rain drove it into the ground. Marcus raised his hands once again into the air, calling the storm away as quickly he had brought it forth. The winds died down, followed by a slackening of the rain. The cloud mass above blew apart. As Marcus watched the sky above and the first stars shine through the rents in the clouds, he used all of his senses to try to track the quarry.

Nothing. She's already gone to ground. And he was sure he knew where she had gone to ground. Marcus willed the change to come over him, jumping into the air as a man, then flying through the air as a bat. He flapped steadily as he gained altitude, wheeling in the sky until he was headed for the Padillas house. *It ends soon*, he thought. *One way or another.* He would get her when she came out of the house. The Priest would get her while she was in the house. Or she would defeat him as she left. But one of those outcomes would happen soon, and end the chase.

*   *   *

"She's here," said O'Connor, looking over his strike team. *What an ungodly crew for God's work*, he thought. He hefted his large silver crucifix in his hand, gaining comfort from the weight of the icon.

"How you know that, doc?" asked Fred, playing with his pistol in one hand while his other played with the cross hanging around his neck.

"Didn't you think that fog was a little strange, Fred?" said Manny, looking at his cross as if he had never seen one before. Which O'Connor was sure was true after a fashion. He doubted the man had frequented one with belief for quite a while.

"Yeah," said Fred, nodding his head. "But strange fog don't really mean shit, does it?"

"I could feel her in the working of the Fog Magic," said O'Connor, grimacing. "And I could feel the abomination that she called up to power the magic."

"Magic. Vampires. What a bunch of Bullshit," said Fred, looking askance at the priest.

"You don't need to believe, Fred," said Manny, grabbing the bigger man's face in a strong grip. That Fred did not fight back was a testimony to how bad a dude

Manny was. "You just need to follow the directions of the good Father here, just like the boss said we should."

"The cross will have very little power without belief behind it," said O'Connor, holding up his own cross. "She will still recoil from it, but in the hands of a believer it will paralyze her with fear."

"Sorry about that, Father," said Manny, putting his own cross in his belt and pulling a revolver out of a holster. "You get what you got. A couple of sinners trying to help out."

"I wish you'd let me have my gun back," said O'Connor, looking at the pistol that was loaded with the special ammo.

"Sorry, Father," said Manny, holding up the gun in front of O'Connor's eyes. "The boss don't quite trust you with firearms, you know. So I'll just hold on to this tonight."

"Well, remember that the bullets in that gun can hurt her," said O'Connor. "While the bullets in your other weapons will have no effect."

"We'll remember, Father," said Manny. "You just watch yourself and stay out of the line of fire."

O'Connor stared at the man for a moment, wondering if he had been threatened. Would he last longer than the vampire? Or even as long? Again he thought, a deal with the Devil sometimes meant the Devil not only took your soul, but sometimes your life as well.

"Get ready," said Manny, hearing the squawk on the small radio at his belt. "She's here."

Manny grabbed the doorknob, slowly turning it. Then he suddenly threw the door open, running into the hall, the large crucifix held before him, Fred on his tail. O'Connor was caught by surprise for a second. Even though the plan was his, he was not the leader here anymore. But he made sure that he had a firm grip on the cross as he heard the shouts and screams erupt from the hallway.

*   *   *

Lucinda could not hear anything in the hall. For some reason her mind was still in stealth mode, even though she had come here with the intention of murdering all within the house if need be to cut the head of the snake. All except the priest that she knew was in the house. Him she needed to avoid, to somehow get around him while she killed the crime boss.

What am I waiting for? she thought. *If it needs doing I need to do it now.* With that thought she reached for the knob and pulled the door open, stepping boldly into the hall.

"There she is," shouted a man toward the living room side of the hall. Lucinda could now hear several of them, along with the static hum of a noise suppression device. As she turned toward the voice, baring her fangs, she could hear a door behind her open and a couple of men run into the hall. After catching a glimpse of a man with a large cross heading cautiously toward her she turned back to the sound behind her, going into speed mode.

The two men coming from the bedroom were also holding crosses, though the one in the lead also had a revolver in one hand. They seemed to crawl toward her in slow motion, to her heightened speed. She looked back to see that a second man was coming behind the first in the living room, then turned back toward the two from the bedroom, sensing that the greater danger was coming from that direction. She looked at the revolver held by the side of one of the big men, and could feel the threat from it. *Holy bullets*, she thought. High velocity pellets that could hurt her badly if not kill her.

Hoping that it wouldn't the feeling of fright began to overwhelm her. The holy symbols, even in the hands of unholy men, still stirred the terror that was instinctual to her kind. She started to back away from the ones coming down the hall, then feeling the ones from the living room coming close behind her turned that way. The symbols in their hands made her want to flee back up the hall toward the bedrooms. But that path was blocked as well.

Her instincts drove her from fear to rage, an animal rage that she couldn't control. She spun toward the bedroom, seeing the crosses coming toward her, the man with the gun now falling back to trail the other, the pistol held pointed up in the air, ready to come down and fire in a moment.

"We got her," yelled one of the men behind her. Lucinda spun that way with speed, her claws swinging in an arc that pushed the leading arm holding the cross across the man's body. Her elongated fingernails continued on to hit the side of the man's throat, slicing through the skin and cutting the veins below. As blood spurted from the ghastly wound she continued the strike, the nails slicing in behind the windpipe of the man. With an outward pull she took the throat out of the man, seeing his eyes go wide with shock.

The crucifix fell to the floor from nerveless hands as she reached down and grabbed the front of his shirt. A quick pull of supernaturally strong muscles swung the man in the air over her head and past her shoulder. As she spun with the throw she aimed the dying man toward the first of the men coming from the bedroom. She released the body and saw that a new danger had appeared. In the form of the priest, a large silver crucifix held before him.

He has real power, she thought, feeling the strength of the God she had denied in life pulsing from the man himself into the holy symbol. It was a power that could physically harm her, and maybe destroy her. Then the body she had flung was slamming into the leading man, the top of the dead man's head striking the other man in the jaw, then the body come down on the now unconscious man.

Lucinda spun back the other way, hoping that the second man from the living room would be within reach. If she could take him out the way to the living room would be open and she could get away from the deadly priest that she could not bring herself to harm. But the second man hung back out of reach, his cross held in front of him. And a third man was coming up behind him, a large plastic cross in his hands.

A glance over her shoulder showed her the big man with the gun stepping over the bodies of the dead man and the unconscious target that he had taken down. The priest was beside him, moving around the pile and holding the silver cross before him, while his lips moved in prayer. She moved the only direction open to her, toward the living room, where the two thugs with crosses continued to back away.

She couldn't think in this state of mind. She was totally running on instinct, the animal instinct to survive. She was no longer a rational creature, and didn't think why they were moving her along the hallway. She noticed that one of the doors on her left was open, leading into a dark room that was not occupied by a cross wielding thug. But in her panic she did not reason why such a perfect escape route was left open to her.

When she got even with the room she started to angle toward it. With the little bit of reasoning ability she had left she thought of escape, even though she had planned to fight her way through whomever she needed to so the boss would die. But the room felt wrong to her as she got closer to the doorway. A wrongness that threatened to destroy her quickly and irrevocably. She looked into the room, her night vision making the darkened room as bright as day. But beside a table and a couple of chairs she could see nothing within that would seem to be able to cause her harm.

Still the room hurt her, a deep hurt right down to her soul. She felt the panic rise in her just from proximity to the chamber. She turned away, back to the men coming up the hall, from the living room, her instinct telling her to push through them no matter the fear.

"No, spawn of Satan," said the Priest, pushing his cross toward Lucinda. She could feel the power of the holy symbol in the hands of a true believer, even more powerful than the fierce strength of the room. The cross touched her on the left shoulder. Agony lanced through her, as the sizzling of flesh came to her ears, and the smell of burning meat entered her nose.

Lucinda opened her mouth in a silent scream, the pain freezing her in place. She tried to reach over and pull the cross away as it was burning its way into her. But she pulled her hand back as it touched the cross, the tips of her fingers burned like they had contacted a strong acid.

The priest jerked the cross away as he slid more to her side. The pain kept her from reacting at any kind of speed. Before she could move the priest thrust the cross into her shoulder again, this time on the outside. Lucinda squealed, a high-pitched sound that had most of the men in the house covering their ears. But the priest ignored it as he pushed with the cross. Burning through clothes and flesh, the cross hurt her like nothing she had ever felt before, living or dead.

"Move, spawn of Satan," yelled the priest, shoving hard with both hands on the cross. Lucinda did not want to enter the room, but what she wanted didn't matter a bit compared to the pain that pushed her into it. Her feet slid on the carpet as the priest pushed yet again. As her body was halfway into the room she felt her muscles go weak. She fell hard the rest of the way, landing on the wooden floor of the room.

The priest backed away, one hand grabbing the doorknob and pulling the door behind him. Lucinda heard the door click shut, then the lock being engaged, as she tried to struggle up to her knees. The walls of the room beat down on her, with a numbing pain that pulsed through her bones.

What the hell is this, she thought as some reasoning ability returned. She scooted to the exact center of the room, where the painful influence lessened just a bit. She examined the room as closely as she could without leaving the center. There was a blue paint on the walls, ceiling, even over the one window in the room. It was obviously new, freshly painted on. And there was something in it, something holy that pushed her down and left her feeling beaten.

No way out, she thought, a hand going up to feel the burned areas of her left shoulder. She winced as her fingers felt the deep burned indentations that the cross had made. *They will heal, though it may take more than a day.*

Lucinda arranged herself on the floor in a lotus position, determined to calm her mind if not her soul. There was nothing she could do except beat herself up for falling into a trap. Not that it would do any good. And not doing any good it was not something she wanted to engage in. She closed her eyes as she repeated the mantra she had learned years ago in college, relaxing her body. Playing the waiting game that she had no choice in participating in.

* * *

"Good work, Monsignor," said George Padillas, walking out of the safe room he had retreated to when the vampire entered the house. "She's trapped bigger than shit. So what's next?"

"We wait for daylight," said O'Connor, wiping the sweat from his brow. "With luck the sunlight coming through the window will kill her, though I think the paint may make it too faint to do the job. Or we go in and destroy her while she's helpless."

"But she's still dangerous now?" asked Padillas, walking past the priest to put his hand on the door.

"As dangerous as a cornered panther," stated the priest, looking at the discolorations on the cross where it had touched the vampire. "That's why we wait until morning.

She won't have any of her powers, and the rising of the sun will also make her lethargic, an easy target."

"And she hasn't fed tonight, right?"

"As far as I know, Mr. Padillas," said O'Connor, looking intently at the man's smiling face. "I think you were to be her dinner tonight. And we prevented that, so she will get very hungry by the end of the night. But she'll be weak as a kitten in the morning, and no danger to any of us."

"So by tomorrow night she would be very much hungry," said Padillas, putting his hand back on the door. "She would not be able to control herself, yes."

"I think that's right," said the priest. "But why all of these questions. In the morning she will be gone and you will be safe from her, forever."

"That's what I wanted to know, Monsignor," said Padillas, looking back over his shoulder at Manny. "Now make sure he doesn't do anything stupid," said Padillas, gesturing toward the priest.

"What are you talking about, Padillas," yelled O'Connor, as another of the thugs grabbed him and pushed him along the hall. He tried to dig his feet into the carpet and stop himself, but the man just grunted and pushed harder, and he was propelled down the hall. "I did what you wanted and stopped her from killing you."

"Yes you did, Monsignor," said Padillas with a laugh. "Just what I wanted you to do. But now I have other plans for our girl in there. Plans that you might not approve of. So I need you to be put away for just a little while, so I can do what I need to do."

"You're a fool Padillas," yelled the priest as the muscle pushed him down the hall with a firm grip on the priest's shirt. "She'll destroy you. You don't know what you're playing with."

The thug pushed O'Connor into the room the priest was using, following him in and slamming the door behind them. Another man went to the door, turned a key in the lock, and stood in front of it.

"Get rid of Marty's body in the morning," said Padillas to Manny, nodding at the bled out corpse on the carpet. "And clean up the mess."

"What about the priest?" said Manny, pointing toward the Monsignor's room.

"I might need him for a little while longer," said Padillas, a smirk on his face. "I might have some more questions that only our vampire hunter can answer. But after I get what I want you'll need to put him in the bay, somewhere he won't ever be found. After all, I can't have the man who knows it all coming after me, now can I?"

Both men laughed at the inside joke, as Padillas winked at his top man.

"Now I'm going to get some shuteye," said Padillas. "Make sure our girl stays where we have her. And make sure the priest stays away from her."

"Will do, boss," said Manny, looking at the door to the room that trapped the vampire, then at the body of Marty. "I wouldn't want her to get her hands on me. At least not till I'm ready to join you."

Padillas nodded his head as he reached the end of the hall and pulled the door to his own bedroom open. With a wave he walked through the door and closed it behind him.

Chapter 9

Lucinda sat in the very center of the room, trying to stay calm as the hunger began to eat at her. At first the only thing on her mind was the terror that the walls and ceiling of the room held for her. She did not know what the priest had done to the paint to make it anathema to vampires. But whatever he had done he had done well.

About an hour after she had been trapped in the room she heard the sound of a hammer driving nails into a wall, and could feel the vibrations of the blows. She heard the sound of the voices of a couple of men, laughing and joking as the nails were hammered into the windowsill outside of her room. The window grew darker after the hammering stopped, then the voices went away.

So they don't want the morning sun to hurt me, she thought. *Why is that?* Were they planning on using her is some way. As an assassin, or as muscle in Padillas' operation. If so they were in for a surprise. A vampire was no mortal's puppet. Especially a vampire who was dedicated to destroying the men who wanted to use her as a puppet. She would lie to them, cheat, swear her soul to God or Satan. But then she would do what she wanted to do. And what she wanted to do was to kill everyone who lived in this house.

Except the priest, she thought, grimacing at the thought of the man burning her with the large silver cross in his hand. She ran her fingers over the burns, already healing. But because of the holy source of the burns they would continue to hurt for years, even after the flesh had seemed to heal.

The priest was an innocent, even if he misguidedly tracked her and tried to destroy her. He had no evil in his heart. Unlike Lucinda and her kind he would be whisked to heaven on his death. Such a one was forbidden to her, by her own vow. Sure, she could lie to others to get whatever she wanted. But she had promised to never lie to herself, and had pledged to herself that no innocent would die by her hand.

The hunger grew stronger by the minute, a thirst that was worse than days under the desert sun without a bit of water. A thirst that threatened to drive her mad. It gripped her belly, made her muscles quiver, and had her looking around the room over and over again. Looking for the food she needed, even though she knew it wasn't in the room.

Lucinda stood in one fluid motion from the lotus position, the hunger driving her to leave the room, to seek food. But everywhere she turned the force in the walls and ceiling kept her from getting too close. A step toward a wall was met with a wave of nauseating terror. The terror drove her back to the center of the room, where the terror was its least powerful.

The ceiling beat down on her head the whole time. By standing she brought her head closer to the ceiling, and it hurt her head to be close to it. She stayed upright as long as she could, fighting to stay on her feet so she might move from wall to wall. But after a few minutes her head hurt too much. Nausea fought with hunger and nausea won. She plopped back down on the wood floor with a hiss of anger. The nausea retreated to a dull background, and the hunger came back to the fore.

Dammit. I'm damned if I do, damned if I don't. No matter which path she took, sitting quietly or seeking an exit, some feeling attacked her. She felt that any moment she would end up curled up on the floor, in a panicked terror that left her helpless. That drove her mad.

The floor, she thought. She hit the floor hard with her hand, but there was no give in it, even to her great strength. She scraped at the floor with her nails, as they hardened to steel sharp claws. Pieces of wood came up under her probing nails, giving her more of a grip between the boards she was working between. After minutes of work she got her nails deep into the side of one of the boards. With a powerful jerk she broke the board free from the surrounding planks, pulling it free from the floor.

Shit, she thought as she looked at the hard concrete below the hardwood floor. That was something that would defeat her no matter what she did. In rage she flung the board toward the door. It struck hard, but on the flat side, falling from the door without doing anything but superficial damage to the paint. As it hit she thought that it would have been better to throw the board at the painted over window. But it was too late.

The hunger was getting worse, as was the nausea from being trapped in the room with holy objects.   Lucinda pounded her fist onto the boards again in frustration. Then she rolled over onto her side and curled up into a fetal position, riding out the agony of the night. Thoughts of going cold turkey on heroin entered her mind. But heroin shakes would eventually go away.

*   *   *

"What in the hell is he doing?"

"Now, now Father," said Fred, sitting on the bed while the priest stalked the room. "Don't you worry about it. Not a bit. The boss knows what he's doing."

O'Connor stopped in his tracks and turned a baleful eye on the hired muscle.

"What he's doing is playing with things he doesn't understand," said O'Connor, pointing a finger at the man. "And he's likely to get burned. And get all of the rest of you burned with him."

"Father," said Fred, his voice strained as he tried to control his rising anger. "The boss is in charge here. Not you. You're going to bust a gut worrying about things you can't do anything about. So calm down."

"But…"

"Sit the fuck down, Father," said Fred, coming to his feet and stepping over to the priest, pointing a large finger in the man's face. O'Connor looked for the nearest chair and plopped down in it, the big man leaning over him.

"You're going to drive me crazy with all of this pacing and whining," said Fred, emphasizing each word with a poke of his finger in O'Connor's chest. "Now you sit your ass in that chair and keep it there. And keep your mouth shut."

Fred turned and stormed back to the bed, plopping on it to the creak of springs.

"I'll be so damn happy when we get rid of your ass," said Fred under his breath.

O'Connor had done much work with the deaf in his early days as a priest, and had become expert in sign language and reading lips at that time. He had kept up the skill through his life, and had no trouble reading the lips of the big man muttering to himself. *Get rid of my ass*, he thought. He shuddered as he thought about what that might mean. But he had enough sense to not let the man know that he had intercepted the speech.

* * *

Lucinda could feel the rising of the sun as she lay on the floor, curled up into a fetal position and trying to weather the storm of pain that radiated from the walls and ceiling. The hunger was terrible. She was not sure that she could stop herself from feeding on anything that was put in front of her, including the innocent.

Her thoughts went back to years ago, when she was still in thrall to the older vampire that had made her. He would send her hunting most nights, to choose her own victims. But sometimes he would send her to bring back food to satisfy his own longings. And he preferred his food to be young and tender, brimming with life force.

Other times he would bring back a morsel for her to feed on. A squirming baby, crying in terror. The smell of piss and shit and fear. She didn't want to feed on such a tender life. But the hunger would take charge and she would sink her teeth in the new flesh and suck the life from it. Then she would look down at the lifeless bundle of meat and feel a deep sorrow for it. And a deep sorrow for herself, for being the monster that took its life. The baby or child would sometimes show up on a milk carton somewhere, but that was the last anyone would see of it.

One day the master did not come back from a hunt. Just before dawn Lucinda felt as if someone had punched her hard in the stomach. From the groans sounding through the lair she could tell that the other two women in the master's coven could feel it as well. The master was gone, snuffed out like a candle that was no longer needed. And for the first time since she had been turned she felt free to do as she wanted.

As the sun rose and the other vampires went to their rest, in too much shock to do much of anything, Lucinda forced herself to stay awake. As they slept she went to their coffins and drove the rough wooden stakes she had made of boards found in the lair through their chests. They had screamed horribly for a few moments, as their bodies deteriorated to their true forms. Rotting corpses that should have been decades in the ground.

Lucinda had then slept, awakening with the coming night, a terrible hunger laying hands on her. She had gone on a hunt as soon as her eyes had opened. But she had chosen the prey. A man who had just raped a young girl in a dark park. She had taken his blood and his life with satisfaction, sating her hunger while doing the world a service. And she had sworn on that night that an innocent would never again fall to her hunger. A promise she had kept in the years gone by.

She came out of the vision as she heard the doorknob turning. Trying to rise brought no result, as her muscles would not respond to her commands. She could smell the blood in the men who entered as the door opened. Struggling against the fatigue and the weakness brought on by the dawn, she was able to raise her head off the floor with the greatest effort.

There were three men standing by the door. The leader held the large silver cross that the priest had wielded the night before, held in front of him like a shield. She recognized him as the leader of the men who had trapped her last night, and probably the headman in the house. One of the others looked familiar, but in her confusion she could not place him. The third was a complete stranger. She could smell the fear on all but the leader, who radiated a confidence that came from holding the cross.

"I see you're still awake, babe," said the leader, grinning down at her. "And just as helpless as the priest said you would be."

"You sure she can't attack us Manny?" said the man she thought was familiar. "I saw what she did to Harry last night."

"Hard to see how you saw anything, Jake," said Manny, glancing back at the man. "What with you hiding in the living room."

"I wasn't hiding, Manny," said the man with a frown. "I was the backup, waiting to come into the hall if you needed me."

"Then you can be the first this time," said Manny, nodding his head toward Lucinda. "You get around her and grab her other arm. You grab the near arm Gary, and get her up on the table."

Lucinda bared her fangs as the men moved around her. She laughed inwardly as Jake passed her feet by the wall, as far as he could get from her. Manny growled when both men hesitated.

"She ain't gonna do shit, you assholes," he said, walking up to Lucinda and holding the cross down toward her. She tried to squirm away, her instinctual terror of the holy object guiding her. At the same time she wanted to sink her teeth into the neck of the foul-mouthed man who stood over her. But she lacked the ability to do either.

Jake looked down at her, shaking his head, then reaching down to grab her arm. She tried to move her head toward him, to rip into him with her teeth. He let go of her arm as she twitched, then looked sheepishly at his boss. Manny stared at the frightened man, who reached down again and got a good grip on her arm.

"She's so damn cold," said Jake, as he lifted up on her arm, with Gary raising her off the floor.

"What did you expect," said Manny, moving to the table. "She's fucking dead."

"I prefer dead things to stay that way and not move around," said Gary, holding her up as Jake maneuvered around the table and pulled her across. They had her on the table, as she struggled to keep her eyes open.

"Come on in, Fred," said Manny. Lucinda turned her head toward the door to see another of the big men she had encountered in the night come in the room. He held a bunch of tie down straps in his hands. As the other men held her arms out Fred wrapped a tied down strap around her chest, moved under the table, and cinched it tight. Another tie down went around her waist, another around her thighs, then her ankles. The last tie down went around her neck.

"What the hell do you want with me?" asked Lucinda weakly through parched lips.

"I don't want a fucking thing from you, bitch," said Manny, slapping her across the face. "If it were up to me I would stake you and be done with you. But the boss has bigger plans for you."

Fred looped some rope around her wrists, then pulled them together and wrapped it tight. Lucinda tried to struggle, to pull her hands away, but in the strong grip of the man she was helpless. He then looped the ends of the rope under the table and tied it tight.

"She's ready, boss," called Manny after Fred gave him an OK with his fingers. Lucinda turned her head back toward the door as George Padillas walked into the room, a smile on his face.

"You've caused me a lot of trouble, young lady," said Padillas, walking up to the table and looking down on the vampire.

"Not as much trouble as I wanted to cause," croaked Lucinda through weakened vocal cords.

"Oh, no doubt," said Padillas, grinning. "You would have liked to put me into a grave. Without my head. And I want to live, a long and productive life. So maybe we can compromise."

"What the hell are you talking about?" she gasped, her eyes shutting without her control.

"You'll see," he said, patting her cheek. "Tonight. You'll be right there in the thick of things."

Lucinda felt darkness enclose her, her last sight the grinning face of the man she had come to kill. And the last thing she heard was the hated voice.

"Sleep tight, beautiful," came the voice of Padillas. "You have a long night ahead of you tonight."

* * *

"You keep her safe and sound," said Padillas to Manny as he looked down upon the sleeping face of the vampire. "And keep the priest away from her no matter what."

"Why don't we just get rid of him now, boss?" asked the thug. "I could do him in a heartbeat, and then you wouldn't have to worry about him."

"I might need him, Manny," said Padillas, turning toward his lieutenant. "I might need his knowledge. But after I'm done with him you can do what needs to be done. In fact you must do what I want done if I'm not to be looking over my shoulder for the next couple of decades."

"OK, boss," said Manny, nodding his head. "I'll take care of that. And I'll make sure no one bothers you during the, transition period. And I'll make sure you have something to eat when you get up."

"And the people you've talked to have agreed to the arrangements?"

"Did you think they wouldn't?" asked Manny with a grin. "Each and every pimp knows to send a girl here when requested. And to keep a lookout for new blood on the street."

"I see you're looking after me, Manny," said Padillas with a laugh. "And then when you're ready to join me I'll look after you."

"Thanks boss."

"Now I've got some affairs to take care of," said Padillas, pausing at the door. "I need to set up for a lifestyle change, and only have one day to do it."

* * *

Padillas walked from the room as Manny turned back to his three confederates.

"Fred," he said, looking at the biggest man, "you relieve Josh and get back to watching the priest. Don't let him out of your sight and nowhere near this room unless the boss calls for him."

Fred nodded his head and left the room, as Manny turned back to the other two men.

"You guys stay here and watch her. I want two people here at all times. There will be someone at the door. Call him in here if you need to take a bathroom break or something. And I'll have people to relieve the both of you by this afternoon."

"I'm kind of tired already, Manny," whined Jake.

"Well, keep your fucking eyes open, shit head," growled Manny, grabbing the flunky by the front of his shirt. "Or I'll shut them for you, understand?"

"Yes sir," said the stammering man. Manny shook his head as he let go of the shirt and walked from the room. *That's a weak link*, he thought as he walked down the long hall to his room, right next to the boss'. *He might find himself in a new role after me and the boss do our thing. I wonder how he tastes?*

* * *

I wonder what is going on in there? thought Marcus, as he stood on the street watching the Padillas house. *It's a big place, with lots of rooms, so she could be hiding in it someplace.* But it didn't feel right. It felt as if she were still in the house, but not in control.

The elder vampire could feel the rising sun just below the horizon, maybe a minute from appearing. He had wanted to be out here till the last minute, in case she came from out of the house. But she hadn't, and if she did now she would be destroyed.

Nothing for it now, thought the vampire, walking away from the house until he reached a main street. He moved across the street, into the shadows he had scouted earlier, and converted into mist. The mist went down the nearby storm drain and Marcus converted back to human form. He walked along the big storm culvert, heading for his own lair.

Tonight, thought Marcus, as he covered his eyes against the burning light. He would have to sleep through most of the day to make up for the energy he was using now by being up at sunrise. But tonight he would again be posted outside the house, ready for what might come.

* * *

George Padillas yawned as he felt the fatigue that threatened to put him to sleep. And the pain in his gut that threatened to double him over in his chair.

"Are you OK, Mr. Padillas?" said the bank representative who had been showing him where to sign his name on the papers.

Padillas grimaced back the pain, set his face, and smiled at the young woman who filled out her business suit quite delightfully. He nodded his thanks as another employee brought him the cup of coffee he had requested moments before.

"I'll be fine, Sally," stated Padillas to the banker. "Must have been something I ate earlier today."

"Yes sir," said Sally, putting a soft hand on his forearm.

I guess I'll really miss sex, thought Padillas, as he looked from the hand to the handsome face of the woman. *But anything will beat this pain I feel every day. And living forever has to have its advantages.*

Padillas signed the papers that made Manny his signatory, then the e-banking forms that would allow him to manage all of his accounts without having to come out into the light of day.

"So Mr. Manfred Gottleib will have power of attorney over all of your accounts," said Sally, looking at the signed papers, then separating the copies from the original. "I sure hope you trust him."

"With my life," said Padillas, taking the next paper from the stack and signing it. "I'm sure my money's safe in his hands."

Padillas stood up and offered his hand to the young woman, thinking again of how nice it would be to feel her body next to his in bed. He hadn't had sex in over a year, since the cancer had taken charge of his life. And he didn't think he was up to it now either. Besides, this was not a high priced hooker in front of him. She had a wedding ring, though from experience he knew that did not always stop a woman from wanting some strange cock in her.

"Are you sure you're OK, sir," said the woman, rousing Padillas from his thoughts. "You don't look well."

"Just tired," said Padillas, blinking the tiredness from his eyes. "I'll be OK with a little sleep."

Sally smiled as she took his hand in a firm business shake, placing her other hand over the top of his. Padillas' eyes widened as she traced her fingers gently over his palm when he withdrew his hand. Padillas smiled back, shrugged his shoulders and turned away.

So she would have been an easy conquest after all, he thought as he walked through the door of the bank. *Money is the greatest aphrodisiac in the world, followed by power.*

Padillas opened the door to the Mercedes parked in front of the bank and slid into the back seat.

"Where to now, sir?" asked the driver, looking through the rear view mirror.

"Take me to Sister Fannie's," said Padillas, wiping the sweat off of his face as he fought back the nausea. "I want her to tell me what she sees."

"Yes sir," said the driver, pulling the car out into the street and accelerating away. Padillas sat in the back, looking out over the city, his city, for maybe the last time he would see it in the light of day. The Fall was finally here, but that didn't mean much in Florida except for slightly cooler temperatures.

I miss the Winter, he thought, nostalgia taking charge of his emotions. Though he had grown up in Florida, from Greek parents who had settled in Naples in the early part of the twentieth century, he had traveled extensively in the Marines and on summer break in college. Plus, when he had made his fortune he had traveled around the world, skiing in Europe and Colorado, diving in Australia. He still found central Florida to be as close to paradise as anywhere he had ever been. But sometimes it was nice to feel the actual weather of the world.

When I'm well again I will travel where ever I want, he thought. *Though it might not be the same at night. But it's better than nonexistence.*

His thoughts were broken as the car pulled into the drive of a modest house. A hand lettered sign in the front yard told the world that Sister Fannie, reader of fortunes, was open for business. Padillas was out of the car as soon as it stopped and headed up the sidewalk to the front door. He rang the bell and waited for a moment, hoping that the old woman was at home. And that she was not busy with another client. He didn't think that was likely when there wasn't another car parked in the drive or on the street in front of the house.

After what seemed like longer but could have only been a few minutes Padillas heard the sound of someone moving toward the door. The door swung inward just a bit, stopped by a chain that kept it from opening further. A wrinkled black face looked through the small opening. The face smiled, the door shut, and Padillas could hear the sound of the chain being withdrawn from its slot. The door swung wide open again, to reveal the short, heavyset black woman standing inside, running one hand over her kinky gray hair.

"Welcome, Mr. Padillas," said the woman in the accent of the Caribbean. "I did not have you down for an appointment this day."

"I was hoping that you might have some time to see me today, Madame Fannie," said Padillas, flashing the woman a smile.

"Of course. Of course, Mr. Padillas," said the woman, returning the smile. "I had a cancellation, so this is your lucky day. Come in."

Padillas walked through the doorway, watching his feet to keep from stepping on the two or three cats that seemed to orbit the woman wherever she walked within her house. He reached down and ran his hand over the soft fur of an orange tabby and was rewarded with a vibrating purr.

"Mr. Max sure seems to like you, Mr. Padillas," said Madame Fannie, leading the man back to the room that she used to give her readings.

"I've always liked Max," said Padillas, himself a cat man. "He reminds me of one I had a decade or so ago."

"How is the pain today?" asked Fannie, as she shooed the cats away before opening the door to the reading room.

Padillas felt a chill run up his spine as she mentioned his illness. That was what had made him a believer. When three years before this woman had told him that he had a terminal illness growing in his belly. Weeks before even he knew of the illness. The doctors had confirmed it at that time, and given him a year or two to live. *Fooled them, didn't I*, thought Padillas. He had lasted three years, though the pain told him the time was coming, soon.

Padillas looked around the darkened room as he entered it. The small round table sat directly in the middle, the black cloth draped over it as always. Madame Fannie flicked a lighter and lit the black candle in the holder in the center of the table, then turned off the low light that had illuminated the room.

"Have a seat, Mr. Padillas," said the woman as she sat in her own chair. Padillas sat in the offered chair, resting his elbows on the top of the table. "And what can I do for you today, sir?"

"I have come to a crossroads, Madame Fannie," said the man, staring into the light of the thick candle. "I know what I need to do. But I would like some assurances that everything will work out."

"And if I can't find any assurances for you, Mr. Padillas?"

"Then I'll take the truth," answered Padillas. "I may not follow the advice, but I'll listen to it."

"Of course, sir," said the woman, her eyes staring at him across the short space. "You have always been one to follow your own path, even when it was one that would cause great harm to others. Or to yourself."

Padillas felt the thrilling shiver again. The woman did not use tea leaves, cards, or the lines of his palms, the props she may have used on other, more gullible clients.   But Padillas could feel the power in this old woman, power that did not need to be revealed other than through her words.

"So what's the verdict, Madame?"

Fannie stared at him for a while longer. Time seemed to slow, as she looked deeper and deeper into his eyes, like a hypnotist bringing her subject into a trance state. But he knew the woman was looking into his soul, not his mind. And that she would see the truth of the matter.

"I see death," said the woman in a quiet voice. "I see much death. Your death. The deaths of many others. And I see something after death, but not the afterlife that most of us face."

"What is this something?" said Padillas, leaning closer to the woman. "What does it mean to me?"

"Damnation," hissed Madame Fannie, her eyes going too wide to seem possible to the man.   "Eternal and irrevocable damnation. An eternity of Hell, both on Earth and after you no longer walk the Earth."

"But I will still live on?" said Padillas, his right hand reaching out and grasping the woman's forearm in a tight grip. "I'll live forever, won't I?"

"You must leave," said Madame Fannie, pulling her arm out of his grip with surprising strength. "On my soul I can tell you no more."

"Please, Madame…"

"Leave," she said loudly, standing up and turning on the light to its full brightness. "You must leave."

Padillas stood up as he reached for his wallet. Leafing through the bills he pulled three hundreds out and tossed them on the table.

"I don't want your money, Mr. Padillas," said the woman, holding the door open. "I do not want you to return. You are no longer welcome in my home."

"The cats need to eat," said Padillas, ignoring the money as he walked from the room. Max was outside the door and rubbed against his leg as he left the room. Padillas reached down and touched the cat on the head. Max looked up, his eyes wide and teeth bared, a loud hiss coming out of his mouth as he ducked away from the hand.

"They know," said Madame Fannie. "They know of the terrible thing you will choose to become. For the love of God do not do this thing."

Padillas looked over at the woman, slowly shaking his head, then turned to walk to the front door. He pulled it open, then turned back to the woman.

"I thank you for all of your help through the years," said Padillas, looking into the woman's eyes. "I'm sorry we had to part this way."

"I too am sorry," said Fannie. "I fear for your soul. I fear for my soul, if I had anything to do with leading you down this dark path."

Padillas turned and walked quickly down the concrete pathway back to the driveway, feeling like the devil was chasing him the whole way. *Am I doing the right thing*, he thought. But the pain that hit him as he opened the door told him all he needed to know. He did not want to die. He was afraid to die. All of his money couldn't keep him alive. But he could still cheat death.

And she knows, he thought, as the driver backed the car from the driveway to the street. *I can't have that. No one but the trusted few must know that I have died and come back. So she must die. Not tonight, or even the next day, because people might have seen me come in here and link me with her. But soon she must die.*

Padillas lay back in his seat on the way home, smiling as he thought of the end of his pain that would come with this night.

*   *   *

Madame Fannie poured herself a stiff drink of rum and sat down in the comfortable chair in the living room. Max and Sabrina jumped onto the chair and climbed onto her as she took a large chug of the alcohol, then pulled a fat joint of marijuana from the side table and lit up. The old woman took a heavy toke, feeling first the smoke enter her lungs, then the wave of relaxation that swept through her body.

She knew she would not sleep well this night, no matter how much weed she smoked or alcohol she drank. There wasn't enough in the city to cover up the terror of what she had seen in the soul of George Padillas. She had seen death in many forms. She had known that George Padillas dealt in death himself. Both in the deadly drugs he moved into Central Florida, and in the people he had gotten rid of to protect that terrible business. And she had still dealt with the man because his money was good and she could tell herself that she was not furthering his business with her predictions.

But today she had seen different types of death. Death that brought more death, and perpetuated itself down the line, into eternity. Death that came on leathery wings in the night Death that captured the soul and held it in bondage. And she had seen her own death in the soul of the man. Because she knew, and he could not afford to have her know.

Fannie took another toke of the good pot, and held it in her lungs. Max settled on her chest and started purring deeply in his body, the soothing vibrations passing into her. Fannie ran her fingers through his soft fur. Sabrina meowed from her perch on the chair arm.

"Jealous," said Fannie, putting the half joint into the ashtray on the side table and stroking the female Calico. *I'm an old woman*, she thought, playing with the cats. *Death will not be that frightening to me. Losing my soul is frightening. And who will take care of my babies?*

Her three other adult cats bounded into the room at that thought, followed by the two kittens. She had no relatives, no family other than the cats. And she could not stand the thought of the trusting cats ending up in the animal shelter. Or on the street, fending for themselves.

There is hope, she thought, sifting all of the images she had seen in her reading of the man. There was another shadow in the background. A shadow that radiated the same evil as the others, but somehow felt different. A shadow that came out of the darkness and stopped the other shadows before they took the life of an old Jamaican woman. She continued to pet the cats as she settled back into her chair and tried to forget what she had seen.

*   *   *

Lucinda tried to move on the table, feeling the horrible illness that fatigue brought on her, and the terrible hunger that fought its way through the feelings of sickness. The vampire flexed her arms and legs, trying to break the restraints that held her to the table. But she was just too weak to accomplish even that simple task.

"I wouldn't bother," said the man standing by the door, holding a crucifix in his hand. "Those straps can hold a rhino down."

Lucinda turned her head toward the voice, baring her fangs. She could smell the blood of the man, his life pulsing through his veins. She could almost taste the blood in him. The sweet blood that would chase the hunger from her body. That would give her the strength to leave this place.

"You want me, bitch," said the man, who she now recognized as Jake. He walked over to the table, holding the cross before him. Lucinda felt the new terror fighting its way through the sickness and weakness. She turned her face away from the symbol, removing it from her sight.

"Let's see how you like this," said Jake, putting the cross on her forearm. The symbol touched her flesh with a sizzling sound, as she opened her mouth in a silent scream, agony lancing through her.

"God Dammit, Jake," roared a voice from the doorway. Footsteps sounded on the wood floor, and the cross was jerked away from her flesh. She let out another hiss from the pain, but also felt the relief of the cessation of the burning into her arm.

Lucinda turned her head back to see Jake being pulled back by the large form of Manny. Manny twisted the smaller man around by his shoulder and slapped Jake across the face.

"The boss said she wasn't to be harmed. Motherfucker," yelled Manny, backhanding the man. "What fucking part of that didn't you understand?"

"I'm sorry, Manny," whined Jake, putting a hand up to defend his face. Manny knocked it down and grabbed the front of Jake's shirt, pulling the man toward him till they were staring at each other nose to nose.

Lucinda struggled against her bonds. There was food here, enough to satisfy her hunger and more. But she couldn't get to it. She felt weaker than a normal human, much less a hunter of the night. Part of that was the daytime, when her powers were not present. Another part was not having slept in her resting place during the morning. And the third was having gone through the night without feeding. That was the part that was really taking it out of her. And the holy room was not helping all that much, augmenting all of her other illnesses.

"You watch her," said Manny, giving the man one more shake and releasing him. "The boss wants her in one piece and as healthy as she can be. And I want what the boss wants. So do your job, or I'll make sure your ass is dead, motherfucker. Understand?"

"Sure, Manny," stammered Jake, looking from the man to the vampire and back to the man.

Manny stormed out of the room, slamming the door behind him. Jake stared at the closed door for a moment, then back at Lucinda. He jumped at the look on her face; the hungry smile of a hunter that knew you would be in its larder, eventually. Jake started for her, the crucifix in his hand coming up. He stopped a few feet from her, the expressions on his face showing the war of emotions that was going on within.

"You're mine, bitch," hissed Jake, staring down at her. "For what you did to my friend, last night, you're mine. When the boss is done with you I get to take care of you."

"And you're mine," whispered the vampire, staring into the man's eyes, projecting her will toward him. The man looked away under the gaze, anger turning to fear in his eyes. "When I am free of these bonds all of you are mine."

* * *

"You ready for another long and sleepless night?" said Jeffrey DeFalco, looking over at Washington.

"I could do with a little help," said the detective, stirring her coffee with a plastic stick. "I wish the chief would give you some more manpower."

"I'm grateful for what he gave me," said DeFalco, glancing back at the Padillas house. The shadows were growing longer on the ground as the sun started on its path below the horizon. "I could be out here on my own, like in the past. And I'll have to tell you. Every other time I've tried to get this girl through a one-man stake out I've failed. Two of us double my chances."

"But so far also failure," said the woman, nodding toward the house. "At least we know Padillas is in there tonight."

Washington turned back toward DeFalco, a look of alarm on her face.

"But what if she's already gone, and we're wasting our time here?" said Washington, looking down at the briefing sheet she had gotten from the station. "There was no body found last night. Or the night before."

"I don't have anything better to do," said DeFalco, staring at the Padillas house. "If she's gone somewhere else I sure don't know where. And she normally doesn't pull off of a target until that target is dead. So I think my best bet is to stay right here on the probability that she'll be back, until she can verify that Padillas is dead."

"I guess I don't have anything better to do, either," said Tanesha, smiling.

"I think you might have a future in the Bureau," said DeFalco. "You have a good, inquisitive mind. We could use you in the field."

"All I have is a Criminology Degree," she answered. "I thought you needed a Law or Accounting Degree to get in the Bureau?"

"Not always," said DeFalco, looking into her eyes. "We can get you on a scholarship to further your studies. And you can serve as an apprentice in the meantime."

"An apprentice?"

"I need someone to help me in my cases. My pursuit of darkness," he said, putting a hand on her shoulder and looking into her eyes.

"You're not going to let this end if you destroy her, are you?"

"You think she's the only one out there?" he said, looking back into the night. "You remember Tashawn? How he threw the car through the window of the hotel? Well there are more being made like him every day. Every night more of these hunters go out and feed. And in their wake they leave new vampires. Most people don't believe it. But you do. You've seen it. You know it's real. And I can use someone who knows to be on my side."

Washington sat silent for a few moments, thinking over what the FBI Agent had said. Then she shook her head.

"I believe," she said. "I know you're right. But I don't know if I want to spend the rest of my life pursuing a darkness that could turn and eat my soul. To become one of them. Aren't you afraid of that, Jeffrey? That you could fall prey to that which you hunt. That you could end up becoming one of them."

"I don't think that's going to happen," he said quietly. "But no, I can't guarantee it. But someone has to do something about this terror. And except for the priest I don't know any others out there searching and destroying. So that means I have to do what I can do, and not worry about the consequences."

"I don't know if I can't worry about the consequences," said Washington. "I believe in God. But I also believe in the Devil. And I don't want to walk that close to the minions of the Devil, lest I become one."

"Well," said DeFalco, putting the night vision glasses to his eyes to see into the deepening night. "You don't have to make up your mind right now. I'm thankful you're with me right here, right now. And I will be very grateful for your aid in helping me to stop this one vampire."

Washington nodded her head, then picked up her own night vision glasses and brought them to her eyes. She scanned the twilight, sweeping the glasses back and forth; searching for the slightest movement that might mean their target was about.

* * *

"I think you are crazy, Mr. Padillas," said Monsignor John O'Connor, sitting on his bed and shaking his head. "You are trying to make a deal with the Devil. And you should know from the literature that no one makes a deal with the Devil and comes out ahead."

"Monsignor," said Padillas, standing in front of the priest and flashing a big smile. "I really don't know what I have to lose. I'm dying. I think you've already guessed that much. And I have not lived a good and holy life. So I'm going to Hell. There's no doubt in my mind. So do I want to go to Hell tomorrow, or a few months down the road at most? Or do I want to go to Hell much further down the road? Centuries? Thousands of years?"

"That is what Satan promises you," said the priest. "But he is the Prince of Lies. Most who make the deal for eternal life find that they don't get what they bargained for."

"I'm willing to take that risk," said Padillas, again smiling. "Even if it's a crooked game, it's the only game in town. So I'm eager to take my seat and ante up."

"You could always repent, George Padillas," said the priest, standing up from the bed and putting his hands on the shoulders of the man standing before him. "You could ask God for forgiveness, and live your remaining days for his glory. And then you could enter into the Kingdom of Heaven at the end of your days and live eternally in the presence of God."

"Sorry Monsignor," said Padillas, placing his hands on the hands of the priest and pulling them away from his shoulders. "I'm too old and far too set in my ways to make those kind of drastic changes. I think I'll take the easier way out. And I want to be the ruler of my domain, not the servant of another."

"I'll pray for you, Mr. Padillas," said O'Connor, his eyes full of sorrow. "I'll pray that you have a change of heart. Or that God does for you what you can't do for yourself."

"You do that, Monsignor," said Padillas, laughing at the priest. "You do whatever you think you need to do. And I'll do what I think I need to do. Goodbye."

Padillas walked from the room and Fred closed the door behind him, standing in front of the door with crossed arms. O'Connor looked closely at the man, then sat back on the bed.

"You just take it easy, Father," said Fred, grinning at the priest. "It'll soon be over, and you can go back to your life."

He's going to kill me, thought O'Connor. *Fred is my executioner, once Padillas finishes with his task and no longer needs his resident vampire expert. He can't afford to have me around, knowing what he's become. And maybe coming after him.*

"You OK, father?" asked Fred, looking down on the priest.

"You hazard much, my son," said O'Connor, looking up at the big man. "You are following a path of evil that you do not even comprehend. It will lead you into a darkness from which there is no return."

The man smiled back at him, his eyes laughing. O'Connor shuddered as he thought what a nest of vipers he had joined in his single-minded hunt for the vampire. Instead of getting him closer to ridding the world of a beast, he had actually gotten closer to loosing a greater monster on the world.

She, at least, only took her prey from among the evil of the Earth, he thought. He had never known her to kill someone who wasn't deserving of it. Not that anyone was deserving of death, said the priest in him. But the human part of him knew that there were people in the world whose absence would be of benefit to mankind. And those were the people she had eliminated. And made sure that they didn't rise again as a greater evil.

Did I misjudge you? Were you actually an Angel of the Lord in the guise of a demon? And did I use my knowledge to stop you from fulfilling your destiny. And give an evil man control of powers he did not need to control.

O'Connor looked again at the man who was keeping him in this room that was his prison. The man who would be his executioner. And the man who knew very little about Monsignor John O'Connor, and the things he had done in a younger life.

* * *

Lucinda could feel the presence of the night, the sun slipping below the horizon. She could feel the heightening of her senses, the greater strength that infused her muscles. But the strength was not as great as usual. Having not fed the night before, having not rested in her home soil, had weakened her even with the coming of night.

She could hear the voice of her hated target in the hallway, and the answering voices of his henchmen. She could smell his blood, even over the scent of life that was already in the room with her. She bared her fangs as saliva dripped down her chin. She flexed her muscles, her instincts telling her that she needed to break her restraints and go on the attack, to grab and kill her prey. But her muscles were not up to the task, and the tight bonds held her motionless on the table.

The door swung open and there in the doorway stood the prey. Lucinda felt a wave of nausea sweep through her as the hunger took charge and fought through the weakness. Her strength increased and she pulled again at the restraints. But the strength was still not great enough and the restraints seemed to laugh at her effort. She sank back to the table as her strength left her again. The hunger fought against the weakness, but it was an unequal battle. The hunger won in her mind, driving all other thoughts before it. But the weakness won in her body, and she couldn't get at the food that she desired more than life.

And then the prey walked over to her, looking down on her with a smile on his face. She could feel a little bit of fear on him, could smell it in the sheen of sweat that reflected the light from his face. But there was something else. A smell of adrenaline excitement that was stronger than the fear. And deeper, deeper. The smell of corruption, within the guts of the man. *He's already dying,* she thought. *And the fear he feels is not of me, but of death in general.*

"How are you doing tonight, my dear?" said Padillas, his voice slightly weak. The adrenaline in the man's sweat showed that he was probably weaker than his voice showed, and was running on the strength of excitement. "I hope you have enjoyed the accommodations."

"I have been in much more hospitable places," she said in a soft voice. She strained again at the restraints, trying to get at the man.

"No need for that," said Padillas, smiling again. "Oh. I have not been a very good host have I? I haven't offered you refreshments."

"The only refreshment I want would come from your ripped out throat," she hissed, pulling again at the restraints. He was the reason she existed. To end his existence. But he had her in his power.

"Get it over with," she whispered. "I know that's what you want. Why else would you have brought the priest here."

"You have one more task to perform," he said, moving closer to her as he pulled the collar away from his neck.

Lucinda could smell the blood pulsing beneath the skin, hear the pumping of his heart as it drove the fluid through his body. The neck came closer, as the man offered himself to her.

This can't be happening, thought Lucinda, her lips curling back from her sharp teeth. *Why would he let me take his blood?*

She felt his flesh under her lips as she tasted his skin. The hunger was overpowering. She could barely think of anything else but the food that was before her. But there was enough of the rational left in her to balk at the man's willingly giving himself to her.

He wants this, she thought, as her tongue licked over the flesh. *He's dying, and there is no way to save his life. So he wants me to turn him. To make him undead, so that he can live forever. But he doesn't know that he will be my minion, does he?*

"Come on, bitch," said Padillas, pushing his neck down onto her mouth. "What the hell are you waiting for?"

He means to have me destroyed, she thought. *Then he will be a free agent. And a greater evil than he is alive. No. I can't allow this to happen.*

But the hunger was too great. Her throat felt dry, her stomach nauseated, her muscles weak. She knew what could cure all of these symptoms, and it was before her. Her lips curled back again and she thrust her teeth into the neck of the man.

Padillas tried to pull away as the teeth pierced his flesh, his instincts trying to prevent that which he wanted. Then he relaxed, showing Lucinda the willpower of the man. The discipline to get what he wanted, no matter the cost.

She sucked away at the blood that welled up at the wound, her hunger taking control of her. She could feel the tension in the muscles of his neck, knowing the pain that the man was feeling at the beginning of the feeding. Then the muscles relaxed as the victim's pleasure took over his body. She could feel her own pleasure rise as the blood flooded into her mouth and down her throat. The orgasmic pleasure of feeling the life of another flowing into her and strengthening her.

She lost herself in the feeding, feeling the strength filling her muscles. The feeling of filling up, as blood cycled through her stomach and the life force took away the nausea of the hunger. Within minutes she could feel the last flickering of the man's life. His heart was barely beating, and she was sucking hard on the neck, trying to tease the last of the blood from his body.

Wait, she thought, pulling the remaining blood from the body of George Padillas. *I'm doing what he wants. I have to stop this, before he becomes one like me.* But she couldn't stop. Her soul demanded the life, to make her whole again. To heal her. In the frantic hunger, the hunger that had come over her after not being able to feed the night before, there was no way she could force herself to not take the last of the blood of the man. She could feel the heart stop beating. She could feel the lifeless state of the body, empty of the soul that living humans carried within them.

And she could feel something else. The seed that her feeding had planted within him. The seed that would grow in three days to an evil demon soul that would animate the dead body.

No, she screamed in her mind as she bit hard into the neck, ripping and tearing, trying to decapitate the man with her teeth. If she could separate the head from the body the seed would be destroyed and George Padillas would go on a one way trip to the grave.

"Is she supposed to be doing that?" said Jake.

"She's trying to destroy him," said Manny.

Strong hands grasped the shoulders of Padillas and pulled him away. Lucinda dug in with her teeth, trying to hold the man to her. But the flesh was too tender and she felt it ripping free under her teeth. Then the body of Padillas was pulled away from her, and she turned her head to see Manny and Jake dragging the body away.

Manny stopped for a moment and threw Padillas' body over his shoulder in a fireman's carry. Jake looked at Lucinda for a moment, then moved toward her, bringing his right fist up into the air. He swung a haymaker at her head, landing a hard fist on her temple.

Lucinda shrugged off the punch like that of a child, baring her teeth in an evil smile. She tensed her muscles, muscles no longer weak but again filled with the strength of ten women her size. She flexed and pulled and felt one of the restraints begin to part. She pulled harder as Jake backed away from her, the smell of fear rising off of him. She jerked and the weakened restraint parted with a snap. She jerked again, feeling the remaining restraints dig into her flesh. But her flesh was stronger than the nylon of the restraints, and another parted with a loud crack. With a final jerk she snapped the last restraint around her arms, then reach to the straps over her chest. Her clawed hands dug under a strap and pulled it away, then another, until her upper body was free and she could work on her legs.

As Lucinda pulled the last restraint away from her she looked up in time to see Jake pulling the door closed. It slammed with a loud thud as the vampire jumped from the table. She could feel the holy wrongness of the room beating down on her, but with her strength she pushed against it, almost making it to the door. But she was still a creature of the night, and could not long fight against the repulsive power of the holy symbols.

Lucinda fell away from the door and crawled along the floor until she was again sitting near the table. There was no way she could get near enough to the walls or ceiling to get through them. *And in the morning they come back and destroy me*, she thought. Which gave her nine hours to get out of the room, though for the life of her she couldn't figure out how she was going to make that happen.

Chapter 10

"In heaven's name, what is going on out there?"

"Take is easy Father," said Fred, getting up from his chair and moving in front of the door.

O'Connor heard shouting in the hall, even through the thick walls of the room and the almost soundproof door. He thought that was Manny's voice yelling at another man, then the slamming of a door vibrated through the walls. Then more loud voices in the hall. The priest tried to move toward the door, but Fred held his big hands out in front of him and fended O'Connor off, placing his hands on the man's chest. O'Connor reached up with one hand and tried to pull a hand away. Fred pushed, hard, and O'Connor fell backwards, stumbling until his legs hit the edge of the bed. He tumbled backwards, landing on his back on the mattress.

"Don't do it, father," said the man as O'Connor came off of the bed. "I don't want to hurt you."

"Bullshit," mumbled the priest, balling up his fists. "You're going to kill me when that son-of-a-bitch gives the order."

"True," said the big man, reaching a hand into his pocket and pulling out the garrote, grasping one of the wooden handles in each hand as he stretched the guitar string between them. "I guess it's time then, since from the sound of it the boss has done what he wanted to do."

The big man walked lightly on his feet as he moved toward the priest. O'Connor backed away, his eyes darting this way and that, looking for a way out of the room. Fred smiled the grin of a shark, his eyes gleaming in the light.

He's a true psychopath, thought the priest, his mind going back to his studies in psychology. *He will enjoy killing me. I wonder how many others he has enjoyed killing.*

Fred raised the garrote up in front of his face, making sure that his victim saw the method of his execution, trying to make sure that man was terrified with the coming death. He frowned a moment as the priest looked steadily back into his eyes.

Time to use some other of my studies, thought O'Connor. He swung a right fist toward the other man's head, waited until Fred reacted, then ducked his left shoulder and sent a hard left cross into the man's right ribs. Fred grunted, then grunted again as the priest sent another pair of left crosses into the ribs. As the man dropped his arm to cover up his side O'Connor sent a right cross to the side of the head, then a left uppercut under the jaw.

Fred's head jerked back under the blow. He growled as he bit his tongue, then swung a heavy right hand at the head of his tormentor. O'Connor caught the blow on his raised forearm, deflecting it over his head, then swung a right into the man's stomach, following it with a trio of left, right, left into the hard stomach. O'Connor knew however hard the stomach a man could not take a hard punch unless he had been trained to take one, and Fred had been the beater for too long. The air woofed out of the man as the punches landed.

This is taking too long, thought O'Connor. The man was hurt, but he wasn't going down fast enough. And the priest was sure that the someone would eventually hear the noise and come into the room. He couldn't afford to have two or more men to fight against. Already the strain was telling on his older body. *Not like the younger days,* he thought, ducking under another haymaker. He would have taken a mug like this apart when he had fought professionally. Even though he hadn't been the best, only up to breaking into the top ten, a man like Fred had little skill as a real fighter.

O'Connor made another feint, right hand to the ribs that was blocked. But the second punch of the planned combination landed, into the Adam's Apple, hard through the cartilage of the throat. Fred's eyes went wide as he tried to pull air through his crushed windpipe. O'Connor threw a right to the man's temple, then a left knife hand to the side of the neck.

Fred tried to stay on his feet, tried to call out, tried to pull in some life giving air. He failed at all three, as O'Connor sent a flurry of fists into the man's head and body. Fred dropped to one knee, one hand on his leg while the other held his throat. O'Connor sent a right into the man's head, followed by another, then a third. Fred went limp, falling to the floor, gasping as he hit, then going unconscious.

O'Connor knelt beside the man, his hand going to the jugular. There was a faint pulse, but the man was not breathing. He would not last long, and O'Connor's heart told him to stay, to try and help the man, to revive him. His intellect won out, telling him that he had to get out of here or his own life would be forfeit.

Patting Fred down O'Connor found the gun he knew the man would be carrying in his back waistband under the long shirt. It was a Glock. A forty-caliber model just like that carried by the Secret Service and FBI. He jacked the slide back and released, loading one of the ten rounds into the chamber, then pulled the two spare mags from Fred's pockets.

O'Connor had never liked guns. They reminded him of the evil that man did to his fellow man. But since becoming a vampire hunter he had become more than proficient with them. So he held the gun expertly as he checked the door and found it locked. Another search of Fred, who had by now died of asphyxiation, revealed the key. O'Connor unlocked the door, listened for a second, then pulled it open. Sticking his head out into the hall, the priest looked both ways. It was clear, and O'Connor slid out into the hallway, closing the door quietly behind him.

That was when the door opened at the end of the hallway, the one leading to the large master bedroom complex. Jake walked out, his face freezing in shock as he saw the priest standing in the hall, a gun by his side. Jake tried to get his hand into his own waistband, to get his own pistol out, and stopped as he saw the muzzle of the Glock pointing at his face.

"Drop it, my son," said O'Connor, holding the gun steady with one hand. Jake slowly withdrew the pistol from his waistband, a revolver that looked familiar to the priest, and dropped it to the floor. The priest advanced on the man, holding the gun close to his body, not allowing Jake the chance to try to knock the gun away.

"Kick that pistol over here," ordered O'Connor, gesturing with his own gun.

"Don't hurt me, man," said Jake as he kicked the revolver, sending it a couple of feet toward the priest. "You're a man of the cloth, father. You're not supposed to hurt anyone."

"The church allows a man to defend his own life," said O'Connor as he squatted down to retrieve his specially loaded revolver. "And God help me but I value my own life more than yours. So don't make me shoot your worthless ass. My son."

"What the fuck!"

O'Connor heard the curse over his shoulder. He started to turn as Jake made his move. Because of his age. Because of his fatigue, Jake overestimated how fast the priest would turn. O'Connor was able to reverse the direction of the pistol even as he continued to turn. He jerked the trigger, sending a heavy slug into Jake's chest from point blank.

Jake fell back against the door with a hard thump, then slid down toward the floor, leaving a slick of blood on the surface. He clutched his chest with his hands, as his wide open eyes stared at the priest that had just put a bullet through his lungs.

A bullet cracked past O'Connor's head as he continued to turn. He dropped to one knee and brought the gun up in front of him in a two handed grip. He tracked the gun up to aim dead center of the man standing at the end of the hall, another of Padillas' thugs who O'Connor had a passing knowledge of. The man's gun, another big automatic, roared again, and a bullet whizzed by O'Connor's ear.

The priest took a full breath, let half of it out, and squeezed his trigger. He had aimed at the chest, but the big gun had pulled up as it fired. The thug's face exploded into a splatter of blood, and a heavy mist erupted above his head, the edge of the cloud of brains and blood that exploded from the back of his head.

O'Connor's ears were ringing from the booming of large caliber pistols. Still he heard someone yelling from Padillas' bedroom and knew that soon there would be more thugs in the hallway, trying to end his life. With the peace that comes from a connection with God the priest did not really fear all that much for his own life. But he had a mistake to rectify, and little time to do it.

O'Connor ran toward the door leading to the room in which the vampire was confined. His hand grasped the knob and turned, but the knob resisted his efforts and he didn't have time to find the key. Taking a step back he sent two rounds into the locking mechanism, smashing the lock and the wood around it. A swift kick sent the door inward, just as the door to Padillas' bedroom was pushed out, and stopped by Jake's body lying against the door. A couple of curses sounded as people on the other side tried to push the body out of the way of the door.

O'Connor sent a couple of rounds through the door, gaining a yell of pain and some more cursing. Then he went into the room he had prepared to trap a vampire.

Cold animal eyes looked back at him as he stared at the woman, one of his hands pushing the door closed behind him. He placed his back against the door, cringing at the thought of a bullet coming through the wood and into his yielding flesh. He put the fear of pain down, again calling on his contact with the Lord to bring an inner peace even in the midst of so much turmoil.

"Have they sent you to destroy me, priest?" asked the evil creature sitting on the floor.   "Could they not do it themselves, that they had to send their hireling to do their dirty work?"

"I am sorry," said O'Connor, looking down on the demon in the body of a gorgeous woman.   "They fooled me into doing their work.   I was convinced that you were the greatest evil in this city.   I did not know that there was even greater evil, and I sold myself to it."

"So what do you want, priest?" she asked, her angry eyes boring into his.   "Forgiveness?"

"I don't ask for that from such as you," said O'Connor. "But I realize that I have misjudged your intentions, if not your methods, or that which dwells within you."

O'Connor could hear the yelling and cursing, louder as the door was being shoved open down the hall.   *I don't have time for a long conversation of reconciliation*, he thought.   He raised the Glock, watching as she watched him with a smile on her face.   *She knows that this weapon holds no threat to her.   And she knows that I know it.*

The pistol barked in the room.   Three shots, through the window that was painted over with the sanctified paint. Glass shattered outward, as O'Connor ran to the window and ran the barrel around the frame, breaking the last remaining portions of hanging glass.   Looking back at the creature of the night he took a couple of long steps and stood in front of her, putting her between him and the window.

"Now get the hell out of here," he said to her, looking down.

"You're going to let me go?" she asked, sitting in front of him.   "I thought it was your mission in life to destroy me."

"I do not condone your methods," said O'Connor, glancing nervously back at the door. "But you get results. I don't know how you have gotten past the evil that lives within you. Because it would seem to me that Satan would rather you killed the good in the world. But enough of this talk. Leave here. Now."

"I can't, priest," said the vampire, showing him an alarming smile of razor sharp teeth. The teeth she used to feed on the lifeblood of mortals. "I'm still trapped here. I couldn't force myself to go out that window if the Devil himself were chasing me."

"Then perhaps we can provide something that scares you a little more than the Devil," said the priest, reaching his fingers into the top of his shirt, under his white priestly collar. The small cross was attached to a chain, and with a quick jerk O'Connor snapped a link. He held the cross in front of him, almost in her face. "In the name of the Father, and of the Son, and of the Holy Spirit, I order you from this place, demon."

The smile left Lucinda's face, replaced by a look of rage that soon metamorphosed into fear and terror. She scurried back, getting to her feet, her eyes darting for a place to escape and finding none. O'Connor walked forward, the cross held before him, saying a silent prayer as he felt the power of God flow through him and out of his hand, using the crucifix as a conduit. The vampire backed, pain on her face as she approached the wall that was covered with sanctified paint. But the holy power before her was greater.

Lucinda turned and jumped through the air, her instincts taking charge, getting her away from the torment that was before her eyes. She flew unerringly through the opening, knocking the plywood paneling out, her body propelled into the night.

One task accomplished, thought the priest. But he still had to make sure that George Padillas was truly dead. Because as much of a monster as the man was in life, he would be even more of one in undeath.

* * *

Lucinda had felt like she was being torn between two elemental forces when the priest came at her with the cross in his hand. The wall behind her was pushing against her progress backwards like a pulsing of heavy storm waves at the beach. While the cross in the priest's hand was like a laser cutting into her from the front, fierce and intense. One pain was unbearable while the other was intolerable. She started to panic, like a wild animal trapped in a burning forest. And like the panicked animal she darted in the direction that looked the best.

Gathering her legs under her the vampire leapt head first at the window. She intense agony from behind lessened as she flew toward the window, while the unbearable pain in front grew. Lucinda was unable to turn in midair. The only way she could stop herself was to put out her hands to push against the wall on the sides of the window. And that in itself was something that she could not do, because she would have to touch the source of the pain.

So she flew through the window, the plywood paneling ripping from the frame. Her nostrils took in the cool night air, feeling the pain lessen on her head, shoulders, and chest. The agony was released as she left the room, last leaving her ankles and feet. The vampire tucked her shoulders as she hit the ground, then rolled up onto her feet. The pain was gone, the nausea was dispelled, and she felt the strength of the night flood into her body. And she was angry, and the anger needed an outlet, the animal in her demanding a release.

"Goddamn," called out a voice in the yard.

Lucinda turned toward the call, to see another big man with thug written all over him. He was raising a gun, lining it up on her even as she began to move. The gun fired as she sprinted toward him, faster than any mortal could move. It flashed fire and boomed thunder into the night as she ran. She felt the bullet hit her and pass through her, barely slowing in its passage. Another round went through her head, then another through her chest, neither causing any harm.

Then she ran into the man, chest to chest, like a football tackle hitting his target. The flesh that had been so insubstantial to the bullets was oh so solid to the man, and Lucinda wrapped her arms around him as they both went down. As the man hit on his back, the air huffing out of him, Lucinda grabbed the side of his head with her right hand and pushed it over with her supernatural strength, exposing his neck.

Her fangs flashed in the moonlight as she drove her head onto the neck of the stunned man. The teeth pierced tender flesh, then withdrew as her lips clamped down on the curve of the neck and she sucked the flowing blood into her mouth. The life force followed the blood, making her feel strong and savage with the rush of power.

Enough, she thought, as her muscles bulged with the blood flow. She could not wait here long. The priest had driven her from the house to save her. And she could not remain in this place where so many sought her destruction. She reluctantly pulled her teeth away from the side of the neck, twisted the head back around, and sank her teeth into the exposed throat. She could feel the windpipe beneath her teeth as she bit down hard. She then pulled her head back with all of her strength while holding the head down in place. The throat tore under the pull of her sharp teeth, and she ripped it out like a wild beast.

Lucinda sprung to her feet, looking down at the shocked eyes of the dying man. *This one will not return.* Though she had fed on him she had not taken his life in the feeding. As the light went out in his eyes she knew his soul would go straight to Hell. There would be no return, and the body that went into the ground would simply become food for the worms.

A cough behind her made her turn before she even realized it was there. *The priest*, she thought, seeing the man straightening up after coming through the window. She could feel the fatigue in the man. She could smell his fear. But she could also sense the inner strength of the man that would not allow fatigue or fear to stop him from doing what he needed to do.

The urge to attack flared in her. The need to destroy this man who had been on her trail for so long. The man who had trapped her in the house. The house where she had been forced to turn a man she had come to destroy.

Lucinda forced the urge down, overruling her instincts with her intellect. The man was one of the good guys. The innocents that she had sworn to protect with her life. And no matter his mistakes she could not take his life, or she would once again be the servant of evil that she had begun this hellish existence as.

She heard the voices before the priest did, though he was much closer to the source. The voices of very angry men. The door to the room crashed open, loud enough to alert the priest. He looked around, alarm on his face, moving the big pistol he had in his right hand to aim toward the window.

"Run," she yelled at the priest. He looked back at her for an instant, then turned back toward the room. A gun thundered in the house, and O'Connor cringed and ducked. Lucinda was at the priest's side in an instant, one of her hands grasping the cloth of the man's black shirt. With a jerk she threw him away from the window, into the soft grass of the lawn.

"Run," she repeated, looking down at him. A trio of bullets flew through the window, passing through her body.

"Run," she yelled. "Get your ass out of here, priest. I'll take the heat off of you. Run."

O'Connor staggered to his feet, looking confused. Lucinda looked into the room, baring her fangs and snarling at the men who looked at her. All of them recoiled from the ferocity on her face, fear in their eyes. That didn't stop them from firing, as they kept their weapons pointed at her and kept pulling triggers, sending a hail of lead into her.

"What the fuck," yelled one of the men. "We ain't doing anything to her."

Lucinda backed away from the window, glancing to see the priest stumbling over the yard. The glass doors slid open and a hand reached out, large revolver held straight out. The gun roared, sending a spear of flame in the direction of the priest. The vampire ran toward the gun, the world slowing once again as she increased her speed. Her hand grasped the wrist as she saw the hammer moving forward again. She pulled up before the gun went off, sending the round into the sky. With a jerk she pulled the man through the half open door, bending aluminum and shattering glass with the body that flew into the yard.

She could hear the men in the room squabbling, and she knew that in an instant they would be firing into the yard. She could hear other voices in the house and knew that other gunmen would soon be firing from other doors and windows. And the priest was standing by the back part of the fence, where the hole that had been broken through it several nights before was patched with two by fours.

Lucinda ran toward the fence, aiming at an area of thinner boards to the right of the repair. She streaked across the yard, her feet barely touching down before rising again into the air. She knew that to the mortals she was nothing more than a blur, seeming to disappear and appear where she willed. But to her senses she was running as would a normal person, though the rush of the wind around her head was like a windy gale.

Lowering her shoulder Lucinda crashed into the fence, feeling the shock through her bones. Bones of the supernatural creature held. Common half-inch thick wood didn't. The boards splintered under her shoulder, then gave way as she forced herself through. Into the night she continued, tearing the boards away from the two by fours that held them in place.

Lucinda reached out a hand and grabbed the side of the fence, stopping her motion. It felt like the arm was going to pull out of the joint, but everything held and she stopped, pulling herself back into the yard.

"Get out of there," she yelled as she looked back into the yard to where the priest was staring at the new hole she had made. "Get over here and get your ass out."

O'Connor composed himself and ran the few steps to the hole. Lucinda grabbed his arm and pulled him through the hole, taking her time so he could twist around and not hit anything too hard, even though there was some urgency to the situation. But killing the man to save him was not in the plan. A couple of bullets smacked into the wood, breaking through the thin boards and sending splinters into the night air.

Lucinda pulled the priest along, ignoring the pain that was shooting up her arm. He was a holy object in and of himself. And it hurt her to touch him. But if she didn't hurry him away he would be killed by the evil men in the house. Already she could hear more of them running out of the house and into the yard.

"Why are you doing this?" asked O'Connor as she tugged on his arm and hurried him into the darkness.

"For the same reason you could not allow them to destroy me," she answered, flashing him a very human looking smile. "I could not let those monsters destroy you."

The priest staggered, almost falling under his fatigue. *He's almost an old man*, she thought, *trying to play in a young man's world. And it's telling on him.*

Lucinda pulled the man's arm over her shoulder, supporting him as she helped him along. The burning feeling ran along her shoulder and arm. She gritted her teeth against the agony and kept moving forward.

* * *

Marcus' ears perked up at the sound of gunshots from within the house. They were faint enough to be coming from the middle of the dwelling. And there were only a couple of them to start out. As he listened there were more, and the sound of men yelling and shoulders pounding on doors.

Could she be coming out? he thought, watching the house as he circled through the air overhead. That was the only reason he could think of for all of the commotion down in the house. If it had been a simple execution of someone there would have been one shot. Or probably not a shot at all, as fragile mortals could be killed by many means. But more shots sounded as he listened.

Or they might actually destroy her, he thought hopefully. He could feel her down there, the essence of her dark soul. It had been weak in the afternoon and the start of the evening, as if she was trapped and not allowed to feed. Then she had strengthened quickly, as if she had fed. *But why would they feed her.* It didn't make sense. And why had she stayed in the house through the day, unless they had trapped her? And then why hadn't they destroyed her?

Unless someone wanted to be turned, he thought. *And who would that be?* He ran down the list of players that he knew of, and only one made sense. *Padillas. George Padillas wanted to live forever. But doesn't he know he would be a servant of his maker, for as long as she kept him on a tight leash.* He must have known. So he would have ordered his men to kill her.

The giant bat turned through the air, flapping its leathery wings. He bared his fangs in a display that would have been a smile if he were in human form. *But they didn't know that they had trapped a tiger. And she has made them pay for it.*

A trio of shots sounded, along with the shattering of glass. He waited a moment and then she flew through the window, coming gracefully to her feet. He was tempted to go down to her then, to attack while he had her in his sights and she was preoccupied. He fought off the urge. It would be better to wait until she was off by herself, where he wouldn't give away his presence to the powers that be in the city.

He nodded his approval as she tackled, fed on and killed the mortal that had fired at her. Then he frowned as the priest came out of the window and she came to his aid. *That one is dangerous, and yet she saves him from the death he deserves. She has turned into a, what do they call it here, a Girl Scout.*

Marcus laughed at that thought as he watched her burst through the fence and help the priest through. *A Girl Scout who must kill to survive. Not what I think the founders of the organization envisioned.*

He watched as she put the priest's arm around her shoulder and helped him away from the fence. *The strength in her*, he thought. *To withstand what the touch must be doing to her. A shame she must be destroyed. But she must*, he thought, as he flapped off into the night to find a spot where he could confront her.

* * *

"We've got gunshots in the Padillas house," said Tanesha Washington into the radio. Jeffrey DeFalco checked his weapon, then climbed out of the car.

"I think it has to be our girl," he said, looking over at the house. "Tell them to get over here with everything they can get their hands on."

DeFalco ran off toward the house, angling into the left hand neighbor's yard. Washington followed him with her eyes as he disappeared into the shadows on the side of the neighbor's house.

"Dispatch here," came the call over the radio. "We have units on the way there. First backup should be there in less than a minute."

Washington could hear the faint calls of blue and whites in the distance, getting closer with each wail of the high-pitched siren scream.

"Wait till we get there, Washington," came the voice of Detective Lieutenant Jamal Smith over the radio. "Don't go near that house until you have backup on the scene."

"I'm sorry, lieutenant," said Washington, making sure that her mobile repeater was linked to the car radio. "My partner went there and I've got to follow."

Washington pulled her gun and ran toward the yard where she had seen DeFalco disappear. Smith continued to yell in her ear bud as she ran. But she ignored him as she obeyed the number one rule of police work. Never leave your partner uncovered.

*   *   *

"Are you alright, Father," said the vampire, looking at the face of the priest in the near total darkness. Her own vision saw him as a heat source. He seemed to be hotter than was normal for a human. She switched it to amplify the ambient light and looked over his face. He appeared to be pale, and she could hear his heart beating way too fast.

"I'll make it," he said with a strained smile. "I don't know what I'll tell the Pope's representatives, my helping a vampire and all."

"I'm still not sure why you did it," she replied, pulling air into her nostrils to add her sense of smell to the mix.

"I discovered that I was mistaken," said the priest, taking in a deep breath to try and alleviate his fatigue. "I thought I was tracking the most evil creature in the world. Or at least a representative of them. And while I was in

Padillas' house I realized that the greatest representatives of evil were living members of my kind."

The priest shook his head for a minute, then reached up to wipe the sweat from his brow. He looked back at the vampire, his eyes wide.

"You haven't killed anyone who wasn't evil themselves," he said. "You always spare the innocents. And you go to great lengths to make sure the contagion of vampirism doesn't spread behind you."

"I try," she said, lifting his arm back over her shoulder despite the pain of contact. "I hate my own kind. Hate what I have become. But I don't have the will to destroy myself, so I go on as best that I can."

"How did you get that way, my child?" asked the priest as he followed her lead, letting her guide him through the darkness of a large vacant block. "I have never heard of a vampire working for the forces of light. And you can't withstand the symbols of light any more than any other of your brethren."

Lucinda hissed for a moment as the pain of touching the holy man ran up her arm, lodging in the center of her chest. She released him, and the priest stumbled for a moment.

"It even hurts you to touch me," he said, a look of concern on his face. "Yet you have ignored the pain and your own safety to lead me out of the lion's den."

"I could not let you stay behind in that demon's lair," said Lucinda, "after you helped me to get out of there."

"And after I trapped you in the first place," said the priest. "I'm surprised you didn't just let me go to hell in that house."

"I couldn't do that," said the vampire. "It goes against my grain to leave a godly man in the hands of evil. Even if he does have a mistaken sense of duty. I...."

Lucinda stopped talking as she felt the presence of evil enter the darkened vacant block. She looked around the lot, her eyes trying to pierce the darkness that seemed complete. Her hearing strained to pick up sounds, but except for some rodents and a stalking cat she could detect nothing. But her nostrils widened as she picked up the death like stench of her kind.

"What is it?" asked the priest, his own eyes searching the darkness.

"Quiet," she hissed, holding up her hand, straining to pierce the darkness, to tell where her adversary was located. *I could turn*, she thought. *Fly from this place and maybe lose him in the night. But what about the priest?*

"I hope you have some of those anti-vampire weapons on you," she whispered to the priest. "Because in a moment you're going to need them."

* * *

Marcus had hoped that she would leave the mortal behind after she had gotten him out of the house. He should have figured that she would instead have played the Girl Scout and stayed with him until she was sure of his safety. Now he would have to destroy her and kill the priest. Not that he had anything against killing priests. But the killing of a public figure was never good for the kindred.

He has sure knowledge of our kind, though, thought the elder vampire as he crept through the night. *He is one of the loudest voices calling from the wilderness. His end will benefit us, as will hers.*

Marcus sniffed the air, a smile stretching his lips. There was a strong current of fear and panic coming from the house, wafting over his shoulder on the night breeze. She had stirred a hornet's nest tonight, and the bugs she hadn't crushed were moving aimlessly about.

They've stopped, he thought, feeling the presence of the pair in the open field across the road. Gathering the shadows about him like a cloak he flowed across the lighted street, a blot of darkness. He could feel a bit of hunger gnawing at the corner of his awareness. The elder vampire had used a lot of energy in the last two nights, and his body was calling for replenishment. He would use more energy before the night was over, but replenishment lay ahead as well, in the vital force of the priest.

Marcus focused his awareness onto the mortal, smelling the blood that flowed through his body. Listening intently to the pulsing of his veins. The rasping of his breath through his bronchioles. The vampire bared his fangs at the thought of that life entering his own body. As the life of countless mortals before him. But first he had to kill the youngling that stood with him. He pulled his concentration from the mortal and opened his mind up to undead in the field.

She knows I'm here. She isn't sure where I am coming from, so she isn't sure where to run. Marcus pulled himself into the shadows by a stand of trees, deepening their already dark, foreboding appearance. He could feel his own rising excitement at the stalk. The excitement that had made the millennia bearable.

It's time to get on with it, he thought, as he watched the priest sitting on the ground, trying to catch his breath. The female stood over him, her eyes darting around the field, trying to ferret out the threat that was coming for them.

Marcus stepped out of the darkness, dispelling the shadows he had called up as well. He bared his fangs as he strode across the grass, heading straight toward the pair that looked over in alarm.

* * *

"Get behind me priest," hissed Lucinda as she watched the smaller clump of shadows detach from the larger clump. The unnatural shadows flew into the night, and the short man stood out in the open. He showed his teeth in a grimace of menace then walked quickly toward the pair.

"Can you take him," asked O'Connor, coming to his feet.

"Not in a million nights," said the advancing vampire with a chuckle. "She might have the strength to, take me as you say, in a couple of thousand years, priest. But she will never last that long."

Lucinda bared her own fangs as she widened her stance, waiting for the elder vampire to come to her. As she blinked her eyes he was suddenly in front of her, his hands reaching out to grab at her shirt. She brought her own hands up in an inside out move that tried to push his hands away. And met what felt like immovable iron bars. Her hands rebounded off as the elder vampire grabbed the front of her shirt and jerked her into the air.

"You should have known your place, Lucinda," said Marcus, his red eyes burning through her will and into her soul. "You could have been among the best of us, in time. If you didn't do everything you could to foil the plans of the master."

Marcus pulled her close to him then pushed her away, his great strength propelling her through the air. Lucinda landed heavily on her back, thirty feet away. She knew that if she had been mortal she would have been lying on the ground with a broken back. But she wasn't mortal, and she jumped to her feet, hands at the ready to repel the elder vampire.

Like I could stop him, she thought. The elder vampire stood where he had been, his eyes staring into hers. She glanced at the priest who was looking back and forth between her and the other demon. Marcus glanced his way for a moment, then turned his attention back to the younger vampire.

Lucinda thought she would be ready when he started to move. But he was almost to her before she even noticed that he had started toward her. She brought up the unnatural speed of her kind, instantly slowing him down in her perception as she started to run toward him. She almost weighed as much as the ex-Legionnaire in life, and was certain that her momentum could knock him back as hard as she would be hit.

She was wrong. The younger vampire hit the elder and immediately reversed her motion under the force of his charge. She was knocked back, flying through the air to hit a pine tree, wood splintering under the impact as she felt some of her own vertebrae snap, followed by several ribs and an arm.

Lucinda looked around in panic. The bones were already starting to knit, but he was coming after her again. And she would not be able to defend herself in her present state. She raised her one good arm up and started to will on a change, hoping she could get away.

"And what about the good Father," said Marcus, stopping ten feet from her and staring into her eyes. "As soon as you take to the sky I will feed on him. It is always good in the eyes of the master to turn one of God's servants to Lucifer's cause."

"He is a holy man," cried Lucinda. "Keep your filthy hands off of him."

"Then it is up to you to stop me," said the elder vampire, showing her a baleful smile.

Lucinda knew that he would kill her if she attacked him again. But if she let him kill O'Connor without a fight she would not be able to go on. So she couldn't let it happen.

She could feel that her arm had almost healed, and the ribs and back were only a little stiff now. And she felt weaker than she had. Some of the life force that was keeping her going had been used up in knitting the bones. She needed all of the strength she could muster to fight the demon in front of her.

"Well, girl," said Marcus, staring at her, beating her will down with his eyes. "Are you going to try and stop me or not. I will make him scream in terror before I tear his throat out. I will make him feel pain such as he had never imagined."

Lucinda sprang from the tree, her nails turned into talons, reaching for the throat of her tormentor. With a laugh Marcus reached up in a blur and grabbed her wrists. His grip dug into her flesh, and she could feel the bones of her wrists crack under the pressure. A scream rose in her throat. But the anger rising in her mind cut off the scream. She brought a foot up and kicked into the midsection of the elder vampire, pushing hard with her hips, as she had been taught during her short life. She twisted her wrists at the same moment, pulling away from Marcus. Marcus flew backward, his hands flailing as he tried to grab onto her, then falling back to stumble and land on his butt in the dirt.

"Damn you, child," he hissed as he sprang back to his feet. "You caught me off guard with that move, but it will not happen again. I was fighting battles thousands of years before your upstart nation even existed. A thousand years before the Buddhist Monks ever came up with the techniques you just used. And now I will teach you about combat."

Marcus moved, low to the ground in a fighter's crouch. Lucinda threw a sidekick at the elder vampire. But Marcus knocked it aside with a sweep of his hand and moved in. His right fist dropped to his left side, then rose in a sweeping backhand that caught Lucinda in the jaw, knocking her head back.

As she tried to pull herself back to awareness with her ears ringing the vampire grabbed her by the front of her shirt and pulled her close.

"Now you end," he said, staring into her face. "Now I will show you how we kill one of our own. I will drink your blood, and drink your life force from you. And leave your lifeless body here in this field, along with that of the Holy Man you have given your life for. Given your life in vain."

Lucinda struggled, trying to pull away, all thought of scientific fighting gone from her mind in the panic she felt. His grip was strong, and she felt like a child in the grasp of a strong adult as he pulled her close. Her arms bent as he brought his mouth down toward her neck. She felt the sharp tips of his teeth pressed against her flesh, then push through the skin.

A thundering roar sounded in her ears and she felt the elder vampire jerk, then jerk again. He pulled his mouth from her neck, his eyes wide. She looked into the pain that shone in those eyes. Something thundered again, and she felt something pass through her own arm after exiting the body of the ancient monster. It burned like fire, tearing a hole in her arm. Then Marcus picked her from the ground and threw her back. Her back and her head hit again against the tree, cracking bone. She slid down on the trunk toward the ground, blackness reaching up and engulfing her. Her last thought as consciousness passed was that she had failed. She would die and the priest would die, and an ancient monster would continue to stalk the Earth, as a new monster was born.

*   *   *

Marcus felt the painful pellets passing through his body as the sound roared through his head. He jerked his teeth back as another pellet flew through his body, burning a path of agony. He threw the vampire child from him, hearing the crack of bone as she struck the tree, her eyes going blank before they closed and her body fell to the ground.

Marcus turned toward the priest, his eyes taking in the form of the man, crouched into a shooter's stance and the pistol in his hand pointed at Marcus.

"Stay away from her, you hell spawn," yelled the priest, his finger tightening on the trigger again.

Marcus moved in a rush of speed, sidestepping in an instant as the bullet cracked from the gun and sped through the space he had just occupied. The priest turned and tried to line him up again, but Marcus moved out of the line of fire as the bullet passed him by. The elder vampire then ran at the priest, moving too fast for the eye to follow. As the man tightened his finger on the trigger once again Marcus reached for the gun. His fingers gripped over the hand and the slide of the gun, keeping the hammer from moving forward. He could feel the sting of touching the flesh of the holy man. But his powers were at their peak, and the master was with him this night.

Marcus tightened his grip, listening as the priest cried out in pain. The fingers loosened and Marcus pulled the gun away, tossing it into the night. He stared into the priest's eyes, reveling in the terror he saw there. His lips skinned back over his teeth in a feral grin.

"Heavenly Father," said the priest in a croak. "Be with me the night and protect me from evil."

"There is no protection for you priest," said Marcus, grabbing the man's other arm and holding him still. "In three unholy days you will rise as one of my kind. And your soul will be enslaved by the master, as you commit murder every night to feed your hunger."

The fear left the eyes of the priest. Marcus could feel the man's will break free of his.

"I will never serve your master," said the priest in a strong voice. "I will never be as you, no matter what you do to me this night."

Marcus smiled at the naiveté of the priest. The man had his courage. But courage could not stand against the power of an elder vampire, and the contagion he would infect the mortal with.

Marcus reared his head back, then thrust forward like a striking snake. His fangs struck the flesh and pierced into the underlying vein. His lips molded to the flesh of the neck, as he sucked the lifeblood of the mortal into his mouth.

No, thought Marcus as the pain shot through his mouth. A hot agony that burned like the rays of the sun. He could feel the flesh of his mouth sizzling under the heat. Some burned into his throat, and he coughed and hacked, trying to bring it out before it burned through to his heart. *He is truly a Holy Man. Deadly to our kind.*

Marcus pulled his head away and spit the burning fluid from his mouth. He could feel the flames licking at his lips as the blood flew out in a burning stream to the ground. Marcus looked at the priest with hate and fear in his eyes. He tried to throw the man from him, but the strength had left his arms and he felt like the child now. O'Connor grabbed at the vampire's arms, trying to hold him now.

Marcus pulled away with the last of his strength, stumbling back. The vampire continued to spit up the blood that was burning him, his face a mask of agony. Escape was all that was now on Marcus' mind. He turned on his heel and ran into the night, staggering and stumbling from the pain.

Marcus ran for almost a mile, feeling the pain receding as he put distance between himself and the priest. He reached his hands up to his face as he regained his composure. The finger touched burned flesh, and came back to his vision covered in blood as he brought them back down.

He is untouchable to me, thought the vampire. *He was truly a holy man, and not just a pretender as are so many of his kind. And she is protected as long as he is with her.*

Marcus walked into the night, following the scent of a mortal that would yield to his embraces this night. He spotted her ahead of him on the dirty street. A whore, walking the night looking for business. Just the thing to wash the holy stench from his mouth, and heal him body and soul.

* * *

"Are you OK?" asked O'Connor, walking over to Lucinda as she struggled up from the ground.

Lucinda looked up at the priest and saw that he was holding one hand over the part of his neck where Marcus had bitten him. A little bit of blood seeped between his fingers, and Lucinda felt a surge of hunger at seeing and smelling the vital fluid.

"I'll live," she replied, pulling herself to her feet. She could feel the bones were almost knit, the healing almost completed. But the healing had taken much of her energy, and she felt very weak.

"Maybe that was a bad choice of words," she said with a smile. "Seeing as I'm not alive."

"What happened to him?" asked O'Connor, pulling his hand away from his neck wound and looking at his bloody fingers. The wound had stopped bleeding, though the neck still looked like a bloody mess.

"You are truly a holy man," said Lucinda in a hushed voice. "Do you know how rare your kind is?" she said in a strengthening tone.

"There are a lot of priests walking the Earth," said O'Connor, looking into her eyes. "Are you saying that all of them are immune to the attacks of vampires?"

"No," she said, shaking her head. "The great majority of the clergy are just as susceptible to the forces of evil as any other mortal. You are special. You have done something special that elevated you in the eyes of God."

"Giving up the Bishopric," said the priest. "And turning down the chance of elevation to Cardinal."

"So you turned down power to do what you thought was your holy calling," said the vampire. "Do you know how rare a quality that is? Selfless and self-sacrificing."

Lucinda stumbled as she walked from the tree. O'Connor reached out to help steady her, then removed his hands as he saw the pain that his touch brought to her.

"You are not as evil as the others," he said to her. "Shouldn't you have some kind of immunity to things that are holy?"

"I guess it doesn't work that way," she replied, trying to straighten up. "I am a creature of the night, no matter my motivations. So I have the weaknesses of a creature of the night."

"Not one that I intend to hunt anymore," said the priest. "I'll still go after ones like that bastard that bit me. But you are inviolate to me."

Lucinda smiled, then grimaced as a wave of weariness swept over her.

"You need blood," said the priest, a statement of fact. "Would that I could give you some of mine, for what you have done for me tonight."

"I don't want my mouth bursting into flame," said Lucinda, smiling at the priest. "And I make it a point to never taste the blood of the innocent."

"I'm not sure how innocent I am," said the priest, "no matter how holy you think I am. I…"

"Freeze," yelled out a voice in the night. O'Conner turned his head slightly, just enough to see the black woman who had walked out of the shadows, a gun held before her.

"Here we go again," said O'Connor out of the side of his mouth. "And the question is, whose side is she on?"

* * *

Detective Tanesha Washington had come along too late to catch much of whatever excitement had happened in the vacant lot. The sounds of yelling and gunshots had brought her here, wishing the whole time she could get in touch with Agent Jeffrey DeFalco. But he had not answered her on the radio, and she was afraid that the perpetrators would be gone if she waited for Tampa PD backup.

She recognized the priest, O'Connor she thought his name was, standing in the open lot. The woman looked familiar, and something about her raised the small hairs on the back of the detective's neck. *The vampire?* she thought. The one they had been looking for? Then why was she with the priest who had sworn to destroy her? And why did the priest do nothing but stand there talking to her.

"Freeze," she called out to the people as she walked out of the shadows on the edge of the lot, holding her automatic in a two handed grip to cover both people. "Tampa PD. Don't move a muscle."

The priest turned his head a bit and then said something out of the corner of his mouth to the woman. Tanesha was nervous enough to shoot, but kept enough control to notice that the man had not moved his hands.

"Don't you move either, lady," the detective called out as the woman turned a bit to see her. "You may think you are bullet proof, but I've got something in this gun to make you change your mind."

Just shoot her, thought Washington as she looked down the gun barrel at the beautiful woman. *She's not human, so why are you treating her like one?* But years of police work had driven it into her mind to not shoot a suspect that was covered and obeying the officer's commands.

She didn't even see the vampire move. One instant the woman was lined up with the pistol. The next she was standing in front and slightly to the side of the detective. A strong hand clamped down on Washington's, holding the gun in place. The detective shuddered as red eyes looked into hers. It felt as if the eyes were burning into her soul.

Tanesha Washington found herself staring at the creature in fascination, feeling a slight thrill of fear as she focused on the sharp canines within the vampire's mouth. *She's going to kill me*, thought the detective. *I should have shot while I had the chance, and now it's too late.*

"She's a good guy," said the priest. "I recognize her now."

"I can see within her," said the vampire in a faraway voice. "You are correct. She is an innocent and on the side of good. So I will release her."

The vampire stared again into Washington's eyes, boring into the soul of the woman. "I could have killed you in an instant. Remember that when I release you."

Then the vampire was gone into the night, a blur that Washington was not sure she actually saw. She looked around her in shock for a moment, then focused on the priest who had moved over to her. She lowered her gun as she stared open mouthed at the man.

"She is not your enemy," said the priest. Washington could see that he had been bleeding from the neck and pointed.

"Another of her kind," said O'Connor, rubbing his hand over the wound. "One without her sense of honor."

"She's still a murderer," said Washington, looking out into the darkness but seeing no trace of the woman.

"Only to those who truly deserve their punishment," said the priest.

"I thought the church did not believe in killing," said the detective. "In any form."

"It is a sin for a human being to kill another," agreed the priest. "She is no longer human. Would you kill a wolf for bringing down a deer?"

"We're not talking about deer here Father," said Washington. "We're talking about people."

"You sound as if you are not so sure anymore, my child," said the priest.

"But I sure as hell am," came the angry voice of a man from the night. Jeffrey Defalco stepped into the light, his gun in his hand as he searched the darkness. "Did you see her?"

"She was here," said Washington, looking at the man as if she had never seen him before, still trying to recover from the shock. "She was in my face before I could react. And then she was gone."

"You're lucky she didn't kill you outright," said the FBI man.

"I don't think she would have," said Washington, her voice low. "I felt that she meant me no harm."

"As she means you no harm, Agent DeFalco," said the priest, looking into the eyes of the agent. "As she means none of us harm who do not prey upon our fellow man."

"What the hell happened here?" growled the agent. "I thought you were as determined to destroy her as anything. And what happened to my partner here?"

"A great deal of learning," said the priest, nodding his head as Washington looked at him. "I have learned that she is not my target. And I had better leave well enough alone. As should you, Agent DeFalco."

"Bullshit," said DeFalco, shaking his head violently. "She's an unnatural monster and she needs someone to take her out. And I'm the someone."

"Then I'll pray for you, agent," said the priest, looking intently at the man. "I'll pray that you purge the unreasoning hate from your soul, as have I."

"Pray for her soul, father," said DeFalco, turning away from the priest. "Because I'm going to send it to Hell, if it's the last thing I do on this earth."

Chapter 11

George Padillas could feel the hunger gnawing at him as his awareness returned. He opened his eyes to almost total darkness as he reached his hands out before him and touched the cloth covering the top of the box. He pushed gently and the lid of the coffin rose. Padillas breathed a mental sigh of relief that he had not been buried. So far everything seemed to be going according to plan.

The bright lights of the room blinded his supernatural night vision for a moment. Then his eyes adjusted to the light and he saw that he was in his own bedroom, the coffin occupying a section of the floor in front of the big bed. As he sat up in the coffin he saw Manny scramble up from his seat on the other side of the bed and walk quickly over to the coffin.

"Is everything OK, Mr. Padillas?" asked the head man of the house, his eyes nervously moving over Padillas' form.

"I feel different," said the boss, lifting himself out of the box with his arms. "I feel much stronger. And everything seems to be sharper to my senses. Eyes, ears, and especially smell."

As he talked he could hear the heart beating in Manny, the blood flowing through his veins. He could smell the sweet red fluid in the man, the fluid that he craved. He drove the thought from his mind for a moment as he concentrated on his own body.

"There's no pain," he said with a grin. "For the first time in years there's no pain in my guts. I'm cured. Or at least as cured as a dead guy can get."

"You look really good for a dead guy, boss," said Manny, his eyes still darting from the boss to the door to the bedroom.

"What's wrong, Manny?" said Padillas, sensing that the man was very nervous by the smell of him. "What did you let happen? No one knows about me, do they?"

"No sir," said Manny, shaking his head. "As far as the world knows you are still alive and well. No one will know anything when you show up again, except that you were on your boat out in the Gulf. I even sent it out for a couple of days so people wouldn't see it at the marina."

"So what the fuck are you afraid to tell me, Manny?" said Padillas, his eyes boring into the other man's. The new vampire could feel the man's will resist his for a moment, then crumble under the assault.

"Did she get away from you, you shithead?"

"I'm sorry, boss," stammered Manny. "The priest got to her and let her out of the house. And she got him out."

"So the priest and the other vampire know about me, huh," growled Padillas. "So your statement about the world not knowing a thing was a fucking lie, huh."

"The priest won't be a problem, boss," said Manny, wiping the sweat from his face with a handkerchief. "He might tell some people in the church, but I didn't think you would be going to church anyway."

"And what about Lucinda?" asked Padillas, standing over the man, feeling his anger grow at the thought of his Lieutenant's incompetence. "She can have my ass if she gets to me."

"We'll just have to make sure that doesn't happen," Manny said in a squeaky voice.

Padillas' anger faded for a moment as he drank in the fear the other man was feeling. *Fear that I'm causing,* thought the boss with a smile.

"Are you hungry, boss?" asked the man. Padillas could feel the fear and knew that the other man was trying to get his mind off the subject. Padillas could feel the hunger come back into awareness as the question was asked.

"I've got a girl here for you, Mr. Padillas," said the man, trying to avoid the vampire's eyes. "Just like you talked about before you, you know, turned."

Padillas could feel the hunger like a driving force, trying to push all other thoughts out of his mind. He pushed it back down for a second as he thought about what he needed to do.

"I'll eat later," said the boss to his underling. "Now let's go to my office and go over the business."

Manny breathed out and looked like most of the stress that had been eating at him drained out of his body. He stood up, walked to the door and led Padillas into the hall. They walked down the hall and into the living room, the boss throwing greetings at his soldiers, they giving nervous responses back.

Well, what did I expect, he thought. *They know I died. And here I am back from the grave. They know what happened, but it still has to feel unnatural to them.* But not to George Padillas. It felt perfectly natural to him to be walking in this body, feeling strong and fit, with none of the agony that the cancer had visited upon his life. In fact living with the pain of the cancer had been unnatural.

Crossing the living room and walking down the other wing's hallway, the two men came to Padillas' office. Manny opened the door and gestured for the boss to enter. Padillas walked into the large, sumptuous office and looked around, feeling right at home at the heart of his empire. *An empire I can rule for a thousand years*, he thought. *Untouchable by my rivals, or the law.*

As the door closed he turned to Manny and smiled, and the man smiled back, visibly relieved to be back in the boss' good graces. The smile left Padillas' face and he turned a baleful eye on the man, pushing with his will against the weaker will of the mortal.

"You failed me Manny," he hissed, his face turning into a fierce mask. He reached out with his hands that had become talons and grasped the man by the shirt. "A simple task, to get rid of the priest and a creature that was trapped. And you failed me."

Manny grabbed Padillas' wrists with his strong hands and tried to pull the vampire off of him. Padillas knew that Manny was very strong, a weightlifter all of his life. And now it felt as if a weak child were trying to pull his hands away.

"You will never fail me again," said Padillas, pulling the man close. The vampire opened his mouth, feeling the sharp fangs slide against his lips. Then he thrust his head out, aiming his teeth for the tender skin of the neck. The teeth cut easily into the flesh. Manny tried to pull his neck away, to push his head back. But the vampire dug in like a bulldog and ripped open the vein.

Padillas placed his lips over the open wound and let the blood flood into his mouth. The blood tasted sweet and salty at the same time, and he could feel an energy he had never felt from any other food. The man's life force was flowing out with the blood, infusing the vampire's body with strength and vitality. Erasing the hunger that had been driving Padillas wild.

Manny relaxed as the vampire fed. Padillas had heard of this power. That a feeding vampire actually took control of the prey through the actual pleasure of feeding. Strange that something that would kill a man would feel good. He pulled the flowing blood down his throat, then started sucking with force as the flow diminished. Soon he was supporting Manny in his grip as the man's legs buckled.

Padillas could hear Manny's heart begin to slow, to struggle in its effort to pump blood as the pressure dropped. It skipped a beat as the vampire was struggling to pull more blood from the neck. With a final series of strong beats the heart stopped, and Padillas could feel the lifelessness of the body he held. Padillas let go of the body as he stepped back, watching as it fell slack muscled to the floor.

"You wanted to live forever too," he said to the wide eyed corpse lying on the floor. "You wanted to revel in the power that I offered."

Padillas walked over to the wall where he displayed his collection of ancient swords. Grabbing a sheathed katana from its hooks, he turned and walked back to the body. The vampire pulled the long blade from its shark skin sheath. He admired the razor sharp blade for a moment. Then he took the handle into a two handed grip and stood over the body. He raised the sword over his head slowly, then slashed it down in a blur of metal. The blade struck Manny's neck, slicing through muscle and bone. The head rolled off on the carpet, as a small puddle of blood flowed onto the floor.

"Now you can serve the master in his home, Manny," said Padillas, bending down to wipe the fine blade on the dead man's shirt. "In Hell, Manny. In Hell."

Padillas resheathed the sword and returned it to its hooks on the wall. He then opened the door to the hallway and stuck his head out.

"Jake, isn't it," he said as he saw a man coming out of one of the bedrooms opening on the hall.

"Yes sir," said Jake, hurrying over to Padillas. "What can I do for you sir."

Padillas opened the door wide and gestured for Jake to come into the room. The man obeyed, walking through the doorway and coming to a stop as soon as he entered the room, his mouth opened wide.

"I want you to take out the trash," said Padillas, gesturing to the head and body of Manny. "Make sure that it gets dumped someplace where no one will find it."

Jake nodded his head, looking wide eyed at the boss.

"And get a carpet cleaner and go over the rug," said the boss. "Use something that will get blood out."

"Anything else, sir," said Jake in a quivering voice.

"You don't have anything to worry about, Jake," said Padillas, putting an arm around the man's shoulder and chuckling when Jake flinched. "As long as you work diligently for me and don't ever fail me we'll get along fine."

The man nodded, his brow furrowed as his face assumed a worried expression.

"And I need that girl Manny got for me tomorrow night. You can send her away and ask her back this evening. You got that Jake."

The man nodded again, looking back at the body.

"Good man," said Padillas. "I'll leave you to it. I'm going to get a little work done in my bedroom. Let me know when it's presentable in here again."

*   *   *

Lucinda could feel the presence of the new vampire in the house. She was sure that she could mask her own presence from one so young. There was no fear of Marcus this night. *It will take him more than three days to recover from the burning of holy fire that he underwent*, she thought. He would be laired up in darkness for at least a month, and she would be well out of this city and working another by the time he was ready to get back on her trail.

The vampire faded into the shadows as a figure passed along the fence line. Not that she feared any of his guards this night. But they might raise an alarm that would be inconvenient for her purposes. And the police, or more importantly the FBI, might come, and she would have a situation on her hands that she wanted to avoid.

Lucinda brought her hands into the air and concentrated on some of the many small minds that ran through the darkness. She could catch glimpses through their eyes as she gave a mental call. Their squeaks resounded through her ears, getting louder each moment, until...

"Fucking rats," yelled one of the guards, scrambling back from the fence as dozens of the big sewer rats came under the wooden slats. There was more yelling from the yard as the large creatures ran into the yard.

"Don't shoot them, you idiot," yelled another voice. "You want to bring the cops."

"I don't want them getting on me," said the first man.

"Then pick up a shovel or something and start banging on them."

Lucinda smiled as she listened to the chaos she had caused. Enough to keep their attention focused on the ground. She raised her arms into the air and transformed. Flapping over the yard she looked down to see a trio of men swinging away with blunt objects at the rats, missing much more often that hitting. None of them looked up as she flew to the house and landed in some bushes that were in the shadows.

Lucinda transformed back to human form and listened at the window she was nearest to. Hearing nothing for a minute or so, she pulled at the window, breaking the latch with her unnatural strength. Having been in the house before she had no problem with entering the dark room. She soon found herself in a bedroom that was silent as death.

Lucinda took a minute to listen at the door to the bedroom. She could hear distant voices, and a couple of laughs. *Probably enjoying the commotion with the men outside battling rats*, she thought. And far enough away to not notice her as she slipped out into the hallway.

While she was trying to decide which door to try on this unfamiliar wing of the house a door opened suddenly and a man walked out. He stopped in his tracks and stared at her for a moment. Recognition dawned in his eyes and his mouth opened to let out a yell.

Lucinda jumped at the man she knew as Jake, her torturer, extending the fingers of her left hand into talons.

The claw like hand hit the man in the throat, sinking though the soft flesh and into the windpipe below. With a quick jerk she pulled the trachea from the neck. Blood spurted as the man tried to gurgle the yell he had not had time to get off. His eyes widened as his hands went to the ruin of his throat. With legs wobbling the man sank to the carpet, then fell face first to the floor.

One piece of vermin taken care of, she thought, looking down coldly at the slack body. She felt a touch of hunger as she saw the carpet around the head darken with the flow of blood. She ignored it, knowing that the blood of the lifeless was of no use to her. Stopping for a moment she listened. She could still hear the voices from the living room area down the hall. They were still laughing. Meaning that they hadn't heard her murder their compatriot. *Now to find Padillas and take care of this matter once and for all.*

Even though it hadn't really been her fault that Padillas had been created, she still felt some responsibility for making him a bigger monster than he had been. She had been trapped and starved, and the only food offered to her had been the crime boss. For his own reasons of course. There was no way she could have resisted the hunger in that situation. But if she hadn't been as she was he wouldn't have come back.

Moving down the hall she noted that one of the doors seemed a little more ornate than the others. Sniffing the air she could scent the blood in the room, a slightly different odor than that in the hallway. Putting her ear against the door she could hear the rustling of papers. She placed her hand on the knob and turned it quietly, then pushed the door open and jumped into the room. A man looked up from a desk, a frown on his face.

"I've come for you, Padillas," said Lucinda as she pulled the door closed behind her. "Your bid at eternity ends this night, before it really begins."

* * *

George Padillas looked up as the door opened, slightly angered at being disturbed. He had been going over the combined books of several of his legitimate operations, seeing what money he could divert into the clandestine, and more profitable areas. His eyes widened as he caught sight of the woman standing in the doorway. She pulled the door closed behind her and stood there, staring at the man.

Padillas felt like his soul was withering under the gaze of the woman. He tried to open his mouth, to say something that was both brave and conciliatory. His vocal cords seemed to fail him and he stared into those burning eyes.

"Cat got your tongue, Padillas?" said the woman, walking toward the desk in a slow, seductive manner. "I would have thought that you had a lot to tell me."

Padillas reflexively cleared his throat, then found that his vocal cords were working again.

"I had ordered that you would be let go," he said in a halting voice. "If you hadn't have broken out you would have been released, along with the priest."

"You're lying, of course," said Lucinda, her eyes locking Padillas in place. "I can tell when you are lying to me, so you had better tell the truth."

"I'll make you my partner," said Padillas, feeling paralyzed in the chair. He tried to move his hands, to gesture along with his speech. But nothing seemed to work besides his mouth and eyes. "I'll give you a piece of the action. I'll even bring you someone to feed on, every night."

"So you think I am like you," said Lucinda, her eyes darting around the room, then focusing back on the newly made vampire.

Padillas could feel his muscles unlock when she took her eyes off of him. He started to make a move, then froze in place as her eyes came back to him and her burning stare ate into his soul.

"You were more evil than I before you turned," she said. "Now you are ten times more evil. Did you really think I would allow one like you to survive? To spread misery across the planet over the centuries. No, George Padillas. You end tonight, as you should have ended days ago."

Lucinda turned her gaze away from her prey for a moment, letting her eyes roam the room. Padillas felt his will return for a moment. He moved his fingers, then his arms. The woman turned her head from him and he felt that he had control of himself again. But for how long? There was a gun in his desk drawer, but he was sure that it would not even inconvenience the more powerful vampire. He looked at the wall where his ancient weapons were hanging, his gaze focusing on the katana that he had used to take Manny's head. A thought went through his mind. Hadn't he heard that a vampire could be killed by taking its head?

To think was to act, and George Padillas sprung to his feet and ran to the wall at high speed. In microseconds the blade was off the wall and in his hands. He slid the katana from the sheath, dropping the shark skin cover to the floor and grasping the sword's handle in both hands. Spinning on his heel as he brought the blade up over his head, he moved toward the woman who had turned toward him with the same speed he was using.

Padillas looked down, keeping his eyes from meeting those of Lucinda. He could see enough of her body to know where to strike. He brought the blade down, glancing up at the last moment to true his aim. The blade struck the side of her neck and cut in. Padillas felt himself fall slightly off balance as the blade met almost no resistance. Then the sword was through, and Padillas looked up at the face of the woman with a smile on his own.

Lucinda looked at him with a slight smile on her lips. Padillas waited for her head to fall, wondering why it was still on her neck. He could not even see the wound that must be on there. The wound that had to have been created by the passage of her blade through the neck. His eyes widened in shock as the woman shook her head.

"You should have asked Father O'Connor more about vampires, Padillas," she said, her eyes locking on his. "We are nearly invulnerable at night. Normal weapons cannot kill us while we are at the height of our powers."

"But," he said, feeling his fingers weaken and the handle of the katana fall to the floor. "I thought taking the head…"

"During the day, yes," said the female vampire. "This is not a movie, George Padillas. We do not explode into dust when a blade cuts through our neck, or a stake goes through our chest. At night weapons are nothing to us."

She took a step toward Padillas. He tried to move away, but his feet felt like they were rooted to the floor.

"I created you, George Padillas," she said, reaching out with her hands and laying them on his shoulders. "Therefore I control you. You are mine to do with as I please."

Padillas wanted to shrug the hands off of his shoulders. To run from the room and get away from the female. But she was right. As long as she was in his presence she controlled him.

"There is one weapon that above all others is deadly to us during the night," she said. "Do you know what that weapon is, George Padillas? Can you guess how I am going to end you?"

Padillas felt overwhelmed with the fear that she was making him feel. He wanted to scream for help, but his mind was a prisoner of his own body.

"We are the only weapon that can destroy us during the time of darkness," she said, baring her fangs. "A vampire can destroy a vampire, like this."

Lucinda slowly moved her teeth close to Padillas' neck. She breathed a cold breath on his skin, then moved her fangs across the skin. Padillas wanted to pull his neck back, but he couldn't. Then he felt the sharp pain of the fangs piercing his flesh. They withdrew and the soft lips of the woman covered the wound, her mouth sucking strongly.

Padillas could feel the lifeblood flowing from his body into the woman who was bent over him. And with it the life force that was animating his body. He could feel some of his will returning while out of her gaze. He tried to pull away, using his strength against hers. He might as well have been a child struggling to get away from a strong adult. She was draining his strength, growing stronger as he grew weaker.

Padillas' vision started going red as she continued to suck, pulling blood and life from him. *This can't be it*, he thought. *I was supposed to live forever. This can't be it.* Then darkness enveloped him, and he knew that he would not rise again from this darkness.

* * *

Lucinda let the body drop to the floor and stood over it, staring down at the man who wanted to live forever and become the greatest crime boss in the world. *Why would anyone choose this existence?* she thought. *Why would anyone want to become a creature of the night?*

She shook her head as she turned away from the dead meat that had been George Padillas. She had finally taken down the target. Another would rise to take his place. They always did. But maybe the next one would look over his shoulder, and wonder when death was coming for him.

Lucinda lifted the window of the room, opening it to the outside. She stepped back and spread her arms, willing the transformation. Within seconds the dark form of the large bat flew through the window and out into the night.

Epilogue

The Magic Kingdom was hours closed, as was MGM Studios and Sea World. But in some parts of the Central Florida Region the night was a time of continued business.

Lucinda followed the siren call through the night, walking the streets of Orlando. Where the police were heading was normally a place of interest for her. She could see the flashing of strobes on the windows. There were a cluster of police cars, men and women in uniform moving between the buildings while others kept the growing crowd away.

"Nothing to see here, people," said one of the officers, holding her hands up.

"What happened?" asked Lucinda of an elderly black man standing near the front of the crowd.

"Another prostitute killed," said the man, looking back at her. "Most likely by her pimp."

"That happen often around here?" she asked.

"You not from around here, are you?" said the elderly man, looking over Lucinda. She was dressed respectfully tonight in slacks and a sweater, not playing the part of a whore this night.

"No," she admitted, shaking her head. "Just visiting family."

"Well the scum pimps kill their girls all the time," said the man. "Or a John kills them. Not a good business to be in if you want to live a long life."

"No," said Lucinda, watching as an ambulance pulled up on the other side of the street and the medics got out. "But neither is pimping or drug dealing."

She watched as the gurney was taken from the back of the ambulance and set up by the medics. It was then wheeled toward the alley. Lucinda allowed her eyes to roam the building after the gurney disappeared from sight. She could see many faces at windows, looking out on the frightening scene. She could feel the fear in the great majority of them. But there was one face that stood out.

Lucinda focused on the angry face of a big black man, scowling out at the scene. She could feel the rage radiating out of him. His eyes turned as he scanned the street. For a moment his eyes locked with Lucinda's, and she could feel the lust breaking through the anger. And she could guess what he was thinking. Someone to replace the one he had killed that night.

Bingo, she thought, a predatory smile coming to her face. She would meet with him, tonight. Though it would not go as he expected. Not at all.

THE END

About the Author

Doug Dandridge is an ex-professional student with degrees from Florida State University and The University of Alabama, and coursework in Psychology, Biology, Geology, Physics, Chemistry, Anthropology and Nursing. Doug has interest in all of the fantastic, including science fiction, fantasy and horror, as well as all eras of military history. Doug is a prolific writer, having completed 22 novel length manuscripts. He is still seeking a major publishing contract, but has decided that self- publishing is the way to go at this time. His work can be found on Amazon and Smashwords, as well as his own website. Doug lives with his four cats in Tallahassee, Florida, and currently has no social life, as he is too busy writing around his work schedule.

Follow my many characters and settings at
http://dougdandridge.net
Contact me at BrotherofCats@gemail.com
Follow my Blog, Doug BrotherofCats Dandridge at
http://dougdandridge.com

Printed in Great Britain
by Amazon